LOST IN SHADOW

Immortal Warriors Paranormal Romance

CYNTHIA LUHRS

PROLOGUE

644 - Edinburgh, Scotland

I

Upon waking that dismal, cold morning, Colin had no bloody clue it would be his last, and it wouldn't be from the damn plague sweeping across the land.

Hearing footsteps, he lifted his head, the small braids on either side of his temple hanging limply, falling forward into his eyes as his brother approached. "Hamish, what are ye doing here? How did ye get past the guards? T'isn't safe."

"Smuggling? What in the hell were ye thinking, smuggling whisky? Thank the gods our parents have passed. They'd be rolling over in their graves at the dishonor ye brought on our family."

Colin watched Hamish flick lint off his ridiculous velvet jacket before his brother finally deigned to turn and face him. He couldn't move chained to the rough stone wall in the dank, reeking dungeon of Edinburgh Castle, otherwise he'd wipe the look of disgust off Hamish's face. He surmised he didn't look like the heir apparent today.

With nostrils pinched and a disdainful sniff, Hamish looked into the cell. "Bloody cold in here. Looks like there are rats in the straw. Manacled like the common criminal ye've turned into. Appalling. Not very commodious accommodations for a baron, brother."

Green eyes blazing, he thundered, "Why. Are. Ye. Here? You're supposed to be guarding Abigail."

Hamish regarded his brother dispassionately, "Yes, I guarded your loving fiancée quite well this morn as she woke perfectly content in my bed. I say, she is quite the tasty wench. I may not have conquered and killed my way across the continent but seems the ladies find me favorable."

Lashing out against the shackles, the lacerations he'd sustained broke open again as blood trickled down his chest. He snarled as Hamish took a few steps back, "How could my own flesh and blood betray me thus? Ye and Abigail? Of all the women in Scotland, you had to steal mine? The treacherous wench. I should have known that social-climbing bitch in heat would slither up to anything with a prick and gold to spend. Ye deserve each other. Step away from me *brother*, if I get my hands on you, I will show you no mercy when I kill you where you stand. Why did ye do it?" Colin spat.

Hamish's hand shook as he fiddled with the lace collar of his shirt. But he didn't answer.

Filled with fury over Hamish's confession, Colin's thoughts slid around his brain. Couldn't believe he'd been caught.

Everything had been meticulously planned; his men would go to their death before betraying him. He didn't understand how that bastard Huntington, Captain Rawlins Huntington of the Redcoats to be exact, had found him.

Using the Vaults was genius. Not to mention Colin's castle had secret passages leading to a hidden cove where a small ship could dock unseen while the whisky was loaded. Smuggling whisky was a verra profitable business; keeping his snooty, spoiled ass of a brother in lace and frocks, as well as paying for much needed maintenance and repairs to the castle. My god,

Hamish looked like some damned peacock strutting back and forth; Colin's eye twitched with every flouncing turn.

Frowning at Hamish, an ugly thought worked its way into his battered brain. Hamish had betrayed him with Abigail so it made sense he was the one who gave them up to the English Captain. Colin's heart shriveled, turning black, curling in on itself. They were all each other had left in this world. He would never forgive this treachery. Shaking his head to clear it, he studied Hamish.

"Ye never answered me brother," Colin growled in a silky, low, menacing tone. Pulling against the manacles he lunged at Hamish.

Hamish leaned nonchalantly against the wall. At slightly under six feet, he was shorter than Colin by five inches with a lean build and the same chestnut hair and green eyes. Anyone could easily see they were brothers.

Swaggering over to Colin, careful to stay out of his reach, Hamish cocked his head to the side and stated, "I thought ye were the smart one. Haven't ye figured it out yet, brother mine?"

Voice cracking with emotion, Colin sounded defeated for the first time in his life. "Ye. Betrayed. Me. With my fiancé. Ye. Betrayed. Me. To the bloody buggering English."

"Aye brother, I gave Captain Huntington your location. Ye really think I didn't know what was happening? Your men will hang in the morn. Criminals—the lot of them. By the way, the reward was a bonus. 'Twill be a nice addition to the family fortune. God knows I'll need it the way Abigail spends my gold. With you out of the way, I plan to enjoy the rest of my days squandering the family fortune on drink, gambling, and bedding Abigail." Hamish frowned, glancing at his sodden, ruined boots before looking back up at his brother.

"You may have sent your enemies cowering back to their tents simply by taking the field of battle, never defeated—yet I, never having faced combat, managed to ensnare you. I relish this defeat of the mighty Baron Campbell. Where's your precious code of honor now, dearest brother?"

Thigh muscles rippling as he strained against his chains, Colin was gratified to hear one of the bolts scraping against stone. If he could pry one loose, he'd have a fighting chance of escape before the English hanged him.

"Look *brother*, the world's a harsh, brutal place. It's time I have the title, the fortune, and the lass. It's too bad ye'll be dead and won't be able to do a blasted thing about it." Hamish yawned, pulling a dagger from his boot.

In a deadpan, flat tone, Hamish continued, "I have hated ye since we were seven and father said ye were his favorite. Ye think his fall down the stairs when I was thirteen was an accident? I pushed the bastard. He never treated me as anything other than second best to ye. And mother. Oh yes, I poisoned her for loving ye more than me. I was the 'spare heir,' nothing more to them. All of ye sodding idiots thought she'd died of natural causes."

By the gods, with this reprehensible confession his brother had gone stark raving mad. Struggling to break free, blood coursed in fresh rivulets down his muscled body tearing wounds the English had bestowed upon him when they'd tortured him. The gut-wrenching pain was nothing compared to the unbearable ache ripping through his soul at the knowledge his own brother had murdered their loving parents. Colin couldn't breathe, the agonizing pain of their loss hitting him again after so many years, crashing over him in waves.

"Go ahead ye cowardly, craven bastard," Colin roared.

Straining, veins bulging in his arms and neck, Colin ground out, "Fucking strutting peacock, ye can't even fight me like a man. Ye come at me to kill me when I'm chained to a bloody wall? I. Curse. Ye. I. Curse. Abigail. May ye both rot in hell with nary a day of peace for the rest of your miserable lives. Well, go on then, do it."

Colin didn't flinch as his brother came running towards him, dagger held out straight in front—tensing, he waited for the blow. The blade glanced off, carving a bloody ribbon across his chest.

"That all ye've got? Ye wouldn't last a minute in battle, the English would rip you to bloody shreds." Colin taunted his brother. He knew how tough and resisting skin was, it wasn't easy to stab someone.

Hamish's eyes were round with fear. Colin watched him wrap both hands around the dagger, cock his arms back ramming the blade into Colin's chest

He couldn't breathe as the metal bit into him, taking his lifeblood. Gasping for breath, he narrowed his eyes, watching his brother, noting the shaking arms, the sweat dripping from his brow as Hamish leaned hard on the blade, straining, grunting, as slowly, inch by inch the dagger slid deeper into his chest until it stopped—hitting bone.

Hamish paled, his entire body quivering with the strain as he rocked back on his heels, and with a mighty shove Colin heard a crack, bone splintering as the dagger found its mark—straight into his heart. He dimly saw Hamish retching, wiping his arm across his mouth, putting his head between his knees to breathe so he wouldn't pass out—it was a common bodily reaction the first time you killed someone. His heart slowed down, the strong beats becoming weaker, skipping erratically.

"It's my time now, brother. My turn to be baron!" Hamish yelled.

The buzzing in Colin's brain took over, his body shutting down, heart failing, breath coming in labored gasps, Hamish's voice fading out.

"Rawlins, have this bloody, revolting mess cleaned up." Turning on his heel as Colin shuddered, taking his last wheezing breath, blood slowly dripping on the damp stone floor; Hamish slid the ancient ring bearing the Campbell family crest off Colin's finger. He wiped the bloody ring clean on Colin's kilt before sliding it onto his finger and fled the dungeon.

Darkness was closing in, the roaring in his head subsiding.

Colin could hear Hamish talking to someone, a woman—it couldn't be—Abigail come to see him die. He would never trust another, never let another get close to him, and never fall in love again. The pain was intense, scorching its way through his heart, encasing the shriveled black lump in ice. Hamish and Abigail's voices receded, his eyesight failed him—no, not yet—Hamish will destroy everything I've built. There are families depending on me, those who need me. I canna go, not now.

As he faded, the noise took over—like a winter thunderstorm, waves crashing against the rocks and one final dying thought screamed its way through his mind and burst forth, "Damn it to hell. I. Won't. Die."

The shadows came, sliding around the floor and slithering up the walls to swallow Colin. His dying soul fought, screaming out for more time, for another chance, for retribution. Filled with rage, he looked down upon his limp, earthly body. Through the mist and shadow, Colin saw lightning beckoning in the darkness, heard a whisper within the maelstrom—offering him a choice.

I

Present Day - Friday, October 30th - Edinburgh, Scotland

"How about touring Mary King's Close, then the South Bridge Vaults? The Close is supposed to be the best-known, most haunted of them all on the Royal Mile. Who knows, maybe we'll see Annie, the little girl who was killed during the Plague when they walled up the Close with people inside. It'll be spooky fun. Old buildings, dark, dank, falling apart, what's not to love?"

Emily's eyes lit up at Kat's suggestion. Breathing deeply, the air smelled crisp and brisk with a full moon trying to break through the clouds as a light drizzle fell on Old Town. Edinburgh seemed eerie with its cobblestone streets, tall medieval buildings so close at the top, the neighbors could reach out and touch each other, and shadows dancing on the streets, playing hide and seek with the moon as the sky darkened to indigo.

Looking around the old street, mist rising up from the cobblestones, curling around the buildings, the hair on the back of Emily's neck rose, as if unseen hands in the mist caressed her. Shivering in the chilly air, the fog rolling in, she couldn't believe she was actually here.

Back in the third grade, in Charleston, a boy named Dougal, from the Isle of Skye, off the coast of Scotland regaled her with fantastic tales of his homeland. His voice, the way he spoke, rolling his r's, entranced her as she dreamed of warrior princes in a faraway land. When he moved away it broke her heart. Ever since then she'd fantasized about visiting the country. Wandering around the city, exploring the stone circles, all the moldy old castles, and historic buildings, she could barely contain herself from running up and down the street shouting with joy at *finally* achieving her dream.

Standing with hands on her hips, one eyebrow cocked, Katherine "Kat" Chandler was five foot seven, same as Emily, though Kat had long auburn hair showcasing a gorgeous creamy complexion topped off by piercing blue eyes. Red boots, jeans, a turquoise sweater, and an indigo scarf, topped off with a shocking pink coat complemented her striking looks. Sometimes Emily wondered if she needed sunglasses when she was around Kat. The girl always wore bright clothes, carrying an infectious laugh and smile to go with them. Emily didn't care if she faded into the woodwork when she was with Kat. She preferred to be in the background rather than center stage.

Her best friend's outfit contrasted with Emily's worn, faded jeans, grey hoodie, black boots, and sensible, black pea coat. A silk scarf in shades of blue and gray which deepened the gray in her eyes, wrapped around her messy brunette updo, provided a hint of color. The two of them were like male and female birds. The brightly colored male eclipsing the drab female was how the two of them looked standing next to each other. Shrugging, Emily realized Kat was talking to her. She'd been having a hard time concentrating since the accident.

Eyes crinkling, a huge grin across her face, Kat snorted, "Seriously, earth to Emily. I promise to ask any ghosts we encounter to scare Charlie to death, just go on the tour with me, hon. Please?"

Kat could always make her laugh until she cried...heaven

knows she needed to giggle and have fun. They were spending two whole weeks in Scotland after Emily's last boyfriend, who was supposed to be The One, Charlie, a.k.a. the overgrown frat boy, almost killed her nearly three months ago.

"I am so over jerks treating women like disposable razors. Use one up; throw her away, on to the next." Blowing bangs out of her eyes, Emily huffed. "I've had it with guys pretending to be caring and sensitive when all they really want is to screw anything with two legs and a pulse."

The rat bastard was sexting Candy and driving while she herself was sitting right next to him in the passenger seat of the tiny BMW. What kind of a name was Candy anyway? Should have been the first clue. Some good friend she turned out to be. With friends like that who needs enemies? It happened so fast. One minute driving along, the next, Charlie lost control of the car, crashing into a tree. The car rolled on its side into the stream trapping her in the icy water.

The next thing Emily knew, she came to, screaming in the ambulance on the way to Mercy Hospital. Still couldn't believe she had been declared clinically dead for eight minutes before they revived her. Someone must have been watching over her. Gotta love modern medicine. Charlie was basically unharmed, sporting a few cuts and bruises. Emily suffered the worst of the accident, sustaining a broken leg, broken nose, a punctured lung, and broken rib along with numerous cuts from the tree branches. Rehab had gone well. Thank goodness she was healthy and healed quickly, though she still tired easily. The doctors told her it would take a few months before she was back to normal.

Glaring at two kilted men walking along High street, Emily crossed her arms over her chest. "Maybe I'll be an old, celibate spinster with lots of animals, spending my days scaring all the neighborhood kids. They can dare each other to ring my doorbell, which of course will be a creaking, falling down, spooky Victorian house."

"Celibacy? Seriously? Has to be the funniest thing I've heard all month!" Wiping tears out of her eyes, doubled over laughing, Kat tried to catch her breath.

Emily scowled, fiddling with the zipper of her hoodie. "Well, I could be all those things. I really, really need a break from men and all of the drama that goes along with them. Time to get my head together—be myself again. Did you hear trampy Candy actually found someone to marry her?"

Tripping over a cobblestone, Kat's mouth dropped open. "What? To whom?"

"She married some guy she met online. Apparently she was two-timing him with Charlie. They were hitched last month, she's already pregnant. Bet she doesn't even know who the father is."

"Well, at least you didn't invest any more time with him. Hell, think if you married him, he'd be screwing your friends. Except me; I like my men nerdy. That's why I married Fred. I mean, look at him, he's a real keeper. A certified public accountant, very down to earth, adores the ground I walk on. Most importantly of all, he accepts me for who I am—flaws and all. I don't ever have to worry about him. He'd forget to eat sometimes if I didn't remind him, I love his quirks. He's like an absent-minded brilliant professor. I know it's hard when someone we love, someone we think we'll spend the rest of our lives with betrays us, but Emily...not all men are like Charlie," Kat finished, hugging her best friend.

Linking her arm through Kat's, Emily smiled. "You're absolutely right. I'm done crying over that idiot. Let's go have fun."

She snorted as she thought of Kat's adorable bumbling husband. "Hey, Fred is a great guy even if you have to lay out his clothes and remind him he's still in his pajamas as he's leaving the house to meet with a client. You two are perfect for each other."

Looking at her watch, Emily pointed down the street. "OK, let's go check out the Close and Vaults. But no pretending some ghost is grabbing your coat just to hear me scream my head off."

Walking down High street, also known as the Royal Mile, Emily and Kat window shopped, enjoying the stores staying open late to celebrate Halloween weekend while making their way towards the tour.

"Wow! That's something you don't see every day." Kat pointed down the alleyway where a construction crew was working. A piece of pipe was being lowered into a hole in the street. The pipe itself was unremarkable; however the crew was quite remarkable as five of the seven men had on modern-day kilts with pockets to hold their gear along with hard hats and bright yellow vests.

"Seriously, if our construction crews at home looked like that, everyone would have a lovely day," Emily giggled, adding "of course the accent would be mandatory."

"Well sweetie, it doesn't hurt to look. Fred has a huge crush on those Victoria's Secret's models so I figure it's okay for me to appreciate the local scenery." Kat waggled her eyebrows while ogling the Scots as they walked down the street towards the meeting spot for the first tour.

Passing a building with gargoyles carved in the stone, Emily thought she saw something moving on the roof as the pale moon hid behind the clouds again. The drizzle had turned into a light rain, muffling the surrounding sounds. The smell of the stone, rain, and the early winter air made her think of a graveyard. Whispered on the wind, the words drifted to Emily. *Beware the Day Walker...he comes for you.* It was full dark, sinister, the revelers in the street doing nothing to dispel the sense of danger.

Passing the Spotted Hound pub, Emily turned to Kat, "Sorry, what was that about a Day Walker? What the heck is a Day Walker anyway?"

"Girl, I think the night air is going to your head. I didn't say anything. Maybe it was a bird."

Frowning, Emily looked around, but no one seemed to be paying them any attention. Reaching in her pocket, she pulled out the two small potato pies she'd been saving for a snack.

Throwing them to the dog sniffing around the alley, she was pleased when the pup gobbled them up, wagging its tail in appreciation. Pulling her coat tighter, she shivered as the icy wind blew through her. Shrugging, she told Kat, "OK, must have been voices carrying on the wind though it really sounded like a warning. Ugh. Don't look at me like that Katherine Chandler."

Squaring her shoulders, Emily glared at Kat, "Yes. I do believe in ghosts. There has to be more to this world than corporate life in some dreary gray cubicle. Just because we don't see it doesn't mean it doesn't exist. Anyway, we could be back in Charleston, going in to work tomorrow instead of traipsing around one of the most haunted cities in the world!"

"All right sweetie, I'll do anything but please don't talk about work. I'm coming back as a farmer in my next life. It has to be better than writing proposals. At least animals pretend to listen." Kat's horrified look had Emily sniggering. Still chuckling, they queued up to purchase their tickets.

Entering the Close, the tour guide motioned the group closer. The guide's name was Ian, and Emily thought listening to him read the phone book would be incredibly entertaining. She loved a Scottish accent—all those rolling r's and the soft burr, granted he did look a bit scruffy with his black hair over his ears and five o'clock shadow. He was wearing a kilt with a pocket for his cellphone, Doc Martens, and a Celtic t-shirt to complete his look. She had no idea if there was anything under the kilt.

"Mary King's Close is the most famous Close on the Royal Mile with over three hundred years of legends and ghost stories. You may very well encounter your own ghostie tonight. Did you know tomorrow is Samhain? It wasn't always called Halloween. 'Twas the night when wary travelers carved scary faces into pumpkins and placed candles inside them to light the way outside their homes for those unfortunate souls who had the misfortune to be out and about on such a terrible night. The lighted pumpkin lanterns were also to provide protection from any nearby evil spirits." Cackling in a goofy evil voice, Ian went on with his spiel.

Trying not to roll her eyes, Kat looked at her best friend who wore a look of skepticism on her face.

"It is said on October thirty-first, which is also the beginning of the spirit world new year, you can communicate with the spirits. The veil between the world of the living, and the world of the dead, is the thinnest during this time to allow spirits to cross over—both good and evil. Sometimes a spirit gets trapped in our world and can't get back or doesn't want to go back to their underworld. So be ye wary as we enter the Close for it might be a restless spirit who was trapped here last Samhain brushing against ye." Ian whispered, in a fake ominous tone, but frankly, Emily thought he sounded a bit bored, as if nothing exciting ever really happened.

Snickering quietly, Emily and Kat followed the group. A few tourists from Australia, in Scotland for their gap year, claimed to feel hands touching them and hear footsteps, but Emily didn't experience anything at all. She'd bet the Australians were tipsy, making it all up to scare each other. It was an interesting tour, but obviously if there were ghosts in the Close, they weren't making themselves known to her. Oh well, maybe at the South Bridge Vaults. The group left Mary King's Close and walked down the damp streets to the South Bridge Vaults talking animatedly about what kind of supernatural entities they might encounter during the next tour.

EXCITED TO HEAD OVER TO THE VAULTS, WHICH USED TO house all types of trades such as taverns, brothels, and other more illicit trades like smuggling and body snatching; she pushed her bangs out of her eyes and caught up to the group. "While excavating the Vaults, children's toys, dinner plates, buttons, and whisky bottles were found. 'Twas also a place of slum dwellers, prostitutes, and the infamous serial killers Burke and Hare, who sold bodies for gruesome medical experiments whilst prowling these very Vaults." The guide's low, menacing voice echoing off the stone walls made the hair on Emily's arms stand up—she unconsciously moved closer to the group.

Ian continued, clearly relishing the telling of the creepy tale. "Did you know, due to poor sanitary conditions and overcrowding, 'tis rumored the Black Death swept through Edinburgh and these very Vaults? Some of the inhabitants were walled up inside, still alive, never to be seen nor heard from again."

Emily looked around. "People used to live like this? It's bad enough being in an office all day but with no sunlight? And smelly and damp? Makes me okay with a boring, gray cubicle."

"No kidding. I think these rooms are bigger than my first apartment, but of course I didn't have ten plus people sharing my space or using my stuff." Kat shuddered.

"And no security system. Just robbers, murders and thieves... oh yeah, let's not forget the body snatchers. Maybe that's why everyone drank so much whisky, so they wouldn't care." She wrinkled her nose. "Why didn't people cart away the oyster shells after eating? The smell would have killed me. Imagine eating all those oysters. It would be like eating snot. Eww!" She and Kat cringed at the same time.

"I could use some smuggled whisky right about now. I'm freezing my ass off."

Kat raised her eyebrows, smirking, and pulled out a flask.

"I could kiss you for remembering to bring that. No wonder you're so cheerful. Hand it over," Emily demanded.

After a couple of healthy swigs, her cheeks were flushed; she felt the warmth emanating from her belly. Contented and warm, she wandered after their guide, Ian.

She wanted to listen but was lightheaded from the whisky, and her mind kept wandering to Charlie, the latest in a long line of failed romances. Maybe she was destined to live the rest of her life alone. She wondered was it too much to ask for a grown man who cared about her as much as he cared about himself? Whatever happened to the strong, silent types? Now every guy she met was in touch with his sensitive side, wanted to talk about his feelings but never hers, not to mention they all wanted the woman to support them, and owned more hair and skin care products than she did. Seriously, that was wrong on so many levels. Maybe a hot Scottish guy would come along, sweeping her off her feet. After all, they should fit the strong silent type, although with that yummy accent a little talking would be okay. Rolling her eyes, Emily mentally smacked herself deciding to stop thinking about guys that weren't right for her; she'd focus on enjoying the trip.

The sound of metal scraping on metal startled her. Looking up she realized she'd lost Kat along with the group around the corner while she was busy talking to herself.

This tour must have re-enactments. This is so much better than the tour of the Close. She eagerly headed towards the noise to get a better look.

Turning the corner, she skidded to a stop, gaping at the scene before her.

2

The scream dying in her throat, she chuckled; this was playacting, nothing to be afraid of.

Where the hell was everybody? Surely, they wouldn't have started the re-enactment without the group here to enjoy the spectacle.

She leaned against the wall, enjoying the show. Three men were fighting with swords. A flash caught her eye, and she leaned forward to get a better look. She wasn't any kind of expert, other than what she'd seen in the movies, but the play swords looked like honest-to-goodness real swords. With pointy tips.

Two of what she assumed were actors were dressed as English soldiers in full redcoat regalia including scarlet-red coats, white breeches, and black leather boots. Frowning, she noticed the uniforms looked well used, very authentic, although they had to look good to scare the tourists, right? Both men had a feral, uncivilized look about them. Wouldn't want to meet them in a dark alley.

The third man was the one who captured her full attention, causing her to stand up straighter, smoothing her hair with her hands. Dressed as the quintessential highlander in a kilt of blue, green, and black plaid, a white linen shirt with silver buttons, and laced at the top showing off a tantalizing swath of golden-tanned skin. He wore black leather boots and enough weaponry to make any solider drool. He was stunning. Inching closer to get a better look, words failed her. Graceful, lethal, dangerous, and fluid, not to mention sexier than any man had a right to be. Riveted to the spot she avidly watched the three men fight.

It didn't seem fair, two against one, though the highlander seemed to be holding his own quite well.

"Come on now, you bloody bugger, might as well be fighting my wee baby brother. Who taught you to fight —your little sister?" The highlander taunted his opponent.

Grunting, the black-haired, pockmarked English solider ground out, "Screw you Colin, my grandmother fights better than you, blasted piece of shite."

Sucking in her bottom lip, Emily's breath caught. He was a specimen to behold. And that accent was like a creamy, tasty caramel melting in her mouth.

The one called Colin had to be six foot five with a body chiseled from stone. Chestnut-brown hair with lighter streaks of honey glinted in the pale light of the Vaults. The faux torchlights threw eerie shadows onto the damp stone walls causing the shadows to dance across the walls seemingly alive. Colin's hair was down to his shoulders with a small braid on either side of his temple. His muscles flexed with each sword thrust as the men continued to fight while constantly insulting each other.

When Colin scowled at one of his attackers, she couldn't help but notice he had a strong, fierce face, all planes and angles. It was stark and masculine, marred by a scar that ran from his forehead, through part of his eyebrow, down his cheekbone and looked like it ended at his ear. Most men would look hideous by this attack on flesh; however on this man, the scar added to his appeal, though Emily imagined it would intimidate the hell out of most men. He had to be the most striking man she'd ever laid eyes on.

Note to self. Move to Scotland. If all men look like him, I'll die a happy woman.

Trying not to leer, her attention shifted to his thighs. She sucked in her breath sharply, rubbing her damp palms against her jeans, watching his thigh muscles ripple and flex as he parried and thrust with the sword.

The sword was an extension of his arm as he fought off both attackers. Mesmerized by the sight, Emily was rooted to the spot.

As the red-haired English soldier's sword flashed down and caught Colin on his arm, Emily swore the blade sliced through the sleeve of the white shirt.

But that wasn't possible, this was all for fun, wasn't it? The blood seemed real enough as a red stain appeared, stark crimson against the snowy white linen. Unaware of what she was doing, Emily moved closer. Maybe it was one of those fake blood capsules bought for Halloween—though it looked pretty darn realistic.

Catching movement from the corner of his eye, the black-haired solider turned towards Emily, a shocked look on his face; time stopped, an instant later he lunged for her.

Jumping back, falling on her ass, Emily screamed as the sword missed her ear by inches.

"What the hell? You could have sliced me to ribbons. Real swords, seriously? Here's a tip—use fake swords. It's not good to kill the tourists," she screeched.

Stalking towards her, the black-haired solider came at her, eyes narrowed, his blade aimed and ready to strike again.

Scrambling back on hands and feet until she bumped into the far wall, Emily was shaking violently. She froze, paralyzed like when she woke from a nightmare and couldn't move, so terrified the monsters would get her...all she could do was watch as he came closer. When he raised his sword, she cringed, shutting her eyes, hoping it was a hallucination and would therefore disappear, or if it was indeed real, it would be quick and painless.

Nothing happened. She heard a muffled thud, kind of like a sack of potatoes thrown against the wall.

Colin was stunned. The woman could see them; she shouldn't be able to, they were all invisible to any passersby. It was unheard of for anyone to be able to see them without one of their kind wishing it so. An uneasy sensation might brush against a human's consciousness causing them to hurry faster down the street trying to escape the darkness enveloping them. But usually they had no clue Shadow Walkers protected all of humanity from the Day Walkers who preyed upon them. If any human ran into a Day Walker, they rarely lived long enough to tell anyone about the encounter.

The woman cowering in the corner had to be a Yank from her speech. She had on jeans, a black coat, and boots, all of which hid her body. He idly wondered what she'd look like naked. Her long brown hair was laced with golden strands, pulled into a knot at the back of her head, showcasing a face so free of guile it would cause an angel to sin. Clear gray eyes were wide open with astonishment, the sprinkling of freckles across her nose had him instantly aroused.

Colin's jaw flexed, he pulled his lust under rein and threw the sorry excuse for a Day Walker against the wall before finishing him off.

He spared a look at the woman; she looked shell-shocked. Wouldn't have a clue the men dressed as soldiers were rotten Day Walkers. Good...her shock meant he wouldn't have to worry about her moving into the fray and facing harm.

He spun, blades clanging together in a macabre dance as Colin fought the dirty, black-haired Day Walker. With a vicious thrust of his sword Colin tore the soldier's still beating heart from his chest and crushed it in his fist. The soldier crumpled to the ground, exploding into gold dust.

Turning to the woman, to make sure she was OK, he wasn't paying attention when he saw her point.

"Look out!" She yelled, waving her arms.

Spinning around, he was a moment too late as the blasted redheaded idiot stabbed him in the thigh. Colin fell to one knee, muscles starting to spasm as pain lanced through his leg, the sword clattering to the uneven, stone floor.

The man stood over him to finish the deed, "Imagine, me killing the mighty Shadow Walker, Colin Campbell."

"Here, take it!" Heedless of her own safety, the woman had run into danger to hand him the blade he'd dropped. He was flabbergasted she would risk her life for him.

Colin spun the dirk around, thrusting it through the arrogant bastard's eye just in time to miss the sword aimed at his neck. Writhing on the ground, the pathetic excuse for a Day Walker raised his hands in a feeble attempt to fight back.

Pulling the serrated knife out of the man's eye, he stabbed the redhead, ripping his heart out. Like others of his kind, the man turned to gold dust and disappeared without a sound.

Someone was screaming. My God, what a horrific sound. Make it stop. It took a moment for Emily to realize it wasn't *someone*, it was *her* screaming and she couldn't seem to stop, replaying the horror behind her eyes over and over.

Tears streaming down her face, she didn't know what had possessed her to hand the breath-taking man the wicked-looking knife. Wrapping her arms around her knees, she curled into a ball wishing she could disappear into the wall. Her body wasn't listening to her brain; it was as if she was encased in cement.

Run. She kept screaming at herself, but her feet weren't listening.

Legs buckling, Emily fell trying to stand. Managing to slide herself up the wall, she waited a moment to steady herself. Instead of running away like a normal, sane person, she moved to check on the injured Scot the other man had called Colin.

Don't let him kill me. This is where the ditzy girl in the horror movie makes a stupid mistake like going upstairs to check on the noise and gets killed instead of running away out the front door to safety. Don't let me be that bimbo.

There was blood everywhere. Drops were hitting the grey-colored stone, dripping down his injured arm, out of his sleeve to pool on the ground.

Kneeling down, Emily realized he was enormous. He dwarfed her. Irrationally, she imagined his strong arms encircling her, holding and protecting her for all time.

"Oh my goodness! Are you okay? Please tell me this is all staged for tourists, and it's just really, really realistic-looking fake blood? I mean, I don't know what a heart looks like but that looked real to me. The special effects must be awfully expensive. How does the gold dust work? Is there some kind of trap door in the floor?" The man looked up at Emily with the most beautiful clear green eyes she'd ever seen. She put a hand up to her chest, dizziness threatening to overcome her.

"Lass, you're babbling. Side effect of being in shock. You need to leave; others will be here soon, they'll take you when they realize you can see us. I willna be able to protect you from them all," Colin rasped. His accent sent a shiver through her, as his deep, melodic voice snaked down her spine.

"What others? There's no one else here. What are you talking about? Let me get help." Emily started to rise but he stopped her with a hand on her arm. His hand was so big, easily encircling her arm, the calluses on his palm rough against her skin. No corporate-manicured, buffed hand on this one.

"Wait, why did you risk yourself to assist me?" He was puzzled.

Colin felt waves of fear rolling off the woman's body. Not knowing why he wanted to calm her, he hesitantly reached out, tucking a stray strand that had worked itself loose from her prim and proper bun behind her ear. She smelled of sunshine, fresh air, and peaches. He wanted to bury his nose in her neck. Inhale her scent. Gods, it had been so long...centuries...since he had wanted a woman. He ached to have this brave slip of a woman. It had been hundreds of years since he'd felt anything at all, save apathy, anger, and a tiredness which crept through his soul, threatening to destroy him.

The woman froze when he touched her. She looked like a frightened rabbit caught in the paws of a wolf, hoping if the rabbit didn't move, the wolf wouldn't eat her. "I...I don't know why. I just had to. I couldn't let that cretin kill you."

He was touched. Couldn't remember how long it had been since someone had helped him without expecting something in return. His interactions with women over the centuries had been limited to fulfilling a physical need. Women wanted the warmth of his body for a night, and he wanted release, no attachments. Never brought a woman to his home, never spent the night in one's bed. After they were both sated, he'd take his leave. What would it be like to wake up next to her?

"I thank ye for your help. 'Twas a brave thing to do." Running his finger down the side of her face, he tilted her chin, forcing her to look at him.

Colin knew he had to be careful not to steal any of her energy. Taking a human's energy was forbidden. It could instantly age or even kill the human. Shadow Walkers were forbidden from this, but Day Walkers, they preyed on humanity, and taking a human's energy made them stronger. Day Walkers had no care for human life, didn't live by the same rules, eager to kill as many humans as possible to increase their power. Once human themselves, Dayne, the god of light, chose them for how truly terrible they were as human beings. Day Walkers gladly embraced the immortal life, happily serving Dayne in his quest to destroy Shadow Walkers, to enslave humanity and rule the world.

"Don't fear me lass, I won't harm you. They call me Colin." He inclined his head to her.

❦

EMILY SNAPPED BACK TO AWARENESS. "EMILY. EMILY LAURENS, from Charleston, South Carolina." Never let it be said Emily Laurens didn't use her manners in any situation that could possibly arise, after all, she was Southern born and bred.

Her manners fled a moment later as anger set in at being set up. Bet Kat rigged all of this up with Ian in order to help her get over Charlie. She was going to let them have a piece of her mind. Smiling sweetly, fluttering her eyelashes, she twittered, "Of course, your name is Colin. You're some totally hot guy hired to make all the female tourists swoon so Ian gets a great tip and I forget jerk face Charlie. Let me guess, you also wear nothing under your kilt to make it even more enticing in case a breeze just happens to blow your skirt up?" Emily glowered up at Colin.

Smirking he leaned in, placing his hands on either side of her effectively pinning her to the wall as he studied her.

"Don't know who Ian and Charlie are and don't care. You think I'm 'totally hot' and you want a feel up my kilt? Be happy to oblige you, Emily the Yank from South Carolina." Colin let loose a very masculine, self-satisfied rumble.

Great. Her face burned with embarrassment and anger at falling for the joke. The words stuck in her throat, she couldn't think with him standing so close. She wanted something from him, something she couldn't put a name to. Watching his pupils dilate, the heat radiating from his body, she was prey to this dark, lethal hunter. In that moment time stopped, stretching until she thought she'd shatter into a million bits.

"One taste." Colin swore, leaning in to capture her lips.

Before she knew what was happening, Emily's knees gave out. She reached out, grasping Colin's biceps to keep from falling as she surrendered to the kiss.

Something was wet and sticky under her fingers. Breaking off the earth-shaking kiss, she raised bloody fingertips to her face. Oh, fake blood. A tangy, coppery smell hit her nose, her stomach heaved...ick...it was real blood...not fake.

"Somebody, please help, a man's been hurt. Please. Somebody. Hurry. Where the hell is everybody?" Emily unknotted the scarf wrapped around her bun, the long hair falling free, her hands shaking as she wrapped his arm to stop the bleeding. It was bad; the cut started at his bicep, went down his forearm ending at his wrist. It was gonna need a ton of stitches. A ripping noise startled her as Colin tore his other sleeve, tying it around his wounded leg.

"Lass, quiet, before you alert others to us. 'Twill heal soon enough, dinna fash yourself," Colin drawled.

As she started to protest; a crackling noise from the corridor stopped her.

"Thank goodness, help is coming," Emily said as she patted his bare thigh, careful not to touch the injury. The muscles flexed under her touch, solid like the ancient rock surrounding them.

"There's nothing you can do. This happens every bloody year." Colin blew out a sigh and grimaced, "It'll be over soon enough."

"It's about time," Emily raised her voice to be heard down the corridor.

"Leave. Me." Colin grasped her arms, lifting her to her feet as if she weighed no more than a bag of sugar.

Something strange was happening. The air started to swirl, sounding like a thunderstorm was in the room with them. The hair on Emily's arms stood up, the tingling of energy dancing across her skin as lightning flashed.

"What's going on! How can this be happening?" Her entire body was vibrating in response to the freak electrical storm.

Colin opened his mouth but no sound came out. The storm enveloped him. Reaching out for her, Emily shook her head at him in mute horror.

Voices. Shoulders slumping with relief, she turned to the approaching tour group.

"Hey, over here! Thank goodness you're here, this man needs help. He's been stabbed. Where in the hell have ya'll been?" Emily shouted at the tour group who stood goggling at her like she had three heads.

"Didn't you hear the storm? Can't you see him?" It was so quiet you could hear a pin drop. After a moment, she swore she heard giggling. Turning to point to Colin and the freaky storm, she was perplexed.

"What the hell?" Emily muttered.

She looked around frantically. There was no evidence of the storm or that anyone had been there—even the blood was gone. "Well folks, I guess one of our group has encountered a ghost or two." Ian's mouth was turned up in a gigantic grin as he moved closer to Emily.

"This isn't funny any longer. Stop pretending. You don't understand. Colin was really hurt. He needs stitches." Rubbing her temples, a headache started, throbbing behind her left eye.

Kat came over to put her arm around Emily. "Honey, we've only been separated a few minutes. What are you talking about? Did you fall and hit your head?"

"No joking around anymore, okay? Tell me if you and Ian had the re-enactors scare me. I get it, you want to take my mind off Charlie, but enough is enough. There were swords, fighting, lots of blood, a crazy, freak electrical storm inside, and disappearing people." Emily turned around pointing to where the insanity had taken place right before her very eyes. It was as if none of it had ever happened.

"I swear. There were three men fighting with swords. One gravely injured. Two of them died right in front of me. Then a freak storm came out of nowhere and Colin disappeared!" Emily's face was red from shouting, sides heaving, hands clenched into fists.

Kat nervously laughed. "Maybe that second glass of wine instead of dinner or those nips of whisky were a bad idea. Your imagination is playing tricks. Bet it's how they keep the tourists coming back, I swear, I didn't have anything to do with it."

The group whispered and chuckled, talking about the 'crazy American'. Emily let Kat lead her out of the Vaults into the night.

Let them laugh. She knew what she had seen. Would figure out how they vanished. The hell if she was going crazy like aunt LouAnne.

"COME ON, LET'S GET YOU BACK TO THE HOTEL. IT'S LATE; WE both could use a good night's sleep." Kat linked her arm through Emily's.

"Do you think I'm losing it?" Her voice trembled. Quickly brushing a tear away, she avoided looking at Kat, dreading the answer.

"Sweetie, you're one of the strongest people I know, but I'm a little worried. You've been different since the 'Charlie incident', which is to be expected, but I think there's something else bothering you. Look, normally we discuss *everything* ad nauseam but you won't talk to me about the accident or your recovery. It isn't healthy to keep your feelings bottled up inside." Kat stopped her with a hand on her arm, forcing Emily to look at her.

Blowing out a heavy sigh, she hugged Kat. "When I came... back. Being lost for eight minutes, it's difficult to describe exactly what I experienced. I haven't talked about the aftermath because I'm still trying to understand it all. We've talked about Charlie for a thousand hours, it isn't him, it's so hard to explain. I feel like on some deep level of my being, I'm different now, and I just want to figure out who I am and what I'm supposed to learn or do. There has to be a reason I was brought back. Bear with me, and we'll get through it. I'll be okay, don't worry." She hugged Kat and wiped the tears from her eyes. She wasn't ready to talk about the vision or dream, whatever it was called. It was too personal; she wasn't sure if she could share it with anyone, ever.

Reaching into her coat pocket for a tissue and lip gloss, Emily's fingers brushed something cold. Pulling her hand out of her pocket to see what it was, she opened her hand and squinted in the dim light of the streetlamps.

In the center of her palm was a silver button.

Looking at it closely, she could see some type of raised crest.

It couldn't be. This looked exactly like the ones on the shirt of that guy in the Vaults—Colin. How was that possible? But the button proved it. Emily had no idea how he pulled the disappearing stunt, but at least she was certain he was real.

Reassured, she hid the proof from Kat, putting it back in her pocket, vowing to learn whatever she could about the mysterious, sexy Colin and may the stars help him when she found him. She'd give him a piece of her mind for scaring her so badly she almost had a heart attack.

Squaring her shoulders, Emily marched down the street towards the hotel. A niggling thought made her stumble almost dropping the lip gloss she'd pulled out of her pocket. What if it wasn't a joke and something else was going on here? What if he really needed her help?

Find him. Get answers.

"I need a drink to calm my nerves. Let's stop in the lobby bar for a nightcap." Emily snapped her lip gloss shut.

"We might want to cancel our early-morning wakeup call; we

could both use the extra sleep. The circles under your eyes look like bruises. It's been a crazy night, so one drink then off to bed, everything will look better in the morning, I promise." Kat patted her arm.

Lost in thought, Emily didn't notice a man standing in the dimly lit doorway of the pub they passed.

RAWLINS WATCHED HER, HIS HEAD TILTED TO THE SIDE, considering, eyes gleaming with malice.

His men told him of the fight with Colin, how this woman could see them when they had made themselves invisible. Which meant she had died and come back. Captain Rawlins Huntington, formerly of Her Majesty's army, now a Day Walker in the service of Dayne, had heard of people with this ability. It was rumored they had a gift to somehow help Shadow Walkers. There was talk of a curse shrouded in mystery. He'd investigate; see what he could find out. If there was merit to this...possibilities swirled in his mind. His enemy was made up of fierce warriors and he'd be damned if a pathetic human would help one of them.

This was war. The fewer of those shadowy bastards to contend with the better.

Shadow Walkers guarded their secrets zealously, those arrogant assholes, thinking they were above them all simply because those sanctimonious bastards were charged with keeping the balance between light and dark in the world. No fun in that; it was much more amusing to kill the pathetic humans than to protect them.

Walkers were like gods—meant to rule the world. The strong always overcome the weak; the weak meant to serve. The corner of his mouth lifted in a small semblance of a smile. The woman would be a bonus. He was going to kill her. If there was anything to this curse business he'd ensure she couldn't help Colin. And if there wasn't, well, he'd enjoy taking her energy watching her scream as she died. He'd send one of his men to keep an eye on the woman and to kill the friend so he could personally deal with this nuisance.

3

Later that night, stalking through the World's End pub, Rawlins sneered at the pathetic humans scrambling to move out of his way.

He needed a drink, a human to drain, and a good lay, not necessarily in that order.

His man Jackson hadn't found anything of use at the women's hotel other than their names and they were visiting from America on holiday. He was in a foul mood. At least Jackson used his phone to search the web and discovered the one called Emily, had died in an accident before being brought back. Rawlins was right; this Emily Laurens could indeed be the Cursebreaker, if there even was a bloody curse—you had to love modern-day technology.

Sipping a twenty-year-old single-malt whisky, he scanned the pub. Several females were darting glances at him. At six foot three, he was taller than most men, with broad shoulders show-casing a heavily muscled body honed from years of sword work. Rawlins projected a deadly aura that had most men cutting a wide path around him wherever he went, while drawing women to him like bees to honey. Short, dirty blond hair cropped close to his head framed brown eyes so dark they usually looked black.

Lounging on the bar stool, he loved modern-day fashion, no more uniforms for him, he preferred designer all the way. Tonight he was dressed in a black Armani t-shirt, Marc Jacobs black leather jacket, jeans, and black motorcycle boots; he was a predator surveying prey before striking.

The pub was larger than it looked from the outside with the inside divided into the eating area and the bar. The dark paneling, leather chairs, and stone walls gave it an old-world flavor. The tourists flocked to this place. It hadn't changed since he'd been stationed here in Edinburgh over four hundred years ago. Rawlins remembered fighting at Flodden Wall. Part of the wall was incorporated into the pub's foundations, a section of which used to be part of Old Town's defenses. Of course at the time, the pub was barely a ramshackle building serving soldiers alongside all kinds of riffraff and other infamous clientele.

Letting his eyes wander over the patrons of the pub, Rawlins scanned the crowd for a delicious female or two to satisfy his hunger. His eyes came to rest on two redheads sitting in a booth in a dark corner of the pub, their heads close together whispering about what they'd like to do to him. Dressed casually, they looked like college kids on holiday, ready to celebrate Halloween, enjoying the weekend without a care in those pretty heads.

Lust coursed through him as he listened to their conversation. All Walkers had preternatural hearing. He could hear every conversation in the pub. Rawlins would take energy where he could get it but especially liked human females, Americans were even better—always so willing, their aggressive energy tasting like a glass of strong ale.

"May I buy you lovely ladies a drink on this festive eve?"

"Oh my, you're English not Scottish." The redhead with brown eyes twittered. Her friend had blue eyes and wasn't a natural redhead, not that he cared. She chimed in giggling, "Her name's Marci, and I'm Mindy. We love foreign accents." Slightly bowing to them, Rawlins leaned in close, "Then let me whisper sweet nothings in your ears milady's."

Marci grabbed him by his jacket and started kissing him, pressing her body against his. He wanted to take her there in the pub, but it wouldn't do to draw too much attention.

The scent of electricity filled the air as Rawlins started to take the human's energy. To the casual observer, it would look like the couple was merely kissing, the woman turned on, limp in his arms. If anyone listened closely enough, they would hear a low-level hum, the same noise heard near large electrical lines. The noise of the pub and stale scent of beer, sweaty bodies, and greasy food covered what was happening. Looking closer, a shimmer radiated between the couple like a mirage on the pavement during a hot summer day.

The kiss turned deadly as Rawlins sucked her energy life-force into him. If he was careful, he would age the human a few years, not enough to be noticeable other than her looking tired. However, a taste whetted the appetites; he would take it all. As the air hummed and shimmered, the girl's appearance began to change. The dark interior would hide anything amiss from curious eyes. If anyone did notice, it would be chalked up to one too many drinks. As Rawlins took her life-force his pulse hammered, blood coursing through his veins, energy building to a crescendo, making him stronger, energy filling body and soul.

Marci's skin began to change, becoming thin as paper, mottled with age spots, dull and leathery. Inside her organs aged, slowed down, and started to fail. Her hair began to turn, the gray flowing down her once-red hair like a rock landslide, until it was completely white. The skin on her face began to sag, wrinkle, and show sun damage. Once taut, young, flawless skin was now old beyond recognition, her lips cracking, thinning, and losing their youthful fullness as her energy life-force seeped from her. He took it all, dispassionately watching her youth and beauty fade like a summer green leaf, now brittle and worn by the passage of time, crackling to dust. Gasping her final breath, feebly trying to pull away, Marci's heart slowed and pumped no more. Going limp, he supported her weight, easing her down on the banquette next to them. Any who happened to walk by would simply note a woman who'd had too much to drink, passed out in the corner. The darkness would conceal the theft.

"Is Marci OK?" Mindy asked, slurring her words.

"She's fine, bit much to drink, she's resting. Now come here luv and give us a kiss," Rawlins purred.

With a bleary smile, Mindy wrapped her arms around his neck. The air around them shimmered with energy and life, seeming to pulse in the air around them as Rawlins finished her off. Placing her next to her friend, the two of them looked like grandmothers, out for a pint at the pub, albeit dressed in college sweatshirts and jeans.

To other humans, it would appear they'd had a heart attack. It wasn't as if there was a checkbox listed on the police report for causes of death that stated "deceased's life-force drained dry."

Sated, content, humming with energy and power, he turned back to the bar to order another whisky.

FINISHING OFF HIS COFFEE, MONROE MACDONALD HEARD HIS police radio crackle. It was a little after eleven o'clock, he should be off shift; however, he didn't sleep much anymore. This close to Halloween there were bound to be altercations, drunken brawls, assaults, you name it, and plenty of crimes committed. Throw in clueless tourists wandering the streets, and it was a recipe for long hours for the entire force.

Was today That Day all over again? He had a bad feeling, twisting his gut into knots. Hell no, he wasn't going there right now. Shut the fucking door in his head, throw away the damn key. Someday he'd revisit that bloody scene, Alice's lifeless body lying in the remains of St Anthony's chapel within Holyrood Park. One day he'd find out who killed her and why, but today was not that day. Today he had a job to do.

Monroe responded to the call. Hell, he could use a couple of dead bodies to distract him tonight. The thoughts eating his brain wouldn't do any good other than causing him to down a bottle of whisky, ending up with a bitch of a hangover in the morning.

A police officer for more than ten years, he loved the city. Born in Glasgow, his widowed mom moved them when he was in primary school. While he loved his birthplace and cheering on Celtic, he knew Edinburgh like a lover knows the scent of their beloved.

All of her imperfections and flaws. He knew them all and carried a deep-seated need to protect his city.

Scotland, like England and Ireland, relied heavily on cameras for security and keeping an eye on its citizenry. Looking around, he noted the pub conveniently didn't have any cameras. There was one hanging by a frayed cord, useless. Sighing, he shoved his hands through his hair in frustration, stalking inside the pub to the crime scene.

An officer approached the taped off area of the pub. "The medical examiner's here, Shamus. You and Monroe ready for him?"

"In a minute mate, Monroe needs a few." Shamus turned to Monroe. "The ME's here, finish it up. You know that dobber Fergus will have your ass in a sling if you muck about with his body."

Monroe jerked his head at his partner to show he'd heard and went back to studying the scene. He'd talked to the wait staff and numerous patrons. No one remembered seeing the women come in or serving them. It had been a busy night; the match was on the telly so most folks eyes were glued to the screens. A tourist on his way to the bathroom called it in. The guy noticed one of the women was wearing a UCLA sweatshirt, his alma matter. When he'd stopped to say hello, he saw they were dead. The guy didn't notice anyone with them.

"Thank you all for your time. Make sure the officer has your name and where you can be reached if we have further questions.

You can go." What a waste of time. He scowled. Not just one dead grandmother, two. Yanks by looking at them. They were propped up against the banquette as if resting. What was it with Yanks dressing decades younger than they were? He couldn't fathom why you'd want to dress like you were twenty when eighty was fast approaching in your headlights, but hell, what did he know? He was lucky if he remembered to shave and put on clean clothes in the morning.

Approaching the vics, his heart started pounding, beating out of his chest, as his nose picked up a long-forgotten scent, waking the animalistic part of his brain, causing it to sit up, sniff the air and roar in fury.

That smell. Monroe would never forget the unmistakable scent. Burnt into his brain, imprinted into his nostrils, seared into every fiber of his being. This particular scent could only be described as sex in the morning overlaid with something burnt, sickeningly sweet. Not leaves or wood, almost the smell of an electrical fire but not quite. This was something darker, *evil*.

Evil electricity? I must be losing my bloody mind.

Putting his shaking hand against the wall, Monroe took deep breaths trying not to pass the hell out. This scent was exactly the same as what he'd smelled finding Alice murdered on That Day. How many killers smell like energy? It had to be the same bloody bastard. He'd be damned to hell and back before he let the prick get away again.

How he could have forgotten...didn't matter it had been ten years, the smell was as fresh in his mind as if only a moment passed.

"Oy, earth to Monroe. What the hell, mate? You know this bird?" his partner, Shamus asked him. "You look like you've seen a ghost."

He had no bloody idea.

"Naw, I'm pure brilliant. Bad curry at lunch or something." Monroe pushed away from the wall and bent over the bodies without touching anything. The suits got their panties in a wad over that sort of thing, he bent to the hair. Why, when they were dressed so young, wouldn't they dye their hair? Maybe white was in fashion. He didn't know or keep up with the latest in women's hair and fashion; after all, he wasn't some navel-gazing emo ass. Still, something was eating at his brain; he was missing something important; it kept sliding around, slightly out of reach, if only he could remember.

Shamus kicked Monroe with his boot. "Let's go. Some Yanks at the Balmoral had their room ransacked and we're closest, I told dispatch we'd take it even though we're homicide not robbery."

Monroe nodded. There was nothing for him at home. The longer the day, the better in his book. His pathetic apartment was breeding dust bunnies, he'd run out of clean dishes since he never bothered to wash what was in the sink. Murder, robbery... all he needed was a nice assault to finish out the night. Then maybe he could grab a decent few hours' sleep without the nightmares. Starting to rise, he stopped dead. There...amongst the white hair, coated on her earring...was the clue he'd been looking for these past ten years.

4

"Let's head up to the room, order some tea, and relax by the fire, I'm exhausted." Kat yawned, watching Emily.

Seriously, Kat was looking at her like she was some kind of rare, exotic bird about to fly away or as if she might run screaming from the room at any moment—well, it was a possibility. Emily sighed, "Really, I'm perfectly fine, the drink helped calm my nerves. I know what I saw. If it was a joke, then it's not very nice. The blood looked awfully realistic. That guy was hurt. There's something weird going on."

"There's no such thing as ghosts. Odd phenomenon is almost always explained by science. I wish fairytales were real too, goodness knows I could use a fairy godmother but I'm worried about you."

"Well, that guy may not have been a 'ghost' but you have to admit it was strange."

Kat shook her head. "Absolutely, it was odd, but don't let it mess with your head. That's all I'm asking."

The sting of Kat's words was taken away by her smile, and Emily knew she was silly for believing in fairytales. But if she gave up believing then it would be like admitting there was nothing else out there, which simply was not acceptable.

"All I want to do is take a bubble bath in that amazing claw foot tub, sip a cup of tea and chill."

"Sounds like heaven." Emily groaned, thinking of soaking in the gigantic tub, allowing the hot water to ease her sore muscles. Their room boasted a large, real fireplace, not one of those gas imitations they had at home, the sitting rooms gave off a cozy atmosphere with the plush velvet chairs positioned in front of the fire. From the sitting room there were two doors each leading to a bedroom decorated in deep indigo for her and burgundy for Kat. The bathroom décor matched the bedroom. The modern furnishings in the old building complemented each other. They had splurged, using all of their airline miles. Since they both traveled quite a bit for work, they had saved up a boatload of miles...might as well use them for first-class tickets and a five-star hotel. After all, this was a once-in-a-lifetime dream trip.

Entering the room they stopped dead on the threshold, mouths agape. The room had been ransacked. While the fire crackled merrily, the rest of the room looked like a tornado had come through. Cushions were tossed on the floor, chairs overturned, all the lovely modern sculptures smashed into pieces, ground into the plush carpeting. The doors to their bedrooms were wide open. Through the open doorways you could see clothing thrown all over the room, dresser drawers tossed with abandon onto the floor, the bathroom mirrors shattered, and toiletries scattered on counter.

Calling the front desk to report the break-in, Emily saw the worried glance Kat couldn't hide. "Don't flip out, I'm fine. What's one more crazy thing to cap off our drama-filled day?" A discreet knock at the door interrupted her.

"Mrs. Chandler, on behalf of the Balmoral hotel, we are dreadfully sorry. The authorities are on their way. Another room is being made ready. The room is one of our larger suites. Complimentary during your stay with us. Please accept our apologies for this dreadful unpleasantness." The hotel night manager wrung his hands, fretfully looking around at the extensive damage to the once-elegant room.

A smart rap on the door was followed by the bell hop ushering in two uniformed police officers. "Pardon me, Officer Monroe MacDonald and Officer Shamus O'Malley have arrived."

"Please show them in." Standing in the center of the room, Emily watched the officers walk around the room. The one named Shamus was short and stocky with brown hair and eyes. His nose looked like it had been broken more than once. Other than that, he had clean-cut features. He was frowning as he noted the damage.

"Monroe, you notice anything odd about this? Can't put my finger on it but something's off."

Walking around the room, Emily could see the one called Monroe didn't miss anything as he took in the chaos. Clearing his throat, Monroe addressed Kat, "Ma'am is anything missing?"

"That's just it officer, nothing is missing, not my jewelry, iPhone, or anything. It's rather strange, isn't it?"

Kat wrinkled her nose, "Maybe the thief was startled and ran away before he could take anything. Who knows? We just want to move to a new room, get a good night's sleep and put this unpleasantness behind us."

Pacing around the room, Emily's skin itched, stretched too tight across her back. Everything was off. She couldn't stay still as she walked in circles in front of the fireplace, trying not to step on pottery shards, thinking. Very strange things had been happening since the accident. At the time, she'd chalked them up to the trauma and drama of everything, but now...she wasn't so sure. She watched Monroe as he looked around their room talking to Kat. He had golden-blond hair and turquoise blue eyes that were at odds with his gruff voice, and a big screw-you attitude. The guy was big, maybe six-two if she had to guess. How strange the face of an angel was attached to a body that screamed big bad wolf. This guy would probably prefer to punch first, ask questions later. She took a step back from him. He must've had women lining up for a night with him. The combination of a pretty face and bad boy aura would draw every woman across Great Britain to his bed.

"Are you missing anything, Miss...?" Monroe glanced at his notes.

A dimple appeared in his left cheek when he was concentrating. It had a devastating effect on his face...forget the face of an angel; try the face of some long-forgotten god of old. Emily grinned, thinking he would hate being called attractive. There was something rough and ready about this man. Incredibly attractive, but while she could appreciate a gorgeous man, he didn't do it for her. Rather like admiring a beautiful painting or sculpture—because you admired it didn't mean you wanted it. Nope, a certain Scotsman named Colin did it for her.

"Ah, Miss Laurens," he said, finding his notes. Moving closer to her, he approached like he was walking on eggshells, worried she'd break down in hysterics.

Rolling her eyes she told him, "Please, call me Emily. No, nothing is missing. Why would someone ransack our room then not steal anything?" Taking her hand out of her pocket to tuck her hair behind her ear, she felt like a guilty teenager lying to her parents.

Monroe's pleasant, bored expression changed in an instant, darkening, sending a momentary fission of fear through her as he caught sight of her clothing. "Miss Laurens, why is there blood on your shirt and a rip in your jeans? Have you been injured?"

"Um...well...oh. We were on a tour earlier of the South Bridge Vaults, and I fell. Guess that's how I tore my jeans." Cutting her eyes to Kat, she gave her a look, warning her not to say anything.

Crossing her fingers behind her back, she told him this lie, backing up a step as he narrowed his eyes.

"Miss Laurens, I don't see any blood on your knee through the rip in your jeans so I'll ask again, how did you end up with blood spattered across your shirt? Looks like you were too close to a knife fight and caught the blood spatter as someone was stabbed. That about right?"

Stalling to come up with an answer, Emily could tell he'd had it with her. His words punched out like a hammer hitting nails. "Did. Someone. Hurt. You?"

Pulling a chair upright, Monroe practically pushed her down as he examined the rip in her jeans, face red, hand clenched at his side. "Miss Laurens, some jerks think it's OK to hurt a woman. I've seen it a hundred times. A woman goes on a date, things get rough, the dickhead hits her." She watched him struggle to stomp his temper down while he scowled at her.

Her mind was a big fat blank. She couldn't think of anything to tell him that sounded remotely reasonable.

In a low tone, Monroe actually growled at her, he was such a friggin' savage.

"Tell. Me. Now."

"Officer! That's quite enough." Coming out of her room, Kat reprimanded him. "Emily's had a trying day as have I. This has gone on long enough."

Monroe didn't acknowledge Kat. Just sat there staring at her. Eyes drilling into her, searching for answers.

"Kat, it's okay. I'll tell him what happened. Go ahead and pack." Feeling her face heat up, Emily tried not to break down and cry. *Please, not in front of him. Get me though this; I swear I'll never eat another brownie again.*

"Fine. You won't believe me anyway." She crossed her arms over her chest, glaring up defiantly at him, curled up in the chair as if the flimsy wood could protect her.

Leaving out the voice she'd heard on High Street, warning her of something called 'Day Walkers', she told him what happened in the Vaults with the men, fighting, ripping hearts out of chests, gold dust, and the disappearing.

"The entire tour group laughed at me...teased me about seeing ghosts, but I know what I saw. Are you going to laugh at me too?" Bracing herself for laughter, she looked up at Monroe through her eyelashes.

He was quiet, too quiet. She leaned up from her chair to get a closer look at Monroe. He was as white as a ghost. There was a fine sheen of sweat on his face.

What exactly did he know?

"I'm not laughing at you, though you must admit it's a rather difficult story to believe, not to mention you admit you had been drinking. Our eyes play tricks on us sometimes, especially when there's poor lighting. You'd already been thinking about ghosts so it's not implausible your mind would make something up..." Monroe started to continue when Emily jumped to her feet, hand out in front of her to stop him from talking.

"...so you saw what you wanted to see," he looked at her open-mouthed.

Indignant, she came to a stop inches from him, poking him in the chest and raising her voice, "Oh no, don't you patronize me, buddy. I'm going to find this man and get to the bottom of this."

"Please let me finish, Miss Laurens. I do believe something happened. This is a promise: I will find out what's going on. Some sick bastard won't get away with running around slicing people up in my city. You, Miss Laurens, will do no such investigating. Leave this to the authorities. Do you hear me?"

Gah, he was so demanding. She'd tell him whatever he wanted to hear, and then she'd do what she wanted, like she always did.

"Fine. We have sightseeing to do anyway. I'm tired, are we done here?" She sniffed.

"Shamus? Let's go. Mrs. Chandler, Miss. Laurens, terribly sorry for the break-in. We'll file a report and let you know if we find the idiot who did this. It was most likely university kids engaging in pre-Halloween pranks." Monroe nodded to both women, leaving his card with them in case they remembered anything else.

5

Saturday, October 31st

Emily yawned, "Did you sleep OK? I kept dreaming someone broke into our room to steal our shoes and purses. Then I was dreaming about trick-or-treating. Do you remember when we were five—I was a fairy princess and you were a box of cereal? I think we snagged the biggest haul of candy ever that year. Then the raccoon I rescued from the neighbor's dog ate it all. In my dream, the raccoon went trick-or-treating with us. Bizarre right?"

"I slept like a baby, crazy I know. We've gotta have a calmer day than yesterday. No more break-ins or drama." Kat looked over to see what other patrons in the parlor were having before turning her attention back to the menu and deciding on an omelet.

"Hmmm...think I'll have Earl Grey Tea and the porridge with whisky. After all, a girl's gotta fortify herself against the cold. At least we can say yesterday was exciting. Anyway, the Close was okay, but I thought the Vaults were really interesting. Can you imagine having to live like those poor people or being walled up alive?" Emily shuddered, wrinkling her nose.

Kat looked up from her plate, "By the way, I think someone had a little too much to drink last night, you lightweight."

Emily started coughing as tea came out of her nose, "I was not drunk Katherine Anne Chandler. I know what I saw. Colin was real."

"Oh, Colin is it? What, ya'll have a date for coffee later today?"

Kat had been her best friend since Emily was five, but sometimes she could be so snarky Emily wanted to wring her pretty neck.

"Snicker all you like but I'm going to find out more about him. If he's some re-enactment guy trying to scare me, he's getting a piece of my mind—he will bleed, for real this time. That was soo not funny." Emily made a face at Kat, and they both burst out laughing.

"Should we hit the museum today? I heard they have some fantastic abstract paintings, and it will keep our minds off of everything that's happened."

"Only if we can take the midnight tour of Edinburgh Castle tonight," Emily pleaded.

"Fine, but first, we're going back to the Vaults to find out who the re-enactors are, then we're tracking down Colin so you can see he's just some scruffy Scottish guy in a kilt. Not a ghost, and he won't have an injured arm. Then we're off to the museum, a nap, followed by a quiet dinner, ending with your midnight Halloween tour." Kat finished her omelet while Emily snorted.

"What's so funny?"

"You are so bossy, not to mention, I think you forgot lunch in our busy schedule." Emily giggled.

Sniffing, Kat paid the bill as they headed out to enjoy the gray day.

TURNING ONTO HIGH STREET, THEY FOUND THE TOUR GUIDE, Ian, in the ticket booth adding up figures on an old-school calculator.

"Excuse me? We were here last night and wanted to find out who the re-enactors were. They were really good," Kat said.

Ian scratched his head, a puzzled look on his face. "We don't use re-enactors on the tours." His face brightening, he said "I remember you two. You encountered the ghosts."

"No, this guy's name was Colin; he was in a kilt, black boots, and white shirt. He was with two other guys dressed as English soldiers with the redcoats and swords?" Emily pressed.

"No lassie, you musta seen a ghostie. You are right lucky, not many see three ghosts at once." Ian sounded wistful, Emily wanted to smack him, but he seemed sincere about there not being any re-enactors so she and Kat would have to figure out who Colin was on their own.

"Thanks for your time." Kat told him, pulling Emily away.

"Wait, tell me more about what you saw, I've been working here for two years, have never seen an actual ghost materialize, let alone fight in front of me, it must have been brilliant," Ian begged.

"Another time, we're on a very busy schedule today, and it's about to storm, bye," Kat tossed over her shoulder as they left.

Rolling her shoulders, Emily looked around her. Someone was watching them. A malevolent wind swirled around them, picking up her scarf, blowing her hair into her eyes. Lightning blazed across the sky causing the hair on her arms to stand up. The air crackled and hummed with electricity. Her gaze was drawn to a darkened doorway. A shadowy figure moved, startling her. Jumping at the sound of thunder, Emily looked to the doorway again...the shadow vanished.

WANDERING THROUGH THE MUSEUM, KAT SPENT HOURS soaking up the abstract paintings while Emily wandered aimlessly; stopping to look at whatever caught her eye. She loved Rodin and the Impressionists but didn't really get the dreary, dark paintings depicting dead animals or people screaming in torment.

Who would want this gruesome stuff on their walls? If there's art hanging on my walls, it's got to be cheery and beautiful, not full of angst and sorrow, the world is harsh enough.

Planning to quickly get through the depressing hallway she headed for the next gallery depicting Scottish history as the lights blinked on and off—must be the approaching storm. She moved on, skirting a tour taking place, wandering amongst the art, half listening to the guide. Approaching the end of the gallery, Emily tripped and landed in front of...HIM!

"Miss, are you alright?" the guide helped her up, and after making sure she was okay resumed her spiel.

Emily couldn't believe it. Moving closer, she read the information placed next to the painting of the guy from the Vaults.

"He was quite the handsome devil, wasn't he? Come closer everyone. This particular painting was done in the mid-1600s. It depicts a baron at his castle, Ravensmore, situated in the Highlands of Scotland. Lord Colin Campbell restored the gardens. He was ahead of his time, utilizing many existing early Roman features to provide the castle with running water, steam heat, and bathing chambers. What's notable is the baron, it was rumored, liked to partake in a bit of harmless smuggling in order to finance the costly renovations to the castle. Unfortunately, he was caught, tried, and convicted of smuggling.

"During his imprisonment in Edinburgh Castle, he allegedly was murdered by his younger brother, Hamish, for besmirching the family name, while awaiting his death sentence. Taking the title, Lord Hamish, went on to marry Colin's fiancée, Abigail, and is rumored the two were carrying on a torrid affair during the time she was engaged to Colin. Hamish's second castle,

Castle Gloom, mysteriously burned, killing Lord Hamish while Abigail was away visiting relatives. 'Tis said Ravensmore and Edinburgh Castle are haunted to this day by Lord Colin's ghost. He died without producing an heir, and the castle was sold numerous times before a distant relative purchased it and restored it. It's privately owned now but is supposed to be quite lovely. Well folks, that's all for the tour, there are some nice trinkets available in the gift shop."

Emily couldn't breathe; trembling, she backed up, reaching for the bench to sit down before she fell over. She was looking up at *him*. Even more breathtaking in the painting than she remembered from the night before. Feeling dizzy, she sat, lost in thought staring at Colin until Kat found her.

"Hey, I wondered where you wandered off to. Are you all right? Whoa. You're pale as a ghost, looks like you're going to throw up or something. Maybe you shouldn't have had whiskey in your porridge for breakfast."

"Kat, it's Colin," Emily rasped.

"Who? Hey, you're shaking. Put your head between your knees and breathe. They'll probably throw us out if you get sick. Kat fussed.

"Colin, from last night. The guy who was fighting and got hurt," Emily stammered.

"The guy in the painting. Is the same guy you saw fighting. Last night in the Vaults?" Speaking very slowly, Emily heard the skepticism in Kat's voice.

"I swear it was him. Why could I see him and no one else could? Why didn't you all hear the noise?" Emily was puzzled.

"Oh honey, I don't know, maybe it has something to do with what happened to you." Kat sat next to Emily. "I'm not saying I believe you saw a ghost, but you obviously saw something. I'm trying here, sweetie."

Putting her head in her hands, Emily was taken back to that awful day. *I remember falling into darkness, then being in a long dimly lit hallway filled with different-colored doors. The gold door was locked;*

she hoped it wasn't the door to heaven keeping her out. Looking around, happy a red door wasn't open since that might be hell, she tried the blue door. It swung open onto a peaceful forest. She walked for a while coming to a waterfall surrounded by a small pool ringed by majestic Oak trees. Sitting on a rock overlooking the pond; she was at peace. Content to stay there forever, listening to the music of the wind blowing through the trees, the birds singing, bees happily buzzing around the flowers, and the tinkling of water over rocks, as if the very water itself was singing with joy.

A woman appeared out of the mist on the water. Ethereal. It was the only word to describe her. Moving towards her, she could see the woman had long silver sparkling hair, bare feet and was dressed in a simple white gown made of some kind of diaphanous material. Incredibly beautiful and serene, it was hard to tell her age. Her face kept changing from young to old. Emily couldn't remember anything other than the woman telling her she was the goddess Terya, mother of the Earth and mother to the old, forgotten gods. Terya told her it wasn't her time yet, she had to go back and do...something. The thought teased her, flitting away whenever she tried to remember what it was she had to do. If she could only remember... What she did remember was the goddess telling her she would be forever changed, able to see those who hadn't or couldn't move on, one foot forever in Shadow.

The next thing she remembered was coming to in a brightly lit hospital, screaming. Later as she was leaving, she decided it was all a hallucination brought on by the accident. Goddesses and gods didn't exist anymore, no matter how much she might have wanted them to.

Pulled back to the present by the sound of Kat's voice; Emily told her, "He wasn't a ghost. I touched him; it was his blood on my shirt. I wasn't going to show this to you..." Pulling a button out of her pocket, Emily handed it to Kat. "From his shirt." Gesturing to the painting, "Matches the ones on his shirt exactly."

Kat frowned as she looked from the button to the painting on the wall. "They do look alike but it could be a popular design.

I wouldn't put much stock in it, bet you can find these in every store in town.

"I need to go to Edinburgh Castle, then to Ravensmore. Ravensmore is supposed to be lovely; we can spend a couple of days there."

"Who could say no to that face? Now I can see how your parents let you bring home every stray in town. Well, we have a lot to do today before we take the midnight tour, pack, and try to navigate Scottish roads in the morning, so let's get moving." Kat helped Emily up as they walked out of the museum.

Heading down the steps, Kat stumbled, falling. The crunch seemed so loud to Emily, it took her a moment to realize Kat was screaming, holding her leg.

"Hell, this can't be happening" Kat screamed. "I think it's broken. I can't move. What am I going to do? How could this happen, I always hold the handrail, it's been drummed into me at work. We can't even cross the damn street without a crosswalk sign. I swear someone pushed me, but there was no one there." Kat moaned, tears running down her face and sweat beading on her upper lip. A crowd gathered around offering assistance. "Please, anyone, my friend is hurt." Emily looked at the crowd, willing them to help. A young couple whipped out mobile phones, "don't worry, we're calling now."

Emily knelt beside Kat holding her hand making shushing noises. "It's okay, help is coming. Hang in there, sweetie."

Emily didn't know how to tell her...*someone*...shoved her. She'd seen some guy dressed in a suit push her friend, but when she looked again, he was gone, vanished. No one else had seen him. Why did she?

❦ 6 ❦

Colin came to spluttering as a bucket of cold water was thrown in his face. Opening the eye that wasn't swollen shut; he looked around, he was back in the dungeon of Edinburgh Castle. Bloody hell, he was chained to the wall. His wrists and ankles were chafed where he had struggled against the cuffs.

He swallowed hard. Every year on the anniversary of his death, he had to relive it to signify his rebirth as a Shadow Walker. Hell, couldn't Thorne come up with something less painful? Thorne was the god of shadows. It was he, in the darkness of the Shadow realm, who offered Colin the choice to become a Shadow Walker. As he had unfinished business, he gladly made the bargain, accepting the curse, swearing to protect humanity from the Day Walkers and became immortal, keeping his soul—the soul is the energy life force in us all. It is what remains behind when someone dies and isn't ready to move on to the next realm.

Damnation, how many hundreds of times, every year at Halloween, had he been killed? The betrayal hurt more than the dying, screw the physical pain, he hardly noticed it. The depth of the deception ripped out his heart every bloody year. Seeing his brother wield the knife to end him, knowing Abigail was part of it, never got any damned easier. Why did they have to relive their deaths every year? Thorne could be one sick son of a bitch; this part of the curse he could live without.

Bile rose in his throat. It all came crashing back.

"By the gods, finish the damned thing!" Colin bellowed. He was tired of standing still posing for the fussy painter. His fiancée, Abigail wanted a portrait of him. He loved to indulge her so he agreed. He didn't realize it would be the same morning he had a deal to complete. Maintaining the ancestral castle was bloody expensive so he supplemented income by making and smuggling whisky.

It was made on the estate in an unused building, out of sight. The malting room smelled delicious like freshly baked bread from the kitchens. The brew had to be tended at all times. From the making to the smuggling someone had to ensure the process and recipe was followed. Not to mention looking out for customs officers and other bloody thieves.

Colin would load his ship full of illegal goods and sail to the Leith docks. From there the goods would be taken to the Vaults in Edinburgh. He stored the whisky there to let it age rather than keeping it on the estate. Safer that way.

Finally, the painter finished. He was late, didn't bother changing.

"Colin, you'll ruin that shirt. You should change before you leave for Edinburgh." Abigail scolded as she came into the solar. "You know you'll just get it filthy and rip it. Why don't you change, darling?" She asked him looking up, fluttering her lashes.

"Abigail, darlin', I'm late—if I ruin the bloody shirt, I'll buy another." Colin kissed her soundly escaping from the room.

It was a quick journey to Edinburgh by ship. He didn't want to miss the tides. Ships were the best way to evade Customs. Having good relationships with many a captain didn't hurt. The captain would take the spirits to the Vaults and in return for his risk be paid in coin and drink. Usually Colin went to Edinburgh afterwards to check on the stock or do business in the city, but this time he wanted to go along to check the route and crew members. There had been a close call a few weeks back. He wanted to ensure the operation was still safe.

The journey was uneventful, the weather perfect, even if it was cold outside. Late fall was a glorious time of year with many interested parties to purchase his whisky. More than the previous year. The alcohol was popular across Scotland and England. He'd recently shipped some to France for a gentleman he met playing cards.

Arriving at the dock, Colin supervised the unloading and transfer to wagons by the light of the moon. It was a full moon, winking out from the clouds; it would provide plenty of light to make the journey. This batch of whisky would age in the vaults for a few months before being sold as a cheaper brand. The casks that had aged for ten, fifteen or twenty years were stored in other locations in the hills around the estate where they couldn't easily be found but could be tended as needed. It was risky but necessary to produce a higher price and finer quality. Tonight, one batch was destined for England. He quirked a brow thinking how ironic it was that the customs officers were English, and this whisky was going to some English toff. Seemed hypocritical to him, but what the hell did he know?

Colin, along with two hired hands, loaded the barrels in a hidden room in the Vaults. Giving a few bottles to the denizens of the Vaults kept them turning a blind eye to his activities. The bribe also helped ensure none would turn them in to the Customs officers. The other batch of whisky should already be loaded on a ship bound for London in the morning.

"Milord, did ye hear that? Sounds like someone's coming," Angus looked around nervously. In an instant, all of them were surrounded by Redcoats.

"Run lads, I'll hold them off," Colin yelled, pulling his sword, charging towards the blasted soldiers.

An uppercut to the jaw brought him back to the present. Powerless to change the tableau in front of him; it always played out the same. Over and over, each year on the anniversary of his death.

An image of clear gray eyes and the scent of peaches made him tense, looking around. He smelled Emily's scent. He was shocked when she'd seen him at the Vaults, interacted with him when he hadn't willed it. Like all Shadow Walkers, he had heard there was a way to break their curse...but never gave it much thought. Given up believing in the true love, soul mate bullshit a long, long time ago. Women were more mercenary then men ever thought to be. He'd met so many women over the years, enjoyed brief encounters though none of them had seen him without him willing it...until her.

Could Emily, with her intoxicating scent that went straight to his balls, be the one mentioned in the curse...he wondered... might this year be different? If she was his soul mate and able to intervene, then everything had changed since they met at the Vaults.

He didn't want to be bound to this unknown woman, give her power over him. Wouldn't give that power to any woman again, didn't care if she failed and he became a wraith, doomed to the in-between. But hell, he wasn't such a bastard he'd doom her to never finding true love and living the rest of her life alone.

His head was going to explode thinking about this. Colin would never risk betrayal again. Gods, he hoped she'd go on her merry way, forget him. Leave him to his fate. He couldn't be her soul mate. No matter a piece of him wanted to protect her, hold her close, tear apart any who threatened her. It couldn't be. He would shut those feelings down.

There was nothing for her, only loneliness and despair if she tried to help him.

❧

"I FOLLOWED YOUR ORDERS, THE FRIEND, KAT, IS LEAVING today, back to the states with a broken leg. So the other one is alone, easy for you to get to without interference." Jackson told Rawlins.

"You pushed her down the steps? What the hell were you thinking? I said get rid of her and that's interpreted as push her down the steps—you didn't even take her energy? We don't need any bleeding hearts amongst our ranks." With that, Rawlins ripped Jackson's heart out with his serrated dagger as the newly turned Day Walker disintegrated into pale, gold dust. Wiping his hands on his gray Calvin Klein slacks, "Figures, you want something done right, you bloody well have to do it yourself. I'll take care of Miss Emily Laurens."

He dematerialized out of the Day Walker realm back to Edinburgh.

"Honey? I have something to tell you. I was going to wait until after the trip but since I'm going home today, I wanted to see your face...I'm pregnant!"

Emily squealed. "Oh, that is such fantastic news! When are you due? Oh my gosh, are you OK with the fall and all?" Emily was thankful Kat was going home. Something odd was going on, and she didn't want her to get hurt worse than the broken leg.

Coming from a small family consisting of her and her brother, Emily always wanted a big, boisterous family of at least five or six kids. Sighing, she thought about how much she missed her parents. They'd been killed in a boating accident when she was in college, but all her earlier life they always knew the right thing to say to make her feel better. It was only Matt now, and while he tried to be there for her; he was a professional fisherman, always away. Emily tried not to worry but kept fearing he'd end up in a boating accident as well. She thought at twenty-eight her time was running out to find a suitable prospect. She'd better get a move-on or she'd be lucky to get married and have one kid let alone five or six. Pushing aside her fears and melancholy thoughts, feeling genuinely happy for Kat starting a family, Emily focused back in on the conversation with Kat.

"So many questions! Let's see, I'm only three months so you have plenty of time before the little one calls you Auntie Emily. We're trying to decide if we want to know if it's a boy or girl, and yes, I'm fine. The leg hurts like hell, but the baby is fine. Don't worry."

Striding across the airport lounge, Monroe stopped in front

of the two Americans. "Miss Laurens. Mrs. Chandler. It seems we meet again under rather unfortunate circumstances." Kat had broken her leg, which normally wouldn't have the police involved except Emily had called him, saying someone deliberately pushed her friend, even though neither her friend nor the witnesses had seen anything.

Clearing her throat, Emily addressed the stern officer. "Officer MacDonald, I don't want Kat to hear me but I know what I saw. I'm only telling you; I know no one else will believe me. You may not either." She'd hesitated before calling him however, he seemed to be hiding secrets of his own, and she had a feeling he might be able to help her find out what was going on.

"I'm not saying I don't believe you, but you must accept it is rather difficult to believe a man pushed your friend down the steps then simply disappeared, wouldn't you agree?" Monroe cocked his eyebrow, crossed his arms over his chest, and stared at her, waiting for her to speak like she was some dog who would jump at his command.

"Yes, to anyone listening to our conversation, it would seem like I've knocked a few marbles loose. Do what you want with the information." She turned to settle her friend in the wheelchair.

"Have no fear, Miss Laurens, I will get to the bottom of this and apprehend those responsible. Don't forget our agreement—stay out of the investigation." Monroe shot Emily a hard look.

"Thank you, Monroe. I feel safer already." Emily knew she hadn't answered him; there was no way in hell she'd stay out of this. Oh no, she was going to find Colin, so she smiled and told him what he wanted to hear. "Of course, I'll stay out of it. Going to finish sightseeing then return home and forget all this unpleasantness." She smiled up at him as she started wheeling Kat to her gate.

Guilt washed over her as she thought about what happened to Kat. It was somehow her fault. Wiping her eyes, she tried not to cry.

Kat had insisted the trip shouldn't be ruined for both of them.

Poor Kat. All the color had been washed from her face. She was wearing sweat pants, a ratty sweatshirt, her hair in a scrunchy, and no make-up. For Kat to look so awful, Emily knew she was in a lot of pain 'cause the girl wore make-up to the grocery store. Best thing would be to get her back to Fred.

When everything falls apart, we need the one we love, no one else will do.

"Go, I'm fine. Please promise me you'll enjoy yourself. For goodness sakes, the trip is paid for, so try and have some fun. I know how hard it will be without me, but you'll survive. You have to finish finding out about Colin." Kat's eyes crinkled as she gave Emily a small smile.

"I didn't think you believed me." Emily stopped to look at Kat.

"Well, I'm still not sure what to believe, but that's why I'm married to Fred and you're running around Scotland after a ghost-but-not-ghost Highlander who fights English Redcoats while his portrait hangs on the wall in the Museum. That about sum it up, sweetie?" Kat reached up to hug Emily. "Be careful. You really don't know anything about him; he could be some lunatic. You can't rescue all the strays."

Smoothing Kat's ratty ponytail, Emily grinned; remembering the first time she and Kat met. New in school, she showed up with a blue glitter backpack and saw Kat had purple glitter; they hit it off immediately.

On the way home from school, she saw a filthy, ugly, dog following them, led the dog home, washed him and demanded he stay. After the bath, the mongrel was still ugly but clean and smelled like some fruity shampoo. Emily named him Hal, short for Halloween. Her parents were used to her bringing home strays. They usually tried to find a home for the animals, otherwise they'd be living in a zoo. She remembered Kat telling her her parents were cool to let Emily bring home a stray dog. She'd even rescued a fallen owl, she named Hoot. The owl flew to school each day and waited for her.

Kat grabbed her hand. "Don't fuss; I'll be waited on hand and foot. Heck, I'll probably gain ten pounds by the time you get back. Please be careful. I'll be worried every day until you come home. Emily—a stray dog is one thing, a stray man is a whole 'nother ballgame, sweetie." Emily kissed Kat goodbye and watched as she was wheeled away.

7

Meandering along the Royal Mile, Emily saw a shop advertising hand-woven apparel. Browsing the racks, she found a fantastic royal purple, turquoise, pink, and green shawl Kat would love. Next on her list was whisky for Fred. "May I help you, Miss?" The shopkeeper was an older gentleman who looked like he enjoyed a few nips himself.

"Please, I would like to send a few bottles of whisky back to a friend in the States." Emily perused the spirits. She enjoyed a drink, but didn't have a clue how to tell good from okay booze.

"Ah, a Yank. Where are ye from, lassie?"

Sighing, Emily smiled at the shopkeeper...that accent was divine. "Charleston, South Carolina. My friend's husband loves whisky, and I don't have a clue how to pick something he'd enjoy. Could you recommend one of your favorites?"

Taking her up and down the aisles, he told her about the various bottles. Emily stopped in her tracks, eyes drawn to a bottle with a castle on the label.

Ravensmore.

"Lass, ye have excellent taste. Ravensmore whisky dates back to the 1600s. The tale is the baron of the castle brewed the spirits in secret to keep up his lands. He was reported to the custom's officers and sentenced to die for smuggling; however, the baron was murdered in his cell the night before his execution. A later heir took the illegal operation legit, and for the past century anyone can legally buy the stuff." He finished his tale, holding out two bottles to her.

Talk about déjà vu...the hair on the back of her neck stood up as a chill slid down her spine.

"What a fantastic story, how amazing the same whisky is still being produced after all these hundreds of years. My friend will love it. Could you ship the bottles for me?" Paying for the lovely amber-colored liquid, Emily headed out to finish buying gifts.

The shops were open late to celebrate Halloween weekend, many people starting early, running around in costumes having a raucous good time. Emily smiled at them as she wandered the streets, window-shopping, eventually making her way to Edinburgh Castle for the midnight haunted Halloween tour. It wouldn't be as fun without Kat, but she needed to find Colin, help him. Shaking her head, Emily entered Edinburgh Castle as the tour was starting.

"...there are two solitary and eight large cells for keeping prisoners. Ye'll also see a pit where lions were kept and unruly tourists fed to them." The guide paused, waiting for the laughter of the group.

"'Tis also rumored there are secret escape tunnels though no one ever escaped from the castle. Enjoy the extra time to wander about as ye like...but beware."

Grabbing a lukewarm Pepsi from the café, she headed down to the dungeons. Wanting to spend some time there, imagining what it must have been like.

While Emily looked over every square inch of the dungeon, the last of her group moved on. They had heard of someone seeing a ghost up near the chapel and ran to find out what was going on. Alone, she moved back to the last cell in the dungeon. Hearing a rustling noise and grimacing to think it might be a rat, she cautiously watched where she stepped. She loved animals, but rats freaked her out.

"Hello, is anyone there? I can hear you. The guide is on his way, I'm not alone."

There were voices coming from the cell on her left, what she heard turned her blood to ice.

Colin.

"Fucking strutting peacock, ye can't even fight me like a man. Ye come at me to kill me when I'm chained to a bloody wall? I. Curse. Ye. I. Curse. Abigail. May ye both rot in hell with nary a day of peace for the rest of your miserable lives. Well, go on then, do it."

"No! Stop! Don't touch him!" Without thinking Emily threw her drink to the ground, shoving the man aside as he was about to stab Colin in the heart.

She blinked as the guy vanished into thin air. What was it with disappearing men? Maybe she was still back in the hospital in Charleston, in some kind of coma and wasn't here at all. Pinching her arm hard, she yelped, *nope, real enough ... that would leave a bruise in the morning*.

The smell of peaches and sunshine—Colin's head snapped up, inhaling deeply, he remembered her scent, it invaded his senses.

"Lass, what are you doing here? How did you find me?"

Damn it all to hell. The hourglass had started, he knew now without a doubt...Emily was his bloody Cursebreaker. One week. She had one week to save him before they both were doomed. He was so weary of his endless existence. On the positive side, if they failed, and he turned wraith—he'd have quiet. Escape from the noise. There was one small, pretty problem...he couldn't let this vibrant, enchanting woman be alone for eternity. She deserved someone to love her. Not him—he was damaged beyond repair—but someone who could love her the way she deserved. Must be some way to spare her. He'd have to go before Thorne...hell; the god was as likely to strike them both dead if he was in a foul mood as he was to listen to Colin.

He was never prepared for the emptiness, the loss of self, as his power drained from his battered body, leaching out, the air swirling around him, shimmering silver. All Shadow Walkers were helpless during the anniversary of their death. None of their powers worked; most times they were grievously injured, making it easier for Day Walkers to hunt and kill them.

'Twas one thing to be powerless for the usual twenty-four hours every year, but a full week? Bloody hell, he'd have to take her someplace safe before any of the Day Walkers discovered what had happened.

He coughed up blood, chest burning with every breath as he ground out, "We have to leave. Get you to safety..." his voice trailed off.

Hell, broken ribs hurt like a bitch, didn't matter if you were mortal or immortal. As far as he knew, no Shadow Walker had broken their curse...head pounding, he figured, why think about "what if," might as well see what would happen in the coming week.

"COLIN? OH COLIN! THANK GOODNESS. I CAN'T BELIEVE I WAS right to look here. Get me to safety? I'm not the one pinned to the wall like a human dartboard." Emily opened the cell door recoiling. He was chained, spread-eagle to the stone. This couldn't be for show. His hair was lank and greasy, his clothes filthy, the sleeve of his shirt stained dark brown. Through the tear in his shirt, she could see his arm, encrusted with blood, angry red lines radiating out from the wound. There wasn't anything in the cell except a bucket...she shuddered to think of having to use a bucket in full view of everyone. As she was thinking about the lack of privacy, the biggest rat she'd ever seen scurried across the floor into the next cell. Stifling a scream, she jumped.

"How do I get you down? We have to get you to a doctor and have that arm looked at. I think it's infected." She moved to his side, brushing the hair out of his eyes, her hand coming away with a silver shimmer. Raising his head to look at her, she could see his lip was split, his face battered and bruised. There was blood on every surface...soaking his clothes, on the floor, spattered all over the walls of the cell. Someone or somebodies beat the shit out of him. He looked awful. Putting her hand to her mouth to keep from gasping, she started to gag from the stench. She would be mortified if she threw up on him. Wiping her face, she tried not to cry at the damage that had been done to him, how one human being could be so awful to another she'd never understood.

"Are ye all right? Seem a bit green around the gills."

"Um, I have a hard time dealing with blood. Something from my childhood."

"Better close your eyes then lass, there's an awful lot 'o it around us." He sounded amused. How could he make jokes when he must be in agonizing pain? She just looked at him like he was crazy. A memory, crystal clear, came to her. Once when her brother was six, he'd cut open his hand playing on the construction site for a new home. In and out, in and out, she thought she could hear the thread pulling, making a squicking sound as it went through flesh and blood, sewing up the wound. All of sudden she saw black spots. When Emily came to, the doctor was chuckling while putting her up on the next bed. He gave her an ice pack for the back of her head. Her brother was fine. From that day on, she couldn't stand the sight of blood.

"The keys are hanging on the wall above the table." Colin rasped as he started coughing, Emily didn't have a clue how she'd get him out of there. This was not possible; she must be having some kind of delayed response to almost dying. She assumed she was hallucinating or having a walking, talking, daydream. This couldn't be real. There wasn't time to get re-enactors down here. *Okay Emily, pull it together and get the damn keys to unlock him. Figure it out later.*

Pausing, she wasn't sure she'd be able to manage Colin on her own, but if she didn't do something, somebody else would show up to kill him or she'd be back in reality on her way to the loony bin for sure. Best not to think about it too long or she'd run screaming from the dungeon; she'd wanted an adventure—looked like she was going to get more than she bargained for.

Trying a number of keys, precious minutes passed before she found the right one. Unlocking the manacles, she winced, seeing his raw and bloody wrists. Reaching out to try and catch him, she knocked over the stool, Colin fell to the ground.

"Oof, I hear somebody, hold milady." Colin motioned to the right where a shadow was moving on the stairs. Getting to his feet, he swayed. Shaking his head as if to clear it, she watched him move silently down the dim corridor, past the other cells. How could he get up, let alone walk with the injuries he'd sustained? Was she imagining him here? Turning around to look in the cell, Emily heard muffled grunts and scuffling. Colin staggered back dragging a scruffy-looking man who appeared to be dead but hopefully was only unconscious.

"Wretched boot licker for the Day Walkers." Colin curled his lip, sides heaving with the effort as he threw the body into the cell and slammed the door shut.

Confused, she looked at him, eyebrows raised to her hairline.

"This human, scum of the earth from looking at him, found out what a Day Walker is, wants to be one, and therefore spends his time playing errand boy for them, hoping to get a shot from Dayne. Immortality is a powerful motivator."

"Sorry...Day Walkers? Dayne? Immortality? I know it's Halloween, but seriously, this is so not amusing in the least. What are you going on about? What the hell is a Day Walker?"

She stamped her foot, hands on her hips and glared up at Colin, even as the term came back to her—that whisper she had heard.

"Lass, we don't have time." Dragging her by the arm, Colin headed away from the stairway deeper into the dungeon.

"Wait, we're going the wrong way, the exit is the other way." Pulling away, she cocked her head, listening. "I hear footsteps; Day Walkers or whatever the hell they are, are coming." Emily's voice was high, almost a squeak.

"Lass, it will be all right. We'll take the tunnel." Colin choked out, staggering against the wall. He was white as a sheet, his skin grey and clammy under the grime mixed with his caked on blood.

Colin needed medical attention; biting her lip in concentration she put her arms around his waist so he could lean on her.

"Maybe this isn't the best time to tell you—I'm a bit claustrophobic." Emily's lip trembled as she tried to put on a happy face. It came out as more of a grimace.

"Don't be afraid. The tunnel runs under the street to the water, called the Nor Loch. Once we get out we'll find an inn. I need to rest and contact someone who can help us." Colin stumbled, wincing. He led them to a corner in the dungeon, far away from the hallway...their only path of escape.

Puzzled, Emily was more than a little ready to give in to a major meltdown when she saw him pushing on a gargoyle's head set into the stone. Astonished, she gaped as the wall swung open revealing spider webs, darkness and the smell of damp stone drifting up to her nose. Open-mouthed, she stopped short, blinking, causing Colin to trip.

"Bloody hell," he spat.

"Sorry, I...I was surprised."

"'Tis okay lass, help me up." Colin sighed.

Helping him stand she took a moment to catch her breath. Moving slowly they started down the steps—into the yawning darkness.

8

Okay, hold it together. It's a hallway without lights. Don't think about being underground in a stone tunnel with no windows, no light, or no way out if it collapses.

Emily could handle elevators if there weren't too many people on them while large crowds gave her more trouble. She'd learned to manage situations that set off her internal alarms. When she was seventeen, she flew to Alaska with her mom and had a major panic attack. The plane was large with two seats, then five and then three. She was in the middle of the five-seater row when all of a sudden the walls started closing in. She couldn't breathe, the seat pressed against her, people were too close, and her whole body started tingling, throat closing up, bile rising—she was going to throw up, had to get off that plane now.

Pulling shut the heavy stone door; they were thrown into total blackness. The tunnel was narrow, and they had to turn sideways to move forward. It was slow going. She smelled the earthen floor, wet stone, and the smell of the past. Almost like the scent of an old library or musty attic. Roots brushed against her face, water trickled down the walls...and the sound of rustling was all around them. The darkness was dense, heavy, pressing in on her from all sides. It was so dark she couldn't see her hand in front of her face. Clammy and sweaty, she tried not to fall to pieces.

"Please tell me that noise isn't rats or some giant crocodile getting ready to eat us." Emily's voice sounded thin and reedy. She was starting to see spots. How was that possible in total blackness? Well, at least it was something to see.

This wasn't good, it was the first sign she was getting ready to faint.

"We have to keep going. You *can* do this Emily. The ones after us will be wondering how we escaped. 'Tis only a matter of time before the entrance to the tunnel is discovered." Colin wheezed.

She couldn't faint, not now. Colin would fall again, further injuring himself slowing them down and they'd get caught by these mysterious Day Walkers. She couldn't imagine what would be done to them if they were caught but it couldn't be good from the urgency in his voice, the injuries on his person. As scary as he could be, if something scared ***him,*** it must be pretty damn bad.

HER ARMS TREMBLED SUPPORTING HIS WEIGHT. HER HANDS were sweaty, and she reeked of fear. Wanting to calm her, to reassure her it would be okay, he soothed, "Lass, hold tight to me. Nothing will harm ye down here. There are no crocodiles in Scotland so don't worry about being eaten by one. I know Yanks have those legends about the sewer systems in New York and other cities, but no worries here in Scotland."

Gods, he wanted to stop, take her in his arms to comfort her, stroke her hair, and tell her nothing would ever hurt her. To tell her he would slay whatever dragons appeared in order to protect her.

He berated himself, stop acting like some whipped boy being led around by the nose and move on. She would betray him like Abigail. He didn't have time for her emotional breakdown; he had to get her out and find a safe place to rest before the Day Walkers caught up to them. *She thinks she's scared now, wait until a group of those bastards show up cutting you down in front of her.*

Taking a deep breath was unwise. Coughing up a lung from the pain, he waited. A moment passed, he started again.

"Emily, there may be rats down here, but if there are, it means there is a way out. Rats aren't going to be trapped; where you find vermin, you find a way to food, water, and an exit. They aren't paying attention to us. Put them out of your mind. Focus on my voice. Listen to me—I'll get you through this. Close your eyes..."

"But...I can't see...anything," Emily stuttered. "Right, that sounded silly." She took a deep breath. "I'm closing my eyes."

Her voice sounded so small and helpless; this brave woman was putting her trust in him. When was the last time a woman had trusted him? How long had it been since he'd let a woman get close. It had been ages since he held someone close, told them he'd protect them from whatever monsters plagued them. Could he do it again? She seemed so vulnerable with those eyes that looked into his very soul. His groin tightened thinking about her full pink lips. She had a habit of biting her bottom lip when she was nervous or worried.

"Close your eyes. I'll tell you a story to take your mind off of the tunnel. I won't let go Emily, I swear it," he promised her.

"Growing up, my brother and I played with some of the village boys. Dougal was a couple of years younger than me, his family had moved from Skye to our village. The lad was always trying to keep up with us, tagging along, chasing after us everywhere we went. One day, we were up at Drummond Keep. It's a ruined keep where we all liked to play King of Scotland, fight wars, you know, stuff boys do. There was a section leading down to the dungeon with a verra narrow opening covered by bars.

"Think of being walled up inside a wall, nothing but a tiny opening covered with bars to see out. We used to lock up our 'prisoners' there and pretend the barred door locked. 'Twas

Dougal's turn to be locked up as the prisoner. We told him to stay there while we went outside to negotiate his terms for release. Never meant to forget about him, but being boys, we were distracted by a stag, went chasing after it, forgetting all about Dougal. It had started to thunder, lightning, and rain, and Dougal, getting scared, pushed the door to get out. A crack of lightning hit the stone, knocking a piece of the keep loose and a large stone fell, barring the door. The poor lad was trapped all night and the next day until we realized we hadn't seen him in a while and went looking for him. When we got him out, he didn't speak for a week, after that he could never abide thunderstorms or small, enclosed spaces."

"The poor guy. I can relate. Thank you for telling me. I'm exhausted. How far is it until we're out of here?" Emily whispered. His reply was cutoff as the ground seemed to shift beneath their feet. The vibration turned into a rumbling, building to a roar as dirt rained down. Colin pulled her into his arms, diving into the darkness taking her with him. He cushioned her landing, taking most of the fall on his back.

Coughing in the cloud of dust enveloping them, Emily tried to get her hands under her to push herself up.

"Lass, I don't mind you grabbing my leg but that's my stomach you've got your elbow buried in. I canna breathe." He grunted.

"Oh gosh, I'm sorry. Are you OK? Hope I didn't hurt you."

Trying to stay still while she patted him all over, her hand landed on his cock. She snatched it away as if burned, mumbling an apology. "Well lass, if I knew it'd only take a little bit of dirt to get you to take liberties with my body; I'd have caved in the tunnel myself when we started down the stairs. Shall I let you slide your hand under my kilt to see if I'm wearing any drawers? Satisfy your earlier question?"

"Oh, you pig!" Emily huffed.

He heard her inhale a lungful of dust, the rest of her retort cutoff as she coughed. Emily frantically reached out, grabbing his arm, "I'm going to faint."

One minute she was talking, the next passed out cold. He laughed to himself, it would serve him right, after more than four hundred and fifty years of immortality, to die of suffocation underneath the ground during the one time he was powerless. The Fates had a twisted sense of humor.

She'd gone down so fast, he sensed it, being too black to see his hand in front of his face. His bloody eyesight was back to human levels. Catching her, lowering her gently to rest on his body, he assessed her for any damage, running his hands over her body. She had strong arms and legs, with a soft stomach. Gingerly touching her neck, he could feel the slow but steady beat of her pulse. Satisfied she would live, he ran his hands through her hair, letting it flow across his forearms, so soft, like silken thread. Colin touched her scalp, no cuts he could feel, ran his fingertips across her brow, tracing her features.

The woman had no idea how mesmerizing he found her, even now, surrounded by dirt and stone, he could faintly smell her scent. Leaning closer, he inhaled deeply, ignoring the burning in his ribs, brushing his fingers across her lips. He shifted to make her more comfortable, she'd panic when she came to, realizing they were truly trapped. It was his fault. Somehow he'd get them out of here; she deserved that much from him.

Feeling around, they were trapped by the cave-in, a wall of debris blocked the way they came—good for keeping Day Walkers out, not so good for escape. Ahead of them, stone had fallen, heavy chunks he could move with his powers, but injured and powerless? It was going to hurt like hell to move them, not to mention not causing another bloody cave-in during the process.

He heard her breathing change. "Welcome back lass, how are you feeling?" Colin rumbled in a low voice.

Trying to move off him, he stilled her in his arms. "Easy now, take a few minutes before sitting up."

"Usually I'm sore when I faint. You're very warm. Did you know you smell like leather and wool and the ocean?" She sounded groggy as she spoke, breath tickling his chest. "I'm sorry. I dreamed the tunnel caved in and we were trapped..." she trailed off.

"Wait a minute, dirt floor, wet. It wasn't a dream; we're trapped under God knows how much stone and dirt. We're going to die down here, aren't we?"

He heard her hyperventilating, trying to scramble to her feet. Pulling her tighter into his arms, her heartbeat racing he did the only thing he knew to do—spoke in low tones, the same he'd use to soothe a skittish horse or wounded animal, whispered nonsense into her ear to slow her heart, calm her.

"Shh, easy. I will get us out of here. Take deep, even breaths, and focus on breathing. In and out, nice and slow. I've got you, lean on me, I willna let you fall."

He heard her breathing slow. She wrapped her arms around his waist, sobbing as she buried her face in his chest.

"I keep thinking about being trapped underground, suffocating to death." Hiccupping, her voice was muffled by his shirt. He stroked her hair, her back, letting her sob. The poor lass had reached her breaking point. She was squeezing his injured ribs so hard he feared she'd break another one. But he didn't want to move her, liked her curled up to him, seeking his warmth, letting him hold her.

Abruptly letting go, he sensed movement in the air, she reached up to find him, cupping his jaw.

"I'm sorry, you helped me and I'm hurting you."

His voice soft, low, he caressed her with words. "I want you next to me. Let me keep you warm."

"And I've ruined your shirt; it's all wet from me crying all over it." She wailed.

Colin started chuckling, he couldn't help it. The laugh rumbled up, rusty from disuse as he threw his head back and roared,

"You're worried about a few tears ruining my shirt, lass? I think the knife and sword slashes, broken bones, filth and blood took care of the 'ruining part'; your tears washed some of the muck out."

"How can you laugh? I'd be curled up in a ball screaming from the pain."

"No time for pain in battle. You lock away the pain; do what needs to be done. Otherwise, you end up dead. Many tried over the years. Though today, a bloody Day Walker might have a fighting chance to kill me seeing as how I'm in such fine fighting shape."

"Wait a minute...I've heard Day Walkers mentioned before—what are they?"

Freezing, Colin knew no one outside of Walkers and their minions knew about them; he'd only just mentioned them to her, how did she know? Was this some kind of new trap the Day Walkers had dreamed up?

"How do you know about Day Walkers? What do you know?" He tried not to scare her, keeping his tone even, listening for a lie.

"Kat, she's my best friend, we were walking down High Street window-shopping when I heard something...it sounded like a voice carried on the wind or in the wind, barely a whisper, it said *beware the Day Walker...he comes for you.*"

"Did your wee friend hear this voice too?" Curiosity laced his voice. By the gods, he hoped she was mistaken, hoped it wasn't some kind of warning. Rawlins was the worst of the Day Walkers, gods help her if he was the one after her...but why would he be?

"Nope, she thought I was hearing things. It sounds crazy, but that's the only way I can describe it. What is a Day Walker? Why do I need to beware? And why is one coming for me? Also, Immortality? Dayne? I need you to tell me what's going on," Emily finished.

"Slow down, lass. There's time enough for me to answer all your questions."

"I'm not usually the kind of person to keep things bottled up. Normally, I get mad, blow up, and calm down just as quickly. That's me, Emily the even-keeled."

He could almost hear her grin as she told him she had a fearsome temper. Shifting his weight, he willed himself to think of cold showers, dying, anything to take his mind off the fact Emily fit perfectly to him, hip to hip, her round perfect ass was under his hands, he moved one up to her back, the other clenched into a fist at his side. Of course he'd be hard as the stone surrounding them, telling himself to think about freezing cold water or anything else but her body, he decided to answer her questions... if she was his soul mate, she deserved to know...well maybe not all of it, but enough.

"First, where is your friend Kat? Won't she be worried and looking for you?"

Sighing, Emily told him about the trip with Kat and the ransacked hotel room. She continued, telling him what happened to Kat, how she saw a man who disappeared after pushing Kat down the steps, breaking her leg, so she had to go home early. She finished by telling him she'd decided to stay, finish the trip she'd always dreamed of, and find out who he was. "So no, she won't be looking for me. I asked her not to call, to focus on getting better, told her I'd call when I left for the airport though if I don't check in, she'll be calling the cops, worried about me."

Not wanting to frighten her, Colin forced himself to breathe normally. Rawlins had to be after her. There was no way Rawlins could know about the curse, was there? "Before I begin this long drawn-out tale, why did ye pinch yourself when you helped free me?" He was curious, wanting to know what made her risk her own well-being to help him.

"I thought maybe I was dreaming—simply imagining all of this. When I pinched my arm, I knew it was real. I couldn't leave you chained to the wall or let that awful man hurt you."

Her sigh blew against his collarbone, sending chills down his spine. The scent of peaches and sunshine warming his frozen heart. "Hmm, it's a valid thought, lass. Come closer to me, you're shivering; it's verra cold down here." Colin pulled Emily closer, slowly stroking her hair.

"Where to begin...the man you saw, he was a Day Walker. Day Walkers are people who were evil human beings, angry, full of malice, not upstanding citizens. When they die, an ancient god, Daync, watches the in-between, selecting the worst of the dregs of humanity to fill his ranks, building an army of immortal Day Walkers to take over the world. Immortality is a powerful enticement for any of us.

"I don't remember any gods named Dayne in Greek or Roman mythology from history class. Who is he?"

Colin could hear her thinking, sorting it out in her mind. "Dayne is powerful, long before the Roman and Greek gods, before the titans ruled, Terya, who is the mother of all gods and goddesses, gave birth to these ancient deities. Time passed, they were imprisoned, forgotten, no one knows why they were imprisoned or who let them out but two of them were set free—Dayne and Thorne."

Grabbing his arm, Emily practically vibrated off his lap. He heard the urgency in her voice.

"Shut the front door! Every hair on my body is standing straight up, this is too strange for words."

Pushing off his chest, he grunted as Emily sat up. She must be talking with her hands from the sudden air movement around them. He tried not to chuckle, picturing her earnest face, wondering if her freckles stood out when she got excited. He pulled his attention back to her.

"I've heard of Terya. In a dream. She told me I had to do something...only I can't remember what it was. All I can remember is she told me I would be forever changed." Her voice trailed off.

"'Tis a verra powerful vision. The goddess favored you.

Maybe was she who warned you to beware. Looking out for you. Though makes me wonder why she's involved..."

He continued his tale. "When a Shadow Walker dies, if we aren't ready to go, have unfinished business or can't move into the next realm for whatever reason, Thorne hears our soul call out, offers us a deal—immortality as a Shadow Walker. We accept and spend our lives living in the shadows, serving Thorne in the quest to protect earth and humanity from Day Walkers and other things that will kick your ass in the night."

"Why do they want to destroy humanity? Can't we all just get along?"

"Day Walkers serve Dayne, they are power hungry and want to enslave humanity as we know it. Evil and rotten to the core, they steal energy from humans to become stronger, usually killing the humans. All Walkers need energy to survive." Colin paused, to let it all sink in. He could hear Emily thinking, wishing he could see the expressions cross her face as understanding dawned and she realized what they were and that she was now involved.

"Whoa, hold the phone; are you like ghosts? I thought ghosts were floating shapes, moaning and shaking chains or appearing at the same place over and over. I mean you're obviously material, you feel solid enough to me." She sounded puzzled, poking him in the arm.

He coughed, tired from the blood loss, his injuries weakening him, though he'd never show weakness in front of anyone. "In a manner of speaking, we are ghosts. There are many different types of 'ghosts'. We retain our soul—the soul is the essence or energy which defines us all. Day Walkers, Shadow Walkers, and other types of 'ghosts' as you know them have different abilities."

"Ghosts...are real. If I believe Shadow Walkers and Day Walkers exist...then logically I have to accept ghosts and all other kinds of supernatural things that go bump in the night are also real. Do I need to worry about witches, vampires and werewolves showing up to chase us too?"

Shifting her to ease the pain on his ribs, he sputtered, coughing and laughing at the same time. "By the gods that's funny. Everybody knows there's no such thing as witches, vampires, and werewolves. They're usually Walkers, demons, fae, or other creatures using the guise to frighten humans."

"Don't sound so smug. How the hell would I know? This is all new to me. Hello!? Still processing the fact the world I woke up in today is not the same world I thought I knew. A little patience please." She was indignant.

Kissing her on the forehead, he smiled. She was feisty. He found he enjoyed sparring with her. "My apologies, milady. Shall I continue?"

She made a sound of assent. Huffing and mumbling under her breath. He thought he made out the words, "hard-headed old pig." Deciding to let her calm down a bit, he went on.

"Poltergeists, orbs of light, the ghostly image of a spirit stuck, performing the same task over and over again. These are the lowest levels of ghosts. They can't harm you and aren't material." He stopped, listening to the sound of stone creaking, offering up a plea to Terya the roof would hold. The workmen he'd seen around the city digging to lay new pipe were causing these old tunnels to cave in.

"Wait a minute, how come I don't see ghosts everywhere? I can see you and Day Walkers."

"Most people have no reason to linger when it's time to pass over. They move on to the next realm to be with loved ones. The movies have made us think there are ghosts all around us, but in reality there are few with the will to stay behind. I love movies with sound. I remember when the first moving picture was shown, people were in awe. Seems like yesterday. But movies aren't reality."

"Makes sense. Charleston is an old city and I never noticed

any ghosts around. So our souls are made of energy...?" Emily's voice was uncertain.

"Yes. All Walkers are created from energy. We are the embodiment of our souls. We look the same as we did before. All plants, animals, and humans are made up of pure energy. Walkers are forbidden to feed off animals or humans by stealing their energy. It ages or kills the recipient."

Colin cleared his throat. "Day Walkers do it anyway as killing humans increases their power. Shadow Walkers use nature, electrical storms, waterfalls, and other natural means to recharge. We can also get energy from very old cities or places. Edinburgh gives off tremendous energy as do all the old European cities. Being made up of energy provides all Walkers the ability to disappear or transform into something or someone else, though transforming is a skill few have mastered. Anyone has the energy to do it, however most humans haven't evolved enough to know how to change themselves."

She laughed. "Recharge? Like a cellphone?" Her body vibrated against him as she giggled. He tightened his legs around her, keeping her close, feeling her heartbeat against his chest. "So if I were a Walker, I could transform into a size-six, blonde Barbie?"

Colin blinked, not understanding, "Don't know what or who a 'Barbie' is. Why would ye want to change your hair, 'tis beautiful. 'Size-six'. Why are women so obsessed with their bodies? Men like a woman with a lovely full arse. We don't want a bag 'o bones in bed with us."

"I think that's the nicest thing anyone's ever said to me."

He started as she reached up and kissed him on the cheek, right on his hideous scar.

"Please continue." She told him, tracing circles on his forearm.

Silk. Her lips were fine silk against his cheek. Every fiber in his being wanted to crush her against him, kiss her senseless, take her on the debris filled floor of the tunnel. He shifted her so his raging erection didn't press against her. At least it was pitch black down here so she couldn't see how badly he wanted her. How she enflamed his desire as he imagined her naked, riding him, calling out his name as she screamed her release. He wasn't an animal, he could control his need for her. Sounding hoarse, he continued, trying to remember what he was telling her.

"Right. Like a mobile phone. Recharging keeps us going as the body, while manifested as flesh and bone, is nothing more than pure energy. If someone figured out how to harness this energy humans and animals would be enslaved forever. You can see why we have to keep what we are a secret."

"Can't you turn into a drill or some other kind of machine and get us out of here?"

He avoided telling her he was powerless. He didn't want to tell her about the curse yet. "We can transform into anything organic. We can't transform into anything nonorganic like a drill, cars, or a building. "When we kill a Day Walker or they kill one of us, we absorb the other's energy and power to become stronger." He coughed, tired. He'd lost a significant amount of blood. Digging in her messenger bag, she found a bottle of water and small baggie of Chia seeds.

"Do Shadow Walkers eat or drink?" Emily held out the water and seeds to him.

"Aye, we eat, drink, sleep, and make love. We don't need to eat or drink, though it will keep us alive if we can't pull energy to recharge; energy is what we need to live. When we are powerless we can't use energy and have to make do with food and drink. I'm rambling, yes on the water. What the hell is in this bag? Pebbles?"

She took a sip and handed him the water. "Seriously, those are Chia seeds, a superfood. The ancient Aztecs used to rely on them for nourishment; they're great for you and taste lovely in a green smoothie."

"I'll eat some of your tiny rocks but no way, no how am I drinking green sludge. Don't care how good it is for me; give me a steak and potatoes any day." Colin poured some of the seeds in his mouth. "They don't taste like anything, kind of sticky."

Murmuring a noncommittal reply, she finished off the chia seeds and tried to stay calm. It was so much to take in. Ghosts, Day Walkers, Shadow Walkers, immortals, whatever they were called. She sighed; her mind struggling to process the information. Something had happened to her when she died for those eight minutes—she was having a hard time actually believing there were such things running around this earth. Wasn't ready to come face to face with anything else that hid in the shadows. This was enough to take in.

So many questions, leaning up to ask Colin to tell her more, the ground started to shake. Crying out, she wrapped her arms around him as something hit the ground next to them. Frantically feeling around him, her hand came to rest on a large piece of stone. Must have come loose with all the construction work.

"Wow that was close. We were almost beaned by that rock... Colin?" Something wet hit Emily's face. Reaching up to wipe it off, she smelled the tang of salt, copper, and something else—the scent of the ocean. Holy crap, it was blood. Touching the left side of his face she felt the warm trickle. Continuing her explorations, she found the gash on the side of his head, near his temple.

Okay, head wounds bleed a lot, doesn't matter if they're serious or a scratch. This can't be happening; I can't be alone without him down here.

Taking deep gulping breaths, she willed her mind to relax. This could be really, really bad. They had to get out of here; he needed help. Shivering from the bone-chilling cold, she started to explore the confines of their prison, looking for some way to escape.

What if he didn't wake up?

9

Sunday, November 1st

"Well, well, well, if it isn't the terrifying Black Bart, or do you go by Robert Bartholomew nowadays? Nobody does long hair anymore unless you're a biker or model. Don't you know it's out of fashion to dress like a pirate? Suede pants, knee high boots, and a puffy white shirt? The Village People called, they want you back. Unless of course you're off to a costume party but then you've got your days mixed up chap, Halloween was last night." Rawlins sneered.

Robert raked a glare over the annoying Day Walker and growled, "If you're here for some girl talk, you got the wrong guy. Yap, yap, yap, by the gods, I'd heard it was possible, but never believed you could actually talk someone to death. Don't think for a bloody minute I don't see those birds back there waiting for you. You can't go around killing humans whenever you please, asshole."

"Sure I can. That's why we have all the fun while you holier-than-thou pricks run around cleaning up after us. Better head over to the docks, I left you a couple of presents—two thugs and I'll leave you two more inside once I'm done out here."

"I'd rather we handle this like gentlemen, more sporting that way. Remember what a gentleman is, Rawlins? At one time you claimed to be one. Pick the weapons. Much more fun that way mate, wouldn't you say?"

Heading to the back door leading to the alley, Rawlins stopped and held the door, "After you, damned whoreson bastard."

Stepping out into the alley, he sensed movement in the air, ducked and turned as Rawlins fist missed his face by inches. Spinning around, he caught Rawlins with a vicious kick to the chest, sending him careening into the metal door. A loud bang sounded as the door dented from the force of the blow. Shaking his head from the impact, Rawlins looked down, picked up a piece of rusted metal and threw it at him like a Frisbee, knocking him flat on his ass. Before Rawlins could finish him off; he vaulted to his feet, catching the bastard across the jaw with a right hook.

Head snapping back, Rawlins didn't have time to react before he landed another punch to the bastard's face and busted his lip open. Fists flying, they were well matched.

While Day Walkers, especially older ones, were tough and incredibly strong; Robert had been fighting since he was a boy, carving a fearsome reputation across England, Scotland, and Wales. Day Walkers had different powers depending on how old they were. Bloody Captain Rawlins Huntington was over five hundred years old with some serious juice from sucking humans dry. Not to mention, with all that energy, he had the power to bloody well fry you with an energy bolt if you weren't careful. Shadow Walkers could do the same thing but any time one of them used an energy bolt, it temporarily drained their powers (unless of course, they'd broken the rules and sucked a human or two dry beforehand) so they'd be helpless until they could recharge in the moonlight, or in the case of Day Walkers, in the sunlight.

You had to watch the bloody Day Walkers or you'd end up

dead and wandering the in-between as a wraith. The good captain had been sucking humans dry for so long, enjoying the taste of energy as one enjoys a fine glass of wine, that he'd never stop, not until a Shadow Walker stopped him—permanently. Robert had to admire the guy's strength and ferociousness, even if he was a prime grade-A asshole.

Without warning two other Day Walkers appeared, attacking while Rawlins stood back. Robert was thrown into the dumpsters lining the alley wall by a bolt of energy. Damn, Rawlins was juiced after feeding on humans tonight. Thank god the thunder was loud enough to disguise the noise they were making in the alley. Wouldn't do for any humans to get curious and investigate.

"Hmm, I guess weapons are out now that we're using energy. That the way of it? All right, let's finish this." Robert taunted them, materializing in front of one of the losers.

Too fast for human eyes to follow, Robert caught the man with an elbow to the nose. A satisfying crunch told him the nose was busted. Spinning, he stabbed the other in the heart with his serrated dagger, ripping it out of his body. Crushing the heart, the Walker burst into gold dust. No worries about clean up. Before Robert could enjoy the satisfaction of dispatching the bugger, the second asswipe hit him over the head with a manhole cover, dropping Robert to his knees.

The cheater jeered as he approached Robert, "Aw, the big, bad pirate, isn't so fearsome after all. Call this a fight? What a waste of time. Guess I'll go inside and snack on a few lovely ladies. Don't bother to get up. I'll finish you where you are, pirate boy." A sword materialized in his hand. Swinging for Robert's head, he connected with...air.

Before he could react, Robert jumped up from a roll, landed on his feet, pivoted and ripped out the loser's heart before stabbing it with his dagger. The Walker disintegrated into gold dust.

That's two less Day Walkers in the world. Dusting his hands against his breeches, Robert looked around for Rawlins.

He watched Rawlins push off the wall, stalking towards him

with twin golden blades clenched in his fists. Materializing an ice blade, no ability for modern-day police to trace them, they were his favorite weapon; he paused, hearing sirens blaring in the distance.

"Another time, Shadow Walker." Rawlins mocked, as he dematerialized back to the realm of Day Walkers.

Three police cars roared down the block into the alleyway behind the pub.

"Stop, don't move," shouted two officers. Robert glanced at them, making eye contact for a moment with one of the cops. Moving into the shadows, he disappeared.

"Hey, did you see that? There were two guys here, weren't there Monroe? Where'd they go?" The younger officer scratched his head.

The one called Monroe pointed out the dented door. "Those were either two strong sonofabitches, or they were high on something. Who knows, in this part of Edinburgh. These tourists think it's safe to wander around at all hours of the night, exploring wherever their fancy takes them. Don't they realize like any city, Edinburgh has dangerous areas to be avoided? Areas where they might only be mugged if they were lucky; killed if someone was having a particularly bad day, like today. Makes me want to shake some sense into the lot of them."

Sensing the change from night to day, Colin struggled to regain consciousness. For a moment, he felt someone holding him, crying over him...before the blackness pulled him under.

Dying. He was dying, his brother's blade embedded in his heart. Trying desperately to take air into his lungs, struggling to live, he heard voices...Abigail's voice.

"Oh my, it smells terrible down here." Abigail shrieked.

"Darling, be careful where you step."

His heart slowing, lungs straining for some small amount of air, Colin knew he was dying. How could Hamish and Abigail have betrayed him? Gladly would he have given Hamish gold and lands if he'd asked; he'd provided a large estate, Castle Gloom, to Hamish upon his betrothal, telling Hamish it wouldn't be long before he had his own wife to love, cherish and make sons with. How little he knew—Hamish was plotting to steal everything. Colin loved Hamish, always looked out for his wastrel brother, protected him. All he received in return was a knife to the heart...his reward for trusting anyone.

"Hamish, my love, let's depart this dreadful place. I want that horrible painting of Colin burned immediately." Abigail stamped her tiny foot and flounced out of the dungeon.

"Rawlins, have this bloody, revolting mess cleaned up." Turning on his heel as Colin shuddered with his last gasping breath, blood dripping on the damp stone floor; Hamish strode out of the dungeon, wiping the bloody ring clean before sliding it onto his finger.

Leaning against the far wall, Rawlins looked disgusted. Instead of calling for the guards to dispose of Colin's body, he removed the manacles, lowering the warrior to the floor. "In another life baron, I think we might've been mates."

Colin was moaning, thrashing about, in the throes of a nightmare while unconscious. On the bright side, at least he wasn't dead. She'd kept him warm against her, promising anyone who was listening she'd give up chocolate, Pepsi, and wine if they'd let him be okay and get them out of here.

Swearing, Colin couldn't hear over the infernal racket. And why was water dripping on him—were they going to drown in this godforsaken tunnel? Sitting up, his head spun.

"Wait, you're hurt. A rock hit you on the head. There was so much blood, I tried to stop it but you wouldn't wake up." Drying her eyes and hiccupping from crying, Emily helped Colin sit up.

"I thought you were lost in the shadows, it's been so long—I can't find any way out, there's an awful scrabbling noise. I think the rats are back. It's terrible having an overactive imagination.

I'm not normally such a mess but I kept thinking the rats would get in and eat us alive." This last bit was said on a particularly unladylike hiccup as Emily pulled herself together.

"Do you think you can stop hiccupping so I can listen for this scratching you heard? Shall I scare you to make the hiccups stop?" Colin smiled thinking how brave she was, taking care of him while she was afraid. She was strong whether she believed it or not.

Listening, he could hear faint noises. This was good; the rats knew how to get out. If he could pinpoint where they were, there was a chance he could find a way to escape. Hell, being trapped while he was injured afforded him some peace from worrying about the bloody Day Walkers killing him while he recovered.

Deciding the noise was coming from the right of them, Colin started digging, removing stone, placing it on the path behind them. If the Day Walkers found the entrance, at least they'd have to remove the stone. They couldn't materialize past it since they couldn't see where they were going. You had to know where you were going or you might end up embedded in a wall. While it wouldn't kill you, it might be a hell of a long time before you got out.

"Let me help." Emily started prying the rock and stone loose.

The bloody stone was heavy; his arms were straining. Pulling a particularly heavy chunk out of the debris, Colin jerked as another rib broke. It must have been fractured and snapped from the strain. He stopped a moment as dizziness and nausea threatened to make him look like a girl.

Gah, damnit to hell, it hurt like a bitch. Focus, you prissy girl, keep going, ignore the pain.

"Ouch!" Emily winced next to him.

Taking her hands in his, Colin examined her fingers; she had snapped off or ripped off each nail down to the quick trying to help remove the stone. "Lass, stop, you've destroyed your pretty nails. I liked the color, reminded me of a bronze shield I once had." Anger filled him; she'd been injured because of him. If she hadn't trusted him, none of this would have happened. She'd never cried out; simply kept digging. She had a spine of steel which he admired.

"They don't hurt anymore."

"You're in shock. Now lean as close to the wall as you can." With a grunt and a heave, the boulder came rolling past her to land at their feet. Air came rushing in, along with the sound of... rats.

"I've never been so happy to hear those dirty little creatures."

Reaching for Emily's hand, Colin first had to wipe his hand and forearm off on his kilt; he must have re-opened one of his injuries, it was bleeding again. He didn't care about the blood, he didn't want to worry Emily.

"It's another tunnel. We'll follow the rats to safety. Take my hand; it's tall enough we can stand up."

In the darkness, he felt her wince as she placed her hand in his. Stopping, he cursed. He should have taken care of her when he realized, not waited. Ripping what was left of his tattered shirt, he bound her hands to cushion the tender fingertips.

"There, there, this will help. Once we are safe, we'll have them tended to. Are you okay?" He stroked her cheek.

"I feel numb."

"Most men would have screamed like girls—ripping a fingernail off hurts like hell." Admiration filled his voice.

She sniffed, "I don't feel very brave."

Turning a corner, air blew in ruffling their hair, the sound of water trickling by their feet, the rats scurrying to freedom. Ahead, he could make out a dim light. Reaching the end of the tunnel, they came to a stone wall. The rats were scurrying out; air and water coming in...there had to be a door here somewhere.

Excitement filled his voice, "Feel every inch of the wall..."

Colin paused for a moment thinking of earlier, her warm hand on his thigh...what it would be like to have her hands exploring every inch of his body. Mentally eye rolling, he continued, "There has to be a lever in the stone we can press to free us."

Exploring every inch of the wall, a thud sounded as Colin pushed in on a stone rosette. Light flooded into the space as Colin pushed with all his might, the heavy door swinging open, leading them outside into the late afternoon.

Sagging with relief, Emily wheezed. "You distracted me so I wouldn't flip out. You're nice when you're not being grumpy."

Hugging Colin tight, she stood on her tiptoes, kissing his cheek. "Thank you."

Desire surging, his control snapped, pulling her tightly against him, he captured her mouth in a demanding kiss, invading her with his tongue, bruising her lips; he wanted to crawl inside her, take her there against the stone wall, on the banks of the water.

Arching against him, she ran her hands over his back and arms, feeling his strength, his wounds—and the blood. A bucket of cold water would have had the same effect. She pulled away, "You're bleeding and badly injured, we have to find help."

"Damn the bloody injuries." Growling at the distance between them, he shook his head to clear it. The worry on her face brought him back to his senses.

"Aye, we need tending, though I'd rather stay here and kiss you senseless. We're close to the Black Swan. It will be safe for a bit, we can get you bandaged up, a hot meal, drink, and then rest. In the morning I'll arrange a ship and we'll set sail up the coast, somewhere safe."

Daylight was fading, the late afternoon shadows would help hide them from prying eyes. There was a path running along the water, ending at the back door of the Black Swan. Robert could help them with a ship. They'd go to Ravensmore. Fury ignited him, thinking of Rawlins and others trying to hurt Emily.

The thought kept eating at him. They couldn't know about the curse, what it meant, could they? He'd cut down every last sonofabith before he'd let any of those filthy bastards lay a hand on a single strand of Emily's hair.

MINE…no one would touch his woman.

10

Arriving at the Black Swan Tavern, exhausted, injured, and dirty, they made their way to a dimly lit table in a back room.

"Colin. Bloody hell, what happened? The two of you look like something the cat wouldn't bother dragging in." Henry, the proprietor of the tavern, welcomed them.

"Here, here, sit down. I'll have a room prepared, let me bring you some food, in the meantime, shall I call a doctor?" He wrung his hands.

"Nothing to worry over, a few scrapes. Would you call Robert? Ask him to meet us here, we need a ship."

"You don't have a phone? How can you not have a phone?" Emily was shocked. She'd been missing hers since the whole dungeon incident. Wanted to buy a replacement as soon as possible.

"Sometimes lass, I wish it was still 1644, I hate technology. Despise all the noise and people rushing to and fro. The past had a rhythm, a cadence—'twas easier in some regards. And yes, I do *have,* a mobile but I don't always carry it with me...when I do, 'tis for my convenience, not to be at the beck and call of others." She watched Colin shove his hands through his hair in frustration. He blinked, looking sheepish, "I concede to you it would be rather useful at this juncture."

She grinned at him. "OK, you made your point. We can pick one up tomorrow." Before she could continue, Henry's wife, Sally, brought them ale, bread, and cheese. "Poor things, you look half dead. Eat, drink, and then we'll get you to your room. I've had bandages, water, and fresh clothes sent up for you."

"Aye, thank you Sally, you're a good woman." Falling on the food like wild dogs, they quickly ate.

"Henry can be trusted. He helps us as his father and his father before, and so on, have done for centuries."

Nodding, with a mouthful of roll, she asked, "Who's Robert?"

"He was called the Prince of Pirates, the most dreaded pirate on the seas before he was hanged at Edinburgh Castle, a few days after I was killed."

With a loud bang, the door was flung open; Emily stopped in mid-chew—the man striding in had to be at least six feet tall. Super-white teeth, long, jet black hair, and his face—he could have graced the cover of any magazine with indigo blue, piercing eyes, he looked like some hedonistic model carved from stone.

"Came as soon as I heard, mate, dreadful bit of trouble from the looks of it...you look like shite." He clapped Colin gently on the shoulder, mindful of his injuries.

The man gave Emily an appraising look, "Allow me to introduce myself; I am Robert Bartholomew of Wales, at your service, Madam."

She stared at him open-mouthed. *Wow, what a charmer.*

"Lass, you look like you're about to fall asleep in the remains of your dinner. Colin—you look like death warmed over, though nothing a night won't cure. Never seen you out to dine with a woman." He smirked.

Emily caught the look Colin shot Robert but didn't know what it meant. Before she could ask, Colin continued. "Robert, this is Emily." Colin introduced her, speaking around a mouthful of cheese.

Yawning, she greeted him.

"Gods Colin, the lass looks like she's about to fall asleep on her feet. Not looking too good yourself, my friend. Want to enlighten me?"

"Not particularly. Let's just say I willna be healing tonight." Swaying on his feet, Colin was losing consciousness as Emily and Robert helped him to the stairs. She'd resisted Robert's offer to carry her.

"Robert, back the hell off." Colin ground out before he lost consciousness.

"So that's how it is, I see. Let me take him, lass. We'll have plenty of time to get acquainted once on my ship."

Moving up the stairs, a buxom waitress blocked their path. "Oy, is he okay? We don't want no drunkards in here. He's not sick is he? The woman, named Mary, peered closer at Colin. Robert stepped in blocking her view from them, "He lost badly gambling and had the piss kicked out of him. Now run along Mary and fetch us some whisky. He's in enough trouble with the missus." Winking at Emily, he turned back to Mary and pinched her bottom. "Come on up later, and I'll show you how appreciative I am." Mary twittered, attention diverted from Colin, and ran off to do his bidding.

"You do realize now they think I'm married to Colin? What will they think when we're in separate rooms?"

"Milady, Colin will have my head if he's away from you, anyways, there's only one room free. Now let's get your wounds cleaned."

The rooms were on the top floor and seemed clean enough, but she wasn't sure what was real and what was hallucination. People always said bad things came in threes, well then, given everything that had happened, things were bound to improve. Tired, Emily wanted to rest, but was she dreaming? Dreams usually didn't come with the smell of unwashed bodies, huge rats, and blood—a nightmare then. She had to face the truth, there was much more in this world than she thought. She'd been thinking about "ghosts" ever since Colin told her what he was, telling her brain to accept the fantastic tale. Not sure whether to be happy it was true or scared to death at what might happen next, she wanted to accept what she had seen and heard. Goosebumps covered her arms thinking about their ordeal.

Her throat closed up, she had trouble breathing. Remembered dropping to her knees with gratitude when they'd emerged from thc tunnel. The walk to the tavern helped calm her a bit, and she was starved by the time they'd been served dinner. She hadn't eaten anything since Halloween night, well, except for a few chia seeds. She was tired, her nerves frayed. Her world had been turned upside-down in the space of a few days. So no wonder she had visions of bed bugs crawling all over her as she looked over the room.

"Wait a minute. Robert? Colin mentioned a ship as well. What do you mean 'your ship'?" Where the heck were they planning to take her?

Colin mumbled something unintelligible. Robert raised his eyebrows and translated. "Apparently you're both in a bit of danger, yes?" She nodded and he continued. "Right. We're sailing to Ravensmore Castle. It's safe there, and whoever is after you will have a rather difficult time figuring out where you've gone. The journey will take two days to get to Colin's home, and he'll want to keep you there a few more days to make sure you're out of danger. I don't see any luggage, lass."

Her shoulders slumped. "My purse, phone, and money were lost between the dungeon and the cave-in. My luggage is at the hotel. We'll need to get it, and I want to make a call to let my friend know I'm OK." She wanted to call Kat to let her know she was fine. Back home she'd never leave on a ship with a virtual stranger—but here, in Scotland, meeting Colin. Things were different. Her entire world changed. She'd navigate it as best she could. Felt she'd known Colin for a long time, it was hard to explain. Anyway, she wanted to visit Ravensmore. Looked like she'd get her chance. Thinking positive thoughts, she decided to make the best of a situation with ghosts and crazy people intent on murder.

Moving into the room, Colin collapsed onto the bed; burning up with fever and semi-conscious. Noticing her hands, Robert sat Emily down in a chair to have a look. "Emily, let me see. We need to tend you first."

"Can't we call a doctor?"

"No, better not, now let me." Sucking in a breath he told her, "I'm amazed you're still standing. Though I think the cut on your cheek adds to your beauty."

Rolling her eyes, she heard him laugh, the big ol' charmer.

Gently, he took her hands in his, the air around her grew warmer, her fingers tingled, silver light spilled out from his hands, and a low electrical hum filled the air. Releasing her hands, he did the same for the cuts on her arms and cheek. Finished, he patted her shoulder, stood and went to build up the fire.

"Best keep this to ourselves, aye?"

Speechless, she examined her hands. Each of her missing and broken nails—healed. Shiny, pink and no longer tender to the touch. Astonished, she looked at him. "How? Is this part of the Shadow Walker thing? But then why didn't Colin do it? I don't understand..."

"He told you about us?" The look of incredulity on his face was almost laughable.

"Yes, it's a long story."

Robert stopped her. "I suppose it is. Though it's starting to make sense. Let's just say Colin would have healed you if he could. The reason is his to tell."

A knock at the door brought Mary with the water and whisky. Robert had a roaring fire going, "Emily, bring the water here, we'll set it to boil. Can ye sew?"

"Oh no, not really, other than making a pillow in school, haven't ever really had to know how."

Robert raised his eyebrows at her, "Funny how the world changes, sewing used to be a skill every lass knew, now, I'd reckon very few know how to sew."

She had to ask, "How old are you?"

"Well, milady, I'm a few years older than Colin, I look pretty damn good for my age, don't I?" He chuckled at her surprised look.

"I, um, well, I, um, just, don't know what, um, to say," she stammered. Jeez, was everyone hundreds of years old? Didn't they make young Shadow Walkers?

She would grow old while he would stay the same. Being a bit vain, it bothered her more than she thought it would. *Best not to worry about it, you don't even know if he's interested in you for anything longer than a night.*

"Don't fret milady, let's get Colin taken care of."

Stripping Colin out of the tattered remains of his kilt, she tried not to look but had to catch her breath. He had broad shoulders, tapering to a narrow waist showcasing muscles that came from hard work and swinging a sword. These weren't gym muscles, no way, sister; these were amazing, corded, rock-hard muscles, and they ran straight to a large cock and heavily muscled legs. Covering him with a towel from the waist down, she quickly averted her gaze from his fantastic package. Staring at the scars covering his chest and stomach, her gut heaved when she realized how many battles he must have seen over the years.

"Like what you see, do you?" Colin came to and peered at her through his inky, long lashes. A wolfish grin on his face. "Keep looking at me like ye want to devour me lass, I'll have to lose the towel and oblige ye." Colin rumbled, low in his throat. She noticed when he was tired, injured, or angry, his accent was more pronounced. She loved his voice.

"Hmmph, I was just noticing all the scars, no need to have your head get any bigger." Emily sniffed, her face flaming, as she prepared the water and cloths to clean his wounds. Robert threw back his head and roared with laughter.

Scowling at him, she busied herself inspecting Colin's arm. It looked awful, encrusted with dried blood and dirt, swollen and bruised. It made her squeamish, light-headed simply looking at it.

"Think I could have a sip of whisky?" she asked voice shaking.

"Now milady, no need to be afraid, it's only a wee bit o' blood. Pretend you're making, what was it? Oh yes, a pillow. You'll have to make do. I have to recharge or I'd help Colin myself. Then I'm off to meet my mates and ready the ship to leave in the morning on the tide," Robert said.

"It's, well, I don't particularly like blood." Emily said.

"Not me should be worried I think. Colin's the one should be worried by your lack of womanly skills." Robert gave him a look, Colin shook his head and grimaced.

"Wait, Robert?" She stopped him from leaving with a hand on his arm, her eyes tearing up. "I don't know how to thank you for healing me." Reaching up, she hugged him.

"Couldn't have your lovely fingers less than perfect, now could we?"

"Robert, quit mauling Emily and get the hell out. Emily just sew the damn thing up and pour me some whisky. I'm tired of hearing the two of you blathering on like old biddies, you're making my head pound." Colin growled at them as Robert shut the door with a bang.

"Fine. Don't get grouchy with me, Mr. Crankypants, I'm the one with the needle, remember?" Emily tried to sound mad, but she was tired. She couldn't blame Colin for being grouchy. She knew his arm must be killing him; couldn't stall any longer after cleaning the rest of the superficial cuts. After a healthy swig for Colin and one for her, she set to cleaning the worst of his wounds.

Colin gritted his teeth but didn't make a sound as she first cleaned his face, removing the dirt and blood, gently cleaning his split lip. He had full lips and even with the bruising and half his bottom lip split, Emily had the strongest urge to run her finger down his face, tracing the scar, it stood out starkly against his pale skin. His head wound was fine, didn't need stitches; his thigh and arm injuries would require lots of stitches.

Moving to his wounded arm she cleaned the dirt and blood. There were bits of rock embedded in the cut. Feeling sick to her stomach, knowing she'd have to remove them, she took a deep breath.

Okay, no fainting, throwing up or generally falling to pieces. Come on now, he needs you, be strong, you can do this.

Listening to the sounds drifting up the stairs—the tavern-glasses clinking, patrons murmured voices, and the fiddler's music helped calm her nerves. "I have to remove the shards of rock from your arm. I don't want to hurt you." Her voice trembled.

"You'll do fine. Pain doesn't bother me, ye willna hurt me. There's no one else I'd rather have tend me."

He never said a word while she removed the debris, an occasional grunt or sharp intake of breath were the only sounds in the silence of the room other than the crackling fire. Stretching, she moved to clean his thigh. His legs were amazing. Strong and well-muscled. Running her hand along the muscles, she heard Colin swear under his breath.

His voice was hoarse, "Lass, if ye don't jab me with a needle soon, I'm going to pull you on top of me and ravish you."

"Oh. As much as I'd like that, you're in no shape to do anything." With one comment, the ornery man almost made her forget what she was doing. One minute he was gruff and grouchy, the next he was teasing her, flirting, or putting her at ease. She knew he was a good guy, rough around the edges with some kind of serious baggage, but he seemed like a decent, honorable man. Emily shook herself. What did it matter? The last thing she needed was another relationship. Hell, her track record was so awful it should be a neon warning sign she found Colin attractive. Given her history, he seemed good, so it was a safe bet he was totally bad news.

Finally finished cleaning his wounds, she moved on to the sewing.

"Okay, this is going to sting; I'm going to pour the whisky on your injuries. Last chance to call a doctor and go to a nice, sanitary hospital with people who know what they're doing..."

"No doctors or hospitals. 'Tis a waste of good whisky if you ask me, but if you insist then go ahead and do it." Colin tensed as she poured it on his thigh and arm, over and over, until the wounds were clean. All throughout her ministrations he never made a sound of protest. Emily couldn't believe the kind of pain he must have endured during his life not to cry out. She would have been screaming at the top of her lungs, yelling for the best drugs the hospital had to offer.

She put the needle in the fire to sterilize it, pulled the thread from the boiling water and took a deep breath. "I'll try and do my best but I've never done anything like this before. I hope it doesn't get infected, this can't be sanitary." Emily couldn't keep the waver out of her voice.

He looked up at her and Emily had to stifle the impulse to lean down and hug him. He looked so vulnerable laying there; she had the strongest urge to protect him, to make the hurt go away. If only a kiss could do that, she'd kiss him from head to toe.

She leaned back to see him intently watching her with the slightest twitch of his lip, but to his credit he didn't say anything. Emily thought she might have stabbed him with the needle if he made a smart remark.

"Lass, just do your best. One or two more scars won't even be noticeable." Colin closed his eyes, waiting.

Taking a steadying breath, she pushed the needle through his skin. The wound went from the crook of his elbow down the underside of his arm, all the way to his wrist. Sweat beaded on her forehead. It was harder than it looked. It was difficult to go through skin, not to mention, the needle made a popping noise as it entered the skin. She could hear the thread making that squicking sound as it pulled through skin, tissue, and blood.

She had to stop, putting her head between her legs to breathe so she didn't faint or throw up. That wouldn't do at all. Shaking, sweaty, and pale, she lifted her head to see Colin trying to lean up on his elbows.

"Are ye okay, lass? Can I help ye? What do ye need?" Colin looked so concerned for her, she almost laughed. He was the one seriously injured, yet he was worried about her. No teasing or laughing, he gently took her hand in his uninjured one and held it.

Looking down at Colin's hand, Emily marveled at how large and strong it was. With callouses set off by tanned rough skin, this was no corporate America hand of the men she typically dated. Those were usually, pasty white, manicured, and doughy. This was the hand of a real man. Solid, warm, and strong. At that moment, Emily thought everything would be all right, as long as Colin held her hand, and that nothing would ever harm her. It was a silly thought, but it comforted her and she said, "Thank you." He didn't say a word, simply rested his hand across his chest, closing his eyes.

Time stood still, the moments stretching out, the quiet, the crackling logs, the warmth of the room seeping in her bones. Pausing in stitching up his arm, she checked on Colin. He was pale, eyes closed, a faint sheen of sweat on his brow the only indication of the pain he felt.

Rubbing her aching neck and shoulders, she stood. Putting the needle in the fire again and pouring more whisky over it to sterilize it as best she could, she laid a cool, damp cloth on his forehead. Moving to sew up the thigh wound, she was thankful it wasn't nearly as long as his arm injury.

Bloody hell, his arm was on fire and hurt like the devil but damned if he'd tell her. He liked her fussing over him. Stealing a look at her through his lashes, he marveled, she was so beautiful with her long brown hair, reaching halfway down her back. He loved her hair, made him want to fist both hands in it as she straddled him while he brought them both to climax. Shades of chestnut and gold caught the light as she moved. Her face was round with full lips, currently in a pout as she tried to concentrate on not stabbing him with the needle. As she leaned over him, he could see her eyes were the color of a winter day, clear gray with a hint of silver and blue and still...she smelled of sunshine and peaches. He'd never look at a peach the same way again. His groin tightened, he shifted to ease it. Gods, he burned for her.

Could he let her into his battered heart, take the chance and trust again?

He felt queasy thinking on the possibility Emily might be the one, the only one for him. He'd pushed aside feeling for so long, it was painful to feel anything other than anger and the thrill of battle. His thoughts shifted. Being powerless was going to cause problems. They needed to get to Ravensmore. He could defend them from there. Until he was sure who was coming after Emily, he couldn't take any chances. Didn't want to risk Captain Huntington finding them while he wasn't at his best for a fight.

Emily cleared her throat, and he realized he'd been caught staring at her. He had his uninjured hand in her long hair, winding his fingers through it. Colin quickly released her hair before she said anything. Finishing up, tying off the knot, he told her to put honey on his wounds to keep them from getting infected and then wrap the injuries with clean linen. Watching her get up, she stretched like a cat, easing the kinks from her back, shoulders, and neck. Disposing of the cloths, she asked him, "Can I get you anything? Some water or more whisky?"

No answer forthcoming, she turned; Colin had passed out, snoring quietly. Something was crawling on his arm. Moving closer to look, hoping it wasn't some giant spider, she could see a fat, lazy, honeybee walking along his arm. Weird, maybe it was attracted to the honey. She liked bees, they were good for everything, she didn't bother them and they didn't bother her. Looking around the room to figure out how a bee got in, not to mention how it was surviving when it was so cold outside, she couldn't tell and was too tired to investigate further. She turned back to Colin, only to see the bee had disappeared as well.

Great, disappearing bees, if there are immortal bees, I'm so outta here, straight to the nearest loony bin, checking myself in.

Dragging her hand across her forehead, she found a wash basin to clean up as best she could. There was no place to sleep except next to Colin. It was a big enough bed, but she worried she'd jostle him, waking him up or rolling on his arm. Throwing her worry aside in favor of exhaustion, Emily climbed in bed next to Colin, passing out into a dreamless, exhausted sleep...

Why am I so warm? I can't move or breathe. Emily started to struggle before she realized it was Colin she was curled up against, a naked Colin. He was warm, his leg draped over her body. Looking down she could see his hand on her breast. Thinking about it made her nipples tighten, her body tense in anticipation of what it would be like to be with him. She could imagine his strong body over hers, raised above her, the muscles of his forearms straining, ready to take her.

Get over yourself, the poor guy had the shit kicked out of him, has terrible injuries, and you're thinking about sex with him, seriously, get a grip you lustful hussy.

Being held by Colin made her feel safe and secure. After checking his forehead to make sure the fever had gone down, she told herself to think about cold showers, wrapped her arms around him, and drifted off to sleep again...

Startled awake by Colin thrashing around in the bed, she put a hand on his shoulder to wake him. He snapped his arm back, hitting her in the eye. Screaming, she sat up as a very naked Colin jumped up in bed.

"Come on Hamish, you fucking arsehole. Get up while I knock your fucking teeth into your skull," he roared. Shaking, he looked around, trying to focus.

"What the bloody hell is going on? Emily? Oh my god, what happened? Fuck, did I do that to you?" Colin came to her side, looking at her eye. "Damnit, it's already swollen. You're going to have a hell of a black eye."

The pain was excruciating. She'd hate to be the guy on the receiving end of his anger. Moving made her head spin so she sat still, watching Colin reach for the basin of cold water. He grabbed the rag, dipped it into the water and pressed it to her eye to reduce the swelling.

"I'm sorry. I was dreaming. When you touched me I reacted."

"It's OK, it was an accident. What was the dream about?"

Colin gave her a sheepish look before putting the cloth on the table. He obviously wasn't going to talk about it. "Who is Hamish?" Emily asked.

Pale and weak from jumping up, Colin fell back on the bed, "Where did you hear that name?"

"You called out in your sleep. Something about fighting with someone named Hamish, your brother, right?" Emily said. At that moment, Colin was spared from answering as the door banged open and Robert strode in.

Taking one look at Emily's eye and Colin's disheveled appearance, Robert said, "Well, it seems you've reached an accord and from the looks of it, spent a rather pleasant evening. Well done Colin. Injured and all yet still able to bed the lady. Hope you didn't rupture your stitches," he leered at them.

11

Monday, November 2nd

A ringing phone startled him awake. Groggy, hung-over, and bad tempered, he snarled into the thing, "Monroe here, what?"

Sitting up in bed, the dim, gray light filtering in through the curtains, every sense was on alert.

Confirmed.

After all this time, thinking he was losing it. This was the clue to break the case he'd been working on during off hours for ten years. Consumed him, drove him to find the truth once and for all. He owed her that much. He might have been a shitty boyfriend who was always disappointing her, but at least he wouldn't fail her when it came to taking down the bastard who'd murdered her.

The lab informed Monroe the DNA sample was tainted. They could identify human DNA, gold, and some other material which couldn't be identified, organic but nothing more. Odd—the dust actually contained real gold. Maybe this stuff was some kind of new expensive body cream with actual gold in it. The Japanese were experimenting with adding gold to all kinds of lotions and creams to make people look better. The tech couldn't be sure, simply a guess based on an advertisement he'd seen in his girlfriend's beauty magazine.

Monroe knew he had something solid now to help him find the bastard who killed Alice. At first he wondered how a guy with gold dust all over himself escaped notice, but then realized, anything went nowadays, people probably didn't even register it.

The lab was able to confirm the dental records on the two college kids. The medical examiner reported this was some type of rare disease bringing on rapid aging or a type of bacteria causing people to appear much older than they were. This news would not be in the report—he was to keep quiet, the ME was doing him a favor telling him since it was the same way they found out the wizened, old body was actually Alice.

Called to the scene of that long-ago day; he'd never believed it was Alice. Didn't matter the body was dressed in her clothes, with her identification, wearing earrings with her initials on them. How could she have aged sixty years in one evening?

Smelling the stench of garbage, he knew a cover-up was in play. News like this would send the city into a panic in today's youth-and beauty-obsessed culture. Wasn't only the Yanks obsessed with looking younger, they'd brought that craziness to Europe as well. It had spread like the Black Plague. Seeing grandmothers in tight jeans, artificially bright hair, high, tight, fake tits, and smooth plastic faces—like mannequins walking around—creepy.

Gut tightening, a nasty feeling went through him; this had to be a bigger problem. IDs not matching bodies, the rising number of missing people, it was all connected.

Hell, can you say serial killer? How would a disaster of those epic proportions play in the press? It was off season now, but soon it would be spring and the tourist hordes would appear, providing easy pickin's for the killer. Time was limited, a brief window. He needed to find the sick bastard.

There would be no court, no law, no bloody reports. He

would give this murderer some good old-fashioned Scottish justice, a vow made all those years ago...one he intended to keep.

❦

"HORSE PISS, YOU TWO WALK ANY SLOWER, IT WILL BE NIGHT and the tide will be gone," Robert groused. Making their way to the Leith docks, Emily noted how busy it was. She loved a harbor town, the cobblestone streets, old buildings, ships coming and going, people wandering around, all the quirky pubs and restaurants, and the smell of the ocean—well there was a fishy smell too but hey, that was part of the whole experience.

At least they'd had time to pick up a few basic necessities and a prepaid cellphone.

"I'll pay you back Colin. Thanks for this. Once we're on board, I'll call Kat to check-in."

Colin arched a brow at her "Ye don't need any bloody money; I'll take care of your needs."

"My men went to pick up your luggage but spotted a couple of minions hanging around the lobby so they left without being seen. Wouldn't do to alert them to the fact you'll be gone a few days." Robert continued, assuring her there were clothes on the ship she could change into. Once they came into port, she could pick up some clothing. A few days at Ravensmore, then this would be all over and her life would go back to normal.

Looking over at Colin, she wasn't sure what she wanted.

Rounding a corner, a gray and black tabby cat with a notch in its ear stopped washing its whiskers and stared at them. "I know people can't see you unless you want them to but can animals see you?"

"Funny thing, most animals know when something 'other' is nearby. Cats especially can see otherworldly creatures and Walkers. But just so you know, we are visible to humans right now. Can't have you walking alone to the ship now, can we?" Robert grabbed a fish off a vendor's stand, throwing it to the cat, who snatched it, darting into the alley to consume the treat.

Walking down the dock to a slip at the far end, a beautiful, historic ship loomed ahead of them.

"Um, guys, isn't that a historic landmark or something? Are we really sailing on it? Is it even safe? Uh, are those real guns?" She wasn't sure about some rickety ship taking them up the coast to Colin's castle.

"Now lass, I like you, but don't be insultin' my lady, she's a fit, working twenty-six gunner, and no, she's not an antique, she was painstakingly rebuilt from memories of my finest ship, the *Fortune*." Robert mock scowled at her.

"I'm sorry Robert, she's beautiful and I'm sure she's safe and sound."

Boarding the *Fortune II,* Emily and Colin were greeted by the assorted motley crew. There was much back slapping and crude remarks exchanged between Robert and his men before he introduced them to everyone.

"Alright now you scallywags, these two are under my protection so leave them be, ye hear? Quit lollygagging, finish loading the goods and let's be off," he bellowed at them. "Allow me to show you to your room. Quarters are tight, so you'll have to share. But that shouldn't be a problem after how well acquainted the two of you have become, should it now?" He leered, showing them to the cabin next to his.

The room was well appointed. A small, but luxurious bed, along with small trunk, dresser and mirror finished the room. There was a tiny bathroom in the hallway. The balance of modern day with the patina from Robert's time, made a beautiful mix of new meeting old. She could imagine Robert, decked out in his finery, surrounded by mounds of stolen gold, jewels, spirits, silk, and of course, a pretty girl or two for ransom draped over his lap or sitting at his feet.

"Might as well get comfortable, will take almost two days to reach Ravensmore if the winds stay with us. Get some sleep, tea's served at four o'clock," Robert told them. Seeing Emily's confused look, he guffawed. "We're not uncivilized, milady. Same as in England, we serve tea every afternoon. You crazy Yanks don't drink much tea, do you?"

"Why yes we do, although we prefer our tea, iced and sweet, with a hint of lemon. I'm from the South, we're not uncivilized either," she sniffed, pointing her nose in the air.

Colin roared with laughter. "No worries, lass. Robert's being an arsehole. Leave her alone; she's had a rough time of it."

Robert winked at her and left them, bellowing orders as the ship set sail.

"I'm going to give Kat a call, let her know I'm OK." Stepping out into the narrow passageway, she dialed Kat's number. Letting her best friend know she was OK, Emily filled her in on part of the story. Something made her feel protective of Colin, not to mention Kat would think she'd lost her marbles if she told her everything. So instead she spun a story, telling Kat partial truths. Even so, she could hear the disbelief in Kat's voice.

"...I'm a little worried about you. Are you sure you shouldn't see a doctor? Make sure everything is OK?"

"Honestly, I'm fine. Going to spend a bit more time with Colin. He's going to show me Ravensmore Castle. I'll call you at the end of the week when I get to the airport."

"Be careful."

"Thanks sweetie." Emily hung up. It was a lie of omission, but she wasn't ready to share the whole story. Had to figure out for herself what was happening before she could even think of telling Kat.

Heading into the room, she called out, "Colin, I'm back. Kat's good. She knows I'm fine. Colin?"

"Here lass, no need to shout." Swaying on his feet, Colin looked pale. She reached up and checked his forehead. He was burning up again. "Get undressed and into bed this instant. You have a fever; we have to get it down. Your arm looks infected too." Emily fussed.

Raising an eyebrow at her, Colin's lip curved up at the corner, "If you want me naked, all ye have to do is ask. I'm more than happy to oblige. We are sharing a bed. It gets cold on the sea and we'll need to be verra close together to keep warm." He waggled his eyebrows at her.

Sputtering, Emily spat out, "You are so arrogant. I don't want my handiwork ruined after I managed to sew something. Fine, get sick and die, I don't care, but don't expect me to stitch you up again. Once was enough." Crossing her arms over her chest, she glared up at Colin.

Chuckling he told her, "Dinna fash yerself lass, I'll let you tend me."

Snorting, she helped him remove his kilt, leaving him in a long shirt, her gaze traveling over him. With a sharp intake of breath, she turned to grab a blanket.

"Wait a minute, why are you taking your shirt off?"

"Well lass, how will you tend my arm if you can't get to all of it? I always sleep naked; will it bother you seeing my unclothed body? Make you want to ravish me?"

"Umm, let me just turn around to give you some privacy so you can get into bed and cover yourself," Emily stammered.

Chuckling, he removed his shirt, tossing it to the floor before flopping on the bed. "All right, you can turn around, I'm decent, well, at least covered up enough to protect your delicate sensibilities."

Emily busied herself picking up his clothes, straightening the room.

"I'm going to take a quick shower, k? I don't want to see these icky clothes ever again." She tucked him in bed, with water and whisky, before grabbing a pair of canvas pants and white linen shirt one of Robert's men provided for her. Heading out the door, she paused, turning to look at Colin.

"How does Robert make his living now? How do you?" she asked, curiosity filling her voice.

"Believe it or not, we're paid in gold by Thorne for being

Shadow Walkers, though smuggling is still a very profitable way to make a living. Robert is quite good at it so that's what he does, a modern-day pirate, without the sword and gunfights unless Day Walkers are involved. As for me, I own Ravensmore distillery, the spirits business is also very profitable. We may be invisible most of the time, but we like our modern-day toys. Not to mention, Robert wanted his ship. And I, Ravensmore. Takes a great deal of money to keep up these old estates. Would scare the staff to hear a disembodied voice asking them to bring the horses around or laughing at the match on the telly. So we make ourselves visible when needed." He winked at her.

"Wait a minute, I thought Hamish owned it. How did you get it back?"

"Curious as a cat, aren't ye? Go on, lass, take your shower; there'll be plenty of time for your infernal questions."

Rolling her eyes, Emily flounced out the door. The hot water was bliss, the soap and shampoo a bit manly but oh, so nice to be clean. Hurrying since she knew there was a limited amount of water, she toweled off, inspecting her fingers. Marveling it was possible to heal someone, she touched each fingertip, thankful Robert had the ability to take away the pain. But why didn't he heal Colin?

Not sure what to do with the disgusting clothing she'd been wearing, she put it in a basket figuring she'd ask later. There were so many questions she needed answers to. Pouring Colin a glass of whisky, she changed the dressing on his arm. The wound looked angry, swollen and not as bad as last night. His thigh was a bit improved as well.

Capturing her hands in his, Colin examined her fingers. "I'm sorry I couldn't do this for you..."

"You said something about being powerless. Why don't you have your powers but Robert has his? Can't he heal your arm and leg?" Taking a drink of water, she sat down at the table, trying to sort everything out. "You'll split your head open thinking so hard. Will be time enough to talk about everything later. I don't need any help from Robert. The wounds will heal. Right now you need to rest. Climb in beside me. I'm cold, you don't want me to catch a chill do you now?" Colin teased.

"Keep your hands to yourself, I'm not sleeping right next to you, you don't have any clothes on. I'll sleep between the two sheets." She primly told him.

He laughed, patting the bed. Emily climbed in beside Colin intending to get answers to her questions, but fell fast asleep as soon as her head hit the pillow. Sighing, Emily murmured in her sleep, moving closer to Colin.

Something smelled delicious. Emily yawned, stretching. She was snuggled up to Colin again. She knew she was attracted to him, wanted to sleep with him but she wasn't one of those women who could have casual sex. Heck she agonized over which accessories to wear and those were just jewelry and scarves. If she was honest with herself, she wasn't sure she was ready to trust someone with her heart again. Hers was still healing, the knife wounds deep. She didn't know if she wanted to take that risk again. Colin had the power to hurt her deeply; she was falling hard and she hadn't even slept with him. Sex would ratchet things up to the next level, one she wasn't quite ready for. Anyway, she'd be crazy to fall in love with an immortal guy, who'd never grow old and was cursed. She needed more answers before she took the next step.

Waking up, Emily realized someone had brought tea while they slept. Not only tea but scones, lemon curd and some kind of sandwich. Emily's stomach protested as she swung her legs over the side of the bed, she heard Colin chuckling. He was always laughing at her. She didn't care, it seemed like ages since she'd eaten, no wonder she was starving.

"Okay, food and drink first, then I want some answers. I saw your picture in the museum, read what it said about your brother and fiancée." Emily tried to sound stern.

Colin pressed his lips together until they were nothing but a thin white line. "My fiancée had it painted. I'd forgotten about it, I guess it ended up there somehow after I was killed."

"Is it true you were imprisoned for smuggling whisky to rebuild your castle?" she softly asked.

Before he could answer, Emily continued. "The guide at the museum, said your brother Lord Hamish, of Castle Gloom, was so angry about the smuggling that he murdered you while you were in chains in a fit of rage over ruining the family name or some crap like that. Doesn't seem fair when you couldn't fight back. I mean, families argue all the time, but they don't usually kill each other. Or was it because of Abigail?"

Seeing the look on his face, Emily went on, "She told the tour group you were engaged and your brother was also involved with Abigail. The rumor is one of them burned your castle to the ground to try and restore the family honor, and that's why Ravensmore and Edinburgh castles are haunted by you."

"Look, Robert and I are immortal Shadow Walkers. I told you we're both more than four hundred and fifty years old. We fight the things that go bump in the night, evil things like Day Walkers and other scary shite bent on destroying humanity. Creatures humans never want to encounter."

Finishing her tea, she noted he didn't really answer her, but she let it go for now. "I'm trying to take all of this in, you have to admit, not only is it difficult to believe, but it feels like we're trapped in some bad movie." Cocking an eyebrow he ground out, "You have no idea what is really out there. Humans go around living their pathetic, boring lives, not having a clue a war's being waged around them every day. Humanity isn't doing so well, the Day Walkers are winning, and some days I wonder why we even bother."

"Hey, I'm trying to understand, but things don't add up."

"There's something I haven't told you. At the Vaults, when you intervened, it changed things." Colin paused as if waging some inner war with himself, deciding what to tell her.

"What exactly do you mean 'changed things'?"

"I've told you who and what we are, who we serve, but I didn't explain the curse. We are all cursed. Every year, Shadow Walkers re-live their death as a reminder of the price we paid to become immortal."

"Curses now too, why am I not surprised?" she looked hard at Colin. There was something he was leaving out, something important. She'd always been good at reading people, and he was hiding something—it couldn't be good. "Whatever it is, it can't be worse than what I've already heard, so get it over with and tell me, you'll feel better." She tried to reassure him. Wondering how terrible it could be if he was hemming and hawing this much.

The slump of his shoulders told her he'd come to a decision; the grim look on his face said it would be bad. Well best to find out now. She hated secrets. Charlie kept too many of them, and it almost cost her her life.

HE HATED TALKING ABOUT CURSES AND WHAT MIGHT BE. HELL, he couldn't even ask Robert to heal his injuries, didn't like anyone knowing he was weak—friends or enemies. He'd rather suffer through.

"The curse states, only one can intervene to change a Shadow Walker's fate, someone who has crossed over into Shadow and come back. The countdown has started, with no way to stop it. A week before it's all over. I'm powerless during this time. 'Tis why I couldn't use my powers to free us from the cave-in or to heal your wee fingers. If within the week we can't end the curse... my soul will be lost, I'll be trapped forever in-between, not living or dying, turning into a wraith. Sentenced to eternal suffering in limbo, gray, soundless, and empty." He raised a hand to stop her questions, best tell her the rest.

"There's more—the gods are cruel, and you pay a price in all this. If you fail, you will be doomed...never finding true love, damned to live the rest of your life alone in the world, dying with no one who truly loves you by your side." He paused before adding, "Look I don't know if I even believe in this curse, well other than re-living my death each year. As far as I know, no one has broken their curse so I don't know what 'intervening' really means. If it's enough you prevented me from dying again or something more. When we're made Shadow Walkers, Thorne gives each of us the same speech regarding the curse but never says exactly what has to be done to break it. The gods are fickle that way. No one knows if this is to keep us in line or there's some truth to it."

Ah, fucking hell. He could see the horror in her face as she processed the information, understanding the consequences of her altruistic act, wishing she'd never tried to help him in the first place. After what Abigail and Hamish did to him, he'd never trust another woman again even one as sweet and kind as she was. Couldn't allow anyone to have that kind of power over him again.

He couldn't let Emily be doomed. If they failed...he'd become a wraith. Hell, how bad could it be? Not like anyone had ever come back to tell them all about the trip to never-never land. At least in the in-between, it was supposed to be quiet. Then again, fate might decide to have elevator music 24/7—he reconsidered —that would be a fate worse than death. See the problem with gods and fate? They never told you straight up what had to be done, instead preferring riddles, myths, and curses. Gave him the mother of all headaches.

"Wait a minute—so maybe we've already broken the curse when I helped you and we just have to wait out the week. What happens when the week is up? Is there some sign, or ringing bell, or something? It's ridiculous you don't know what you have to do to break the damn thing."

"I don't know if we've broken the curse. Maybe, but I would think if we had, I would know."

"Oh Hell's bells. And what happens if we succeed? Does everything go back to normal?" She asked. This was getting worse by the second. Of course she believed in true love, what normal woman didn't? Was it possible she'd really never experience true love if she failed? Anyway, it wasn't fair to have these consequences without telling her before she got involved, or not telling them how to break the curse. There had to be something he didn't know; this was too unfair for words. "I knew I should have paid better attention in those classes on mythology and philosophy."

"If we succeed...hell, no one has done it so all I know is what we've been told. We can go back to our lives. You get to go back to Charleston and live the life you're meant to have. For me, one of three fates: one, I'm human again, spend rest of my now-mortal life as a human; two, I can continue as a Shadow Walker who is no longer cursed. I'd fight because I want to. Or three, we fail, it's all true and I turn into a wraith for all eternity." Watching her face, Colin saw the emotions there. Let her think him a bastard for not saying they should try to be together, let him be a wraith—let her be alone ... at least she would live without being chained to someone like him, someone who'd never fully trust her. She'd find some man who could love her even if she couldn't fully love him back.

12

Leaving the Balmoral, Monroe was concerned something had happened to Emily. She hadn't been in her room for two days, hadn't checked out either. Was possible she was traveling the countryside, but she'd acted determined to find answers to her questions and he was worried. Remembering she had her phone with her, he tried multiple times, kept going straight to voice mail. Enough time had passed to officially list her has a missing person, however, his gut feeling told him not to do it. She had stumbled onto something, part of the same strange happenings he'd experienced. He'd find her, and she'd better be in trouble—if she was at a spa or wandering castle ruins in the Highlands, he'd have her head.

Remembering she'd been at the museum, he started there to retrace her steps. He showed the clerk a copy of her passport photo. The clerk didn't remember her but there were so many tourists coming through it was hard to notice anyone in particular. Monroe had never had much time for museums. He knew his history, didn't see any point in wandering around looking at it all the time. Walking around Edinburgh was a living history lesson every day.

He walked through the galleries, showing her picture to each person who had worked over the past two days. Coming up on the last docent who had worked during the timeframe, he asked about Emily. The docent remembered the American because she fell, and she thought the woman was going to throw up in the gallery. She talked about how the young woman was still sitting on the bench, looking pale and sick, an hour later when the docent finished her tour. The docent had approached but Emily waved her away, claiming she was coming down with something, not to worry, she wouldn't be sick in the museum. The docent shrugged and went to meet her next tour group. That was all she knew as she pointed Monroe to where Emily fell.

Striding over, a wall of portraits caught his eye. The wall was labeled *Scottish Scoundrels* so he started there as it was directly facing the bench.

Well, I'll be damned.

There was a painting of a baron named Colin Campbell—same name of the guy Emily went on about. He moved closer to read the plaque, the hair on the back of his neck standing up. It couldn't be the same guy, but the killer had to be using this identity somehow to target Emily—but why her?

Worried the killer was after her, he had to act quickly. Questioning the docent again, she thought she remembered hearing the Americans talk about going to Edinburgh Castle for the midnight tour.

He'd bet fifty quid Emily went there after getting Kat on the plane. She was a stubborn, tenacious woman. Telling her to leave things alone must have made her furious, so what did she do? Ignored him and continued investigating herself. He'd shake her fillings loose when he found her.

Heading over to the castle, he went through the same spiel. One of the employees remembered her. She had been there with a tour group. He wouldn't have any luck there; it would take too long to find those folks, many of them having moved on to the next city or country on their itineraries. No one remembered seeing her leave, there was so much going on it would be easy to miss her.

It was closing time, so he wouldn't have to worry about tourists mucking about, destroying any clues that might remain. Of course, even thinking a clue would remain after two full days of tourists traipsing about was madness.

Recalling the plaque in the museum, he headed to the dungeons, a perfect place for the killer to lie in wait. Running his hands through his hair in frustration, he was ready to call it a day when he spotted something shiny in the corner of the last cell. Under an old, tattered rag was a phone—with a pink and white monogrammed case bearing Emily's initials. The battery was dead. Examining every square inch of the cell and hallway, he was stumped. Picking up the rag to dispose of it, he looked closer...it was dirty, grimy, with rust-colored stains. He smelled it...a faint coppery tang hit his nostrils. Blood—was it hers? The killer's? Or simply coincidence?

He needed Shamus. His partner had an uncanny ability to track; noticing minute details Monroe might not have seen or attributed to anything suspicious. Knowing Shamus, he'd go along with not reporting Emily as missing; he knew all too well what Monroe's theories were on this case.

Ringing him, Monroe sketched out the details. "Shamus, I need you at Edinburgh Castle. Listen, I found that American's phone but no trace of her. Miss Emily Laurens seems to have vanished from the dungeons...brilliant, see you in thirty." Snapping his phone shut, he decided to head upstairs to the café to grab a cup of coffee.

While he waited, he read the paper, same old shite, different day, and finished up his coffee. Looking up, Monroe spotted Shamus striding across the cafe. "Hey Monroe, where's mine? It's colder than a witch's tit today."

"Thanks for getting here so fast." Filling Shamus in on what he'd found thus far, showing him Emily's phone, they refilled their coffees, heading back down to the dungeon.

Giving Shamus room to do his sniff and find thing, Monroe handled calls involving his other open cases. Moving to the end of the corridor to wait, he leaned against the wall, shoulder knocking into a stone gargoyle. Next thing he knew, it got all sci-fi, creepy as a door opened in the wall. Almost falling down the steps, he swore, "This shite keeps getting stranger and stranger."

Shining flashlights down the steps, they noticed footprints in the thick dust. A man and a woman's. Looked like the woman was supporting the man... Why would Emily help the killer? Unless he wasn't the killer—but then who the hell was he and how was this bloke involved?

Wouldn't find out standing here with his thumb up his arse. Jogging down the stairs, they didn't make it far before seeing the cave-in.

Shamus stopped Monroe with a hand on his shoulder. "The Yank could be trapped. We need to call it in, get some help down here to clear the cave-in. You know we can't risk a civ's life, even you aren't that stubborn."

"Wait a second, one of the old guys upstairs, you know, the one emptying trash...he said he'd worked here for a million years, knew everything there was to know about this place. First we check, see what he knows about secret tunnels. If he doesn't know, then we'll make the call." Monroe didn't want this turning into a circus, needed to keep it quiet, not tip off the killer.

Running up the narrow stairs, feet hitting the treads like a hammer, Monroe sprinted to catch the old geezer before he finished up and left.

"Angus, right?"

"Who are ye, why ye want to know?"

A crotchety old guy, he had to be in his late-eighties if he were a day. Stooped over, with only a couple of tufts of hair over each ear, the guy had the leathery skin of a sailor. Bright, intelligent, brown eyes, gazed out at him as Monroe resisted the urge to pump his fist in the air.

"I could use your assistance. Heard you were the go-to guy

for details no one else knows about this place. That true?" he watched Angus carefully. Seeing his face light up, Monroe resisted the urge to break out in a grin.

"Aye, what ye be wantin' to know laddie?" Smiling, the guy must have been missing half of his teeth, on his left hand, two fingers were gone. Rubbing his hands together, partly to keep warm, partly out of excitement, he told him about the secret passageway.

"Now laddie, ye shouldn't be messin' with that stuff, scare up a lot of old ghosts down there. But aye, there's tunnels all over Edinburgh, some say there's secret tunnels go all the way to Rosslyn Chapel...'tis how the Knights Templar secretly moved the Grail to hide it at Rosslyn undetected. Course ye also need to beware, one of those tunnels leads to a large cavern where all sorts of wicked dark doin's took place. Which tunnel did ye find?"

Seeing the confusion on the policeman's face, Angus elaborated, "Where was the opening?"

"Ah, at the far wall of the dungeon by the last solitary cell. I bumped into a stone gargoyle head and the wall opened, with stairs leading down. There's been a recent cave-in so I was hoping you might know where it comes out? It's important, a young American woman might be trapped down there."

Angus motioned for Monroe to follow him. He led the way to a small room. In the corner was a makeshift desk covered with books, papers, and drawings.

"Aye, I also keep the heat on round here. Now, where is it... ah, yes." Rifling through the papers, he pulled out a leather wrapped folio. Reverently opening it, Angus smoothed the old parchment. Seeing the look on Monroe's face, he clarified, "I didn't steal anything, came across this in a junk shop in the country, didn't know what they had, likely didn't care. Bought it for a steal. Dinna fash yourself boy, I'll add it to the castle collection once I'm done poring over it. Now look here, it shows all the tunnels from the castle. Let's see, that tunnel comes out by the water, at the top of Nor Loch about a mile or two thereabouts from the Black Swan. Best to start from that side if it's caved in here. Damn shame, I'll let folks here know about the tunnel, and they can send men out to clear it. Make a great tourist draw. Though laddie, same as on this side, you'll need to look for a lever or some type of stone you can press to open the door, like ye did with the gargoyle."

The old man put away his drawings and ambled down to the dungeon to have a look at the tunnel for himself. Monroe and Shamus followed. "'Twas fine craftsmanship, building these tunnels. Ye know lads, my ancestor, Angus the first, was hanged here at the Castle. Part of Black Bart's pirate crew. He would have loved this tunnel, maybe he could've escaped."

Monroe sighed as Shamus's face lit up. The guy loved history. Especially anything to do with old ships.

"Black Bart you say? Think I could buy you a pint in exchange for telling me the tale?" Shamus asked.

"Aye, be happy to tell it. I'm here most days, come by 'round closing and I'll tell ye what I know." Angus nodded at Shamus.

Monroe and Shamus bid Angus good day as the old-timer drew on his coat, walking out with them, appearing to be lost in the shadows of his thoughts.

Picking their way down the embankment, towards the Nor Loch, looking for signs, Monroe cursed, slipping in the muck. Shamus spotted it first.

"Oy, this brush is broken; there are footprints, man and woman, in the mud by the path. Might be the ones we're looking for. The entrance should be close."

Behind the hedge was a stone wall with broken branches on the ground, stone rosettes inlaid into the wall in a pattern. Pressing each one, Monroe could feel his excitement building. He was getting closer, he could feel it, knew he was on the right track, closing in. A click told him he'd found the lever. The door swung open. Shining their torches, heading into the darkness, they could follow the footprints all the way to the cave-in. Looking closely, Shamus noted blood on some of the rocks while Monroe picked up two broken fingernails; they looked like they'd been torn from the nail bed. Female from the color.

Good news was they'd gotten out. Not so good news, he didn't know if she'd been harmed, who she was with, if she was with them voluntarily or not, and where the guy was taking her. Angus mentioned the Black Swan; it was an old, historic pub favored by the locals...was said it used to be a well-known pirate hangout. A dirt path followed the Nor Loch. The map he'd seen should lead them there. Would be worth checking out.

Entering the tavern, it was dark, with a thatched roof, scarred wooden tables and chairs, old oak flooring, and a cheery fire giving off warmth but doing nothing to dispel the gloom. Not many tourists, this was more a place for locals, disreputable ones from the looks of it. Looking around they spotted the proprietor.

"Can I help you boys? I'm Henry, owner of the Black Swan." Henry looked at them, wiping his hands on his apron behind the bar.

"Hope so. I'm officer MacDonald and this is officer O'Malley." Holding the picture of Emily out to Henry, Monroe continued, "We're looking for this American. She may have come through here recently, have you seen her?"

"Right pretty lass. No, haven't seen her, not that I can recollect." Henry scratched his head.

"Are you sure? She might have been with a man? Anybody else working we could speak with?" Monroe pressed. He could swear Henry was lying.

"Well, I'm always working, have to make a living. Just me and the missus. Sally? Can ye come here a moment?"

Monroe watched the woman approach. She looked tired and wouldn't meet his eyes

"These officers are looking for an American woman. Think she might have passed through. I told them we hadn't seen her.

Do you remember anyone looking like this lass?" Henry pointed to the picture Monroe was holding.

"Ma'am. Have you seen this woman?" He repeated the question, showing her the photo.

"No, officer, not that I recall. We've been terribly busy, but I think I'd remember a Yank. We mostly get local folk coming through here, not many tourists. Sorry I can't help." Sally told him.

"I'll leave my card in case either of you remember anything or she happens to wander in. Thank you for your time." Monroe handed them his card and motioned Shamus over from the bar.

"Damn it, I know that old buzzard knows something about Emily. He's seen her or heard of her." Frustrated, Monroe hadn't slept well the past night, dreaming of Alice. His nerves were frayed, his temper at the boiling point.

No one else in the tavern could help or would help. Outside, Monroe looked around to regroup. If Emily and her captor had even stopped in the tavern, there was no telling where he was taking her or what he might have planned.

Shamus interrupted his thoughts. "If the bastard has your Yank in his car, we'll never find them without reporting it. Why don't I call it in, start the official investigation?"

"Not yet. Call the rental car companies, see if anyone fitting their description rented a car. The docks are close, let's ask around and if we're at a dead end, then I'll call it in myself. Deal?"

His partner didn't like it by the look on his face but he agreed. "Fine. Let's get moving before the skies piss on us."

It was gloomy, the sky leaden gray, sun straining to break through. Cold, the wind ripped, chilling him to the bone. While Shamus called the rental car companies, Monroe rang the hotel to see if Emily had returned. The hotel confirmed her bed hadn't been slept in, though her room was paid until the end of the week. The front desk clerk assured him it wasn't unusual. Tourists frequently kept their room at the

Balmoral while exploring for a day or two around the countryside.

Striking out with the rental cars, Shamus stopped, buying a couple of hand pies to eat while they walked. Making their way to the docks to ask around, Monroe sensed they were getting closer.

No one had seen the travelers or was saying if they had, so he and Shamus found out which ships had set sail recently and checked each one out. A name caught Shamus's eye.

"Oy, over here. Remember me telling you I was researching what happened to that old pirate ship, the *Fortune*?"

Monroe looked at his partner. Shamus had a gleam in his eye. He was a fanatic about old ships. Spent every moment researching them, building models, reading every piece of history he could get his hands on. Was his partner's favorite hobby.

"What of it?" Monroe groaned, hoping he wasn't going to have to listen to a long drawn out tale.

"Don't you think it's a strange coincidence that Angus's ancestor was hanged as part of Black Bart's pirate crew and now I'm looking at a ship called the *Fortune II*...and the owner is listed as one Robert Bartholomew, which was the real name of Black Bart? His ship was known for trading in illegal goods."

Rolling his eyes, Monroe wasn't convinced. "Probably some old ship fanatic like you. Doesn't mean anything."

"Come on, this unofficial investigation has been nothing but strange. Listen—a ship built and named after an infamous pirate ship sets sail in the right timeframe. The ship is listed as carrying goods, sailing up the coast, making several stops."

"I'm listening." Monroe leaned against the counter in the clerk's office.

"Right. Out of the listed ports, two stand out based on what we know thus far. Inverness and Invergordon." Shamus trailed off.

"Which means the killer could be headed to Ravensmore

Castle." If Emily's story were true, and there was some crazy immortal ghost warrior running around Edinburgh...the plaque at the museum said it was his castle so that seemed a likely place to look.

Monroe hadn't told Shamus they could be looking for a ghost. Shamus might have his back, but a ghost—he'd hound Monroe to see a shrink for sure. Instead he told Shamus the killer might be a crazy re-enactor who deluded himself into thinking he was a baron from the 1600s.

Doubtful the killer or ghost or whatever he was, would go to the brother's ancestral castle, what with the brother murdering him, unless he was also alive? Fuuuuck, it was too much for his tired brain to process. They were behind a day but could make up the time driving, might even catch them as they disembarked.

"See, I told you it was important to know all the old ships and their history. This may break our case wide open, go ahead, thank me now, better yet, buy me a couple of pints. A-n-n-n-d a whisky or two—you might be the brilliant one but you don't know shite about ships." Shamus clapped him on the back.

Great, his partner would hold this over his head for at least the next week. He'd never hear the end of how important it was to know your history. Snorting, he stopped to grab a coffee before heading out.

RAWLINS HAD THE PATHETIC HUMAN UP AGAINST THE WALL, one hand on his throat, the man's feet kicking a frenetic beat against the boards. "I'll not ask again, where were they headed? You know each and every ship in and out of this port, destination included, so speak and I'll consider sparing your life."

He'd already taken a good twenty years from this man, his once red hair, now a dull, lusterless orange. Feeling the added energy coursing through his veins, Rawlins could smell everything around him. He'd had it on good authority from those he paid to watch the comings and goings all over Edinburgh that a man and woman fitting Colin's and Emily's description had boarded Robert's ship. That bloody bastard—after all these years, still causing problems for him. No worries, he'd killed him once, this time he'd make sure the pirate stayed dead. Ripping out his heart would ensure he was nothing but dust. His lip quirked up in a semblance of a smile, turning his attentions back to the human who was now turning a ghastly shade of purple. Letting him drop to the floor, Rawlins placed his booted foot on the man's neck.

"All right, they boarded the *Fortune II* ... it's making multiple stops." The man gasped like a fish out of water, flopping about on the floor, desperately trying to force air into his screaming lungs. Two stops stood out to Rawlins—Inverness and Invergordon. Ah Colin, not so smart after all...headed to the ruins of Castle Gloom or to Ravensmore? Can't be Gloom since I've been making use of the dungeons there. Must be Ravensmore. Rawlins had been in the castle enough times to be able to dematerialize there without worry about ending up embedded in a wall. Easy enough to find out. He'd take the fight to his enemies...put an end to those two once and for all. The woman would be icing on the cake; he'd take her to his bed before draining her. Finishing the man off, he threw the corpse to the corner of the room, dematerializing to rally his troops.

13

Dinner was noisy, chaotic, and delicious. Emily couldn't remember when she'd felt this carefree, after all Colin had told her, she needed to take her mind off thinking about curses for one night. Captain Robert's crew dined in the adjoining room, and she could hear the ribald jokes, stories becoming larger than life, growing exponentially with the amount of rum they consumed.

"Your crew—are they like you?" She thought they were human, but unless she noticed no one else could see them, she couldn't tell if they were ghosts or not.

Chuckling, Robert answered, "No, they're all human. My crew died long ago, God rest their souls. None stayed behind. They all went on to find their peace."

Wrinkling her nose in concentration, she went on, "So how did you find these men?"

Robert looked at Colin, "Your lass is curious as a cat isn't she?"

"Aye, she keeps things interestin." Colin winked at her.

"I hired boys from the families who had perished and so on. The men you see are descended from my first crew. 'Twas the least I could do to help the families who were left behind. All I hire know I'm 'different,' though every now and again I forget to make myself visible and scare the hell out of one of my men." Robert smirked at her and Colin broke out in laughter.

The crew ate in shifts. Robert had modern engines but preferred the old ways, said the rhythm and pace felt more natural to him than the humming of engines. He liked the sounds of the ocean, waves hitting the bow, gulls calling, the rigging creaking with the motion of the ship, the occasional whale sighting, and the dance of everyone knowing their job, working together as a team.

The Captain's dining room was beautiful, decorated in rich shades of burgundy, navy, green, and gold. Sumptuous silk curtains framed the windows, silk pillows adorned each dining chair, the chairs and table made out of rich mahogany with gorgeous carved legs. There was even a china cabinet in the room. The table was set with heavy linens; silver polished to a mirror finish, beautiful fine crystal and of course the china. She adored china, collected it, used it all the time, even to serve pizza on; after all, why save it only for special occasions? Pizza Tuesday could be just as special as Thanksgiving dinner. She never understood why people saved beautiful things, only to use them rarely, if ever. Not as if anyone would look back and say oh, I shouldn't have used that china so much. Surrounding yourself with beautiful things made the world a nicer place which it sorely needed.

The meal was delicious, the wine like velvet on the tongue and the conversation fascinating. Colin kept her glass full, making sure she had whatever she wanted. Seated between the two men, she felt safe and secure. Stealing glances at Colin, he took her breath away—so strong, lethal, and sexy—it should be against the law to have that kind of sex appeal. Discreetly fanning her face, she dragged her thoughts from the warrior beside her to the table; she had to know, "Robert, how does the china cabinet and table stay in place when there's a storm?"

"Good question lass, back in the day, not only were storms an issue but battles as well, so the heavy items are bolted to the walls and floor. Used to be six or seven sets of china packed away in the ship's hold so if we encountered a bad storm or ran into battle with the bloody English, we'd have more. What's a meal without fine china, crystal, and sterling silver?" He cocked an eyebrow at her.

Biting her bottom lip, she thought about it. It made sense, something they should think about in earthquake-prone places like California. Though her grandmother would have a conniption putting screws through her precious antiques to bolt them to the floors and walls; being a fine southern lady, she'd never live on the wild West Coast anyway.

"The china, is it Haviland? It looks like a pattern my friend Kat has. Hers is almost two hundred years old. It's in excellent condition but yours looks new."

"Good eye lass, I traded black pearls from the South Seas for it from Mr. Haviland himself, 'tis been in storage for a time." Leaning back in his chair, Robert settled in to tell the story while Colin poured another glass of wine and rolled his eyes.

"He had recently gone into business, set up a fine factory in Limoges, France, and wanted to give his pretty, young wife a lovely bauble. I was sailing from France back to Scotland with a hold full of goods when he approached me. He was a brave man to enter the pubs lining the docks in Marseilles. They were a rough place then. We came to an accord and made the trade, both happy with the outcome."

The table was cleared, dessert brought in. Rich, gooey, chocolate cake with chocolate ganache on top, Emily was in hog heaven. She groaned in ecstasy tasting the rich confection.

Reaching over, Colin wiped a tiny drop of chocolate from the corner of Emily's lip—she stilled, watching him as he deliberately took his finger and sucked the chocolate off. She swore she could feel it down to her core, insides molten, like the center of the cake.

Laughter brought her attention back to Robert.

"Me thinks you two should get a room—right—you have a room, why don't ye go there and get naked?"

Colin glared, "Shut your mouth before I shut it for you."

Before things could get out of hand, Emily jumped in. "Tell me how you met Robert."

"Aye, Colin, tell the lass, 'tis a fine story. I saved his head from the chopping block numerous times."

Raking a murderous glare over Robert, Colin told her, "He's so full of shite, I saved his arse from the English too many times to count. Will you shut the hell up and let me tell the damn tale."

As the dessert dishes were cleared, wine replaced by cognac, Emily was tipsy. Sated from dinner and drink, warm and sleepy from the gentle rocking of the ship.

"You see Emily, it was verra long ago, my usual Captain had gone down with his ship in a fierce storm, I'd heard of the infamous 'Black Bart' and decided to introduce myself."

Robert broke in, "Aye, we met in a broth...er, in a...well, in a bawdy house. I was finishin' with Lola when I heard a scuffle outside."

"Seriously, you are such a woman; I thought I was the one telling the story—let me tell it already. If you tell it, we'll still be sitting here when the dawn comes. It gets longer every time he tells it." Colin cut his eyes to Robert. "Don't give me the poor, wounded me look. I've plans for the rest of the evening, and they sure as hell don't involve you, mate." Emily giggled, heat flared in her stomach at Colin's words. Looking at him, her face hot, "Please continue. I want to hear the story."

"Getting back to the tale then...there was a scuffle, the English had taken a couple of my lads, as they shouted for me, I came out the door as did Robert. We managed to free the men and escape from the blasted English. Couldn't have them knowing I was the smuggler. After a few too many drinks I hired Robert to transport my merchandise from that day forward. Course, you had to mix up Captains so the English would be kept guessing, but we ran into each other over the years until we both ended up in the one-star accommodations of Edinburgh Castle, bound for the gallows."

Opening her mouth to ask Colin a question, she was cut off when he grabbed her hand, excusing them from the table. "I can see the wheels turning in your head. Thought we'd have a walk after dinner, enjoy the sea air."

Colin practically dragged her from the dining room to the deck. The open air carried a salty tang she could taste. The smell reminded her of him.

"You didn't want me to start asking questions, did you?" She playfully hit his uninjured arm, allowing him to escort her around the deck.

One of the crew members was playing a violin, a haunting melody, as if in homage to the full moon overhead. Stopping to lean against the railing, he asked her why she was in Scotland.

"When we were trapped in the tunnel, you told me you and your friend Kat came to Scotland to 'get away,' what did you mean? Did something happen that caused you flee the country?" Colin asked in a light tone.

Staring up at the night sky filled with stars, the moon hanging heavy, almost touching the water, she thought about how to answer him. Releasing a pent-up sigh, she began, "Well, I was in a relationship with a man named Charlie. What I didn't realize until it was too late was he liked to keep secrets. One of his secrets was another woman; his cheating is what caused the accident. I ended up in the hospital."

"ACCIDENT? HOSPITAL? WHAT HAPPENED TO YOU LASS?" HE growled, jealousy roaring to life...if that bastard had hurt her, he'd tear him apart.

Not looking at him, she continued, "We were driving, he was sexting with her, lost control, and hit a tree. The car rolled on its side into the stream..." her voice trailed off. Giving her a minute, he wrapped his arms around her.

"'Tis okay lass, tell me the rest."

"They told me I died. I was lost for eight minutes. They'd given up...as they were leaving the room to tell my brother and Kat, I came to screaming." She was rigid in his arms as if worried what he might think.

"It must have been a terrifying experience." Trying to ease her suffering, the strain of the memory making her tense, he stroked her hair, tucking the errant strands behind her ear.

"Did you know the stars are made out of tears?"

Turning in his arms, inches separating them, she looked through him, into his very soul with those knowing gray eyes.

"Tell me."

"'Tis said each and every star we see in the night sky, was formed from a tear, a tear made from broken hearts and broken promises. An ancient god and goddess, deeply in love, were ripped from each other, destined to be apart throughout eternity...the tears from Luna's broken heart created the stars in the night sky. She became the moon; Solus the sun, passing each other for a brief moment in time each morning and evening. This is why sunrise and sunset are so beautiful, the tragic lovers, yearning to be together again, knowing it can never be, fill the sky with the colors of their love for each other.

"What a heartbreakingly beautiful story. I've never heard it before, so much better than thinking the moon, sun, and stars are distant planets...though sadder."

Quiet, lost in their thoughts, listening as the violin wove a spell of enchantment on the night air; neither spoke.

"What, no more questions? I haven't heard you this quiet since we met in the Vaults."

"It's so much to absorb, the curse, Shadow Walkers, Day Walkers, immortality; not to mention, I'm not sure what I have to do to help you. It's exhausting thinking about it."

"Maybe you're to help me find that bastard Captain Rawlins

Huntington. Then stay out of the way while I kill him. Hamish betrayed me...not only with my fiancée but to the captain, which also cost me my crew—men who depended on me to protect and provide for them and their families. He knew I kept the whisky in the Vaults, watched to learn when and how I moved it so he could turn me in, allowing the good captain to find me. My own brother conspired with the English while Rawlins left me chained to a wall so I couldn't defend myself against Hamish. He let him kill me." Colin told her, very matter-of-factly; what did it matter now, ancient fucking history, that bridge was burnt and long gone.

"I can't imagine how much the betrayal by your brother and fiancée must have hurt. Betrayal..."

He waved her off, not wanting to go there, "It's the past, more importantly, how are you holding up, processing your new reality? Knowing there really are things out there that go bump in the night?"

Emily pulled a button from her pocket and handed to him. Puzzled he looked at her.

"It must have come off in the Vaults," she told him. "It's how I knew you weren't a ghost, of course, I didn't really know what you were, other than some crazy re-enactor, which made me determined to find you and give you a piece of my mind for scaring the living daylights out of me. When I saw the painting, the shirt you had on, well, it was the same button."

"Aye, it was painted the morning I was arrested."

She wrapped her arms around him, holding him tight, resting her head against his chest. If she only knew...he was damaged, had kept every emotion locked away deep inside for so long—trembled at the thought of letting her in.

Ice cold. Her skin was so cold. He hadn't noticed the temperature dropping, was too engrossed in her. "Let's get you inside, out of the cold." Taking her hand, he twined his fingers through hers, leading her down the stairs to their room.

"Do you want a drink before bed? Um, before we go to sleep I mean," she was breathless.

Seeing her standing there, riveted to the floor, watching him, his nostrils flared, catching her scent as he stalked towards her. This woman captivated him. Inexplicably he was drawn to her, a base need he couldn't put a name to. Reaching out, he caressed her hair. Want...need...desire, filled him, threatening to spill over. Tentatively, she reached up, caressed his jaw, her fingers soft against his stubble, the sensation heading straight to his groin. A simple touch of her hand was all it took, in that moment he wanted to crawl into her skin; mark her for all time.

"Damn the whisky," he choked out.

The room crackled with electricity, a dim silvery light filling every corner and crevice as he dipped his mouth to hers. The clock on the mantle stopped ticking, he felt her breath hitch—before she could take her next breath, he kissed her with savage need.

Taking her into his arms, she moaned against his mouth, holding him tight, losing herself within their kiss. His muscles twitched under her caress, he growled, an ancient predator ready to devour her. Hands moving to his hair, she played with his braids, twining her fingers through them, pressing her chest into him.

"I've never wanted any man like this."

He lifted her up, settling her against his hips, his desire for her evident, his erection pressing against her core. The contact was electrifying. As he licked his way from her earlobe down her neck, she moaned, deep in her throat. The feel of her, wrapping her legs tighter around his waist, he could hold her forever.

Hands cupping her ass, stroking circles with his thumbs, he felt her breath as she panted against his cheek.

Her fingers traced his jaw causing him to flinch as she followed the hideous scar, tracing the jagged line. When he tried to move her hand away, she stopped him. "Don't. It's part of you. I think it's beautiful." His woman was daft to think the scar 'beautiful.' Letting her explore his face, he fumbled, reaching for the dagger. With the rip of fabric, he sliced through the linen pants—she shivered in the cold air as their bodies separated enough for him to pull the fabric from her body, falling to the floor in a heap, useless rags.

"Damned tie was stuck."

Her giggle turned to a gasp, as he grasped her thighs, stroking, palming her arse, the cool breeze blowing in through the window raising goose bumps across bare skin.

"Your skin feels like silk," he rasped, reverently sliding his palms over her skin. Struggling to be closer to him, she reached out, pulling at his shirt. Raising his arms up, he pulled it over his head so she could run her hands over his chest. He was filled with a raw hunger. It had been centuries, hell maybe never since he wanted a woman as he wanted her. Being a Shadow Walker meant never letting anyone get close; he didn't trust women, wouldn't wake up next to one, only letting them take their pleasure from his body, feeling nothing as they came and went over the years. Something about Emily was different from the rest.

Startled, he realized, he wanted to wake up, see her next to him, watch the morning light play over her face, make her laugh —gods, he loved her clear, innocent laugh. He couldn't love her, no way he would cut open his heart. Not ever again after the gut-wrenching betrayal of Abigail, but...he felt something, feelings he couldn't explain or put a name to—if he couldn't love her, he could give her passion. She was a warrior in her own right, overcoming her fear, standing up to him; he imagined how fierce a lover she would be.

The beast within howled, demanding he take her. Giving in to desire, he crushed her lips, invading her mouth, exploring every inch. Skimming his hands across her back, down to her ass, he marveled at what a tight, gorgeous arse it was, couldn't wait to nip it with his teeth, lick each mound down to the crease where ass met thigh.

Feeling her clench her thighs tighter around him, the beast

rumbled, ready to take her as he carried her to the bed, laying her down on the sheets, not breaking contact, skin to skin, scents intermingling as the silvery air grew brighter around them, a low hum reverberated around the room, seeming to come from nowhere, everywhere, as he ground into her, feeling her wetness against his thigh.

"Kiss me harder." She ran her hands up his thighs, under his kilt, digging her nails into his ass. Pulling at his kilt, trying to remove the barrier between their skin, she huffed, "Damnit, I can't get it undone."

Chuckling, he shifted; breaking contact with her body as he quickly removed the kilt, throwing it to the floor. Purring in satisfaction, she raked her nails down his back. His cock jerked against her. Running his hands over every inch of her body—wasn't enough—the rough fabric of her shirt, impeding them from full skin to skin contact, he hissed in protest at the fabric in the way, hearing her gasp as he took the shirt in his hands, ripping it down the front, buttons popping. She was exquisite. Gazing at her, body translucent in the light, he thought he could see inside her, every thought, doubt, and dream swirling around in her head. Hand darting out, she reached for the sheet.

"No, you enchant me, skin so smooth and soft, don't cover up, let me see all of you," he rasped. Awed by this goddess beneath him, he bent his head as if in prayer, before kissing her shoulders, trailing kisses down her arm, licking that tender part of skin under her arm.

His fingers caressed her breast, rolling her nipple between his thumb and finger as it puckered and hardened for him.

"You smell like the ocean." She kissed his bicep then licked it. "Taste like it too." He felt her skin growing warm, the air in the room heating up as they explored each other. Running his hand down her breast, over her ribs, he traced circles on her stomach. So soft. He wanted to sink his teeth into her, devour her. His back arched when she caressed him, cupping his balls, gently rolling them in her hands, lightly brushing his cock as it jerked in response to her touch. Running her palm over the head, he moaned when she touched the drop of moisture there, putting her finger to her mouth to taste him. Her hand was custom made for him, he quivered, thinking no one who came before her meant anything. This was something new. The fates had made her for him. Trailing her fingertips along his muscles, tracing each one, she stopped at his injured arm.

"I don't want to hurt you—your arm is still injured, your ribs need to heal."

"There is no pain, only pleasure." He leaned down to kiss her but she stopped him with her palm on his chest.

"How can you not feel any pain? I bruised a rib once, and it was weeks before I could breathe without wincing."

"Lass, I don't allow myself to feel pain, pain gets you killed, I don't have time for it." Not to bloody mention if he didn't keep those emotions locked away tight, he'd curl up in a ball in the corner crying for his mommy; those memories carried the power to cut him down.

Wanting to lose himself in her, he leaned down capturing a nipple in his mouth, cutting off her reply as he licked and suckled the nipple, feeling it tighten as she arched beneath him, her fingers tangled in his hair.

He slid his palm slowly down the length of her body, stroking her curves and softness, marveling at how amazing her body was, he reached what he was seeking, his fingers stroking her, teasing her. She shifted, wordlessly trying to tell him what she craved when he started grinding his palm against her bud, fingers delving inside her, pumping in and out while his palm kept pulsing against her. Hips thrusting up to meet his hand, she brought her knees up, spreading them wide, giving him full access to her while she fisted the sheet in her hand, twisting it tighter and tighter as her body responded to his touch. His other hand continued to roll her nipple between his fingers as she cried out. Pressure was building inside her, her skin flushed from the heated air as she rocked against his hand.

Enthralled, he moved closer to her, filled with wonder at the sight. Catching her scent, he almost came on the spot

Her knees slammed together. "What's wrong? Why did you stop?"

"Wrong? Not a single bloody thing. My god, you're so beautiful...smell so delicious, so wet and ready for me, I need to taste ye." Dipping his head, he licked her, lapping, over and over, flicking his tongue against her as she writhed in the bed. The tension eased out of her as her head fell back and her knees opened wider, allowing him the access he craved. Sweeping his tongue from side to side, he took her deeper into his mouth, hearing her keen with need. Circling her nub, he latched on; sucking to a rhythm only he could hear, playing her body like a fine instrument. Flicking his tongue, she arched, fisting the sheets. Scraping his teeth gently across her mound, he grabbed her thighs, locking her against his mouth.

Penetrating her with his tongue, she rocked hard against him. "Oh, please don't stop, I'm almost there..." Arching off the bed, Emily exploded as her orgasm rocked her, a second more intense orgasm followed as he lapped and licked every drop, rubbing his whiskers against her sensitive sex, wringing one last orgasm out of her as she finished against his mouth.

Peaches, she not only smelled like them, she tasted like them. Forever, he'd bite into the juicy fruit and think of her.

His control shattered, couldn't wait another second as he thrust into her, filling her to the hilt. She bent her knees deeper to take him in. He belonged inside her. Pleasure unlike anything he'd ever experienced filled him. Thrusting in and out, deeper and deeper, he looked down at Emily, the bliss on her face, almost causing him to spill. "By the gods, you steal my very breath."

Grabbing her ankles and lifting them onto his shoulders to allow him to penetrate her more deeply, he groaned. She was so hot, and wet, and tight, gripping him with each thrust, her thighs shook. He increased the tempo and slid in harder and deeper while reaching his hand back to her...pressing his finger against her cleft, tapping, tapping, tapping. Emily was staring at something, he glanced down at his arms, seeing the hair standing straight up. Their hair was floating in the breeze—before he could make sense of what he was seeing, he felt her tumble over the edge of the cliff, muscles clenching around his cock as she screamed, "Colin."

"Mine." He growled, following her over the cliff, his entire body trembling in ecstasy.

❦

WITHDRAWING FROM HER, TAKING HER IN HIS ARMS, EMILY'S body screamed in protest at the broken contact. Worshipped...it was the only way to explain what Colin did to her. She felt boneless, laying there in his arms while he played with her hair, winding it through his fingers.

Panic rolled over her...she couldn't do this, couldn't let someone get this close, she hardly knew anything about him, and what she did know would send any sane woman running away fast. The sting of betrayal curled around her brain, sending hateful tendrils to her heart—he will betray you, like Charlie betrayed you. Hating the mean, inner critic, she shook her head, willing it to go away.

She'd been tearing down her walls ever since he'd told her of his own betrayals, the pain evident in his voice, the wounds deep, lashing out when he felt vulnerable, she could understand those feelings, respect them. Telling the voice in her head to beat it, she made a decision...to try. Try and trust this warrior, try to let him in, try not to push him away. Believing in following her heart, she wanted this strong, damaged man with every fiber of her being. Let the chips fall where they may, she needed Colin, couldn't imagine being without him. She would only think about now, living in the moment, not worrying about tomorrow or going back to Charleston and leaving Colin, she'd worry about it another day...but not tonight...tonight she would feel.

She snuggled closer to him. Would never get enough of his scent—who would have thought the smell of leather and the tang of the ocean could smell so sexy?

Colin had his eyes closed, breathing deeply. She hoped they hadn't made his injuries worse. He traced lazy circles on her body, she shivered, his touch sending tingles through her.

Something niggled at her memory...

"Our hair was standing on end, like before lighting strikes... come to think of it, why does the air look silver and feel so warm?" she asked puzzlement filling her voice.

"'Tis part of being a Shadow Walker...I told ye we're all made of energy? Well, during sex, we release energy, it manifests as heat and electricity—'tis why our hair stood on end. The silver light is part of our makeup; we serve Thorne who bears allegiance to the Moon goddess so we have silver light or when we are killed, silver dust. The Day Walkers, serving Dayne, who is allied with the Sun god, have golden light and dust. Look how the silver sparkles on your skin."

Wiping a finger down her arm, she was puzzled; her skin sparkled as if she'd put some sort of shimmery lotion on it but the dust didn't come off.

"It won't come off. Will I walk around all the time sparkling?"

Grinning, he told her, "No, it will fade away in a few hours. It happens sometimes during sex. All walkers have to be careful when having sex so we don't steal your energy."

"What do you mean, like some kind of siphoning off or alien suction tube stuff?" Wrinkling her nose in thought, she waited for an answer.

"You have no idea how bloody sexy you are when your wrinkle your nose or bite your lip when you're thinking," he growled at her, leaning in to kiss her.

Stunned. Never wanted any man like this, not even Charlie. She was a desperate pool of liquid need as his touch ignited her.

Breaking off the kiss, he fondled her breast. "No aliens. Day Walkers steal a human's energy which ages them instantly or they keep going and kill the human—it is forbidden to do either but they prey upon the innocent and think the prize is worth it... it makes them stronger, taking in energy. When we recharge, it doesn't make us any stronger—you have to kill another Walker, then you take their energy and become stronger. The lowlife's cheat by stealing from humans..."

Emily interrupted him, holding a hand up in the air, in the universal stop gesture.

"Hold on, stop the presses—AGE THEM? My god, if that got out, it would strike terror in every woman in the world. We fight every day to look young...my mother drilled it into me when I was in high school. This could cause a worldwide panic. No, I think women all over would take up arms to kill the Day Walkers for daring to age them and undo all that hard work. Think about it, an army of angry women, you could rule the world." She snickered, then sobered as she realized, fudge, they wouldn't be able to see them to fight them unless like her they'd been to the other side and back. Oh well, nice idea.

She relaxed, putting Day Walkers out of her mind, thinking of the mind-blowing sex they'd had, she sighed, snuggling closer into Colin's side, leaning up, softly kissing his temple.

He wasn't moving; did she do something wrong?

"Are you OK?" Stroking his cheek, Colin seemed surprised by her affection. Her heart broke...had he been without a kind word or touch for so long?

"Fine, not used to spending this much time with someone—'tis nice."

Emily swung her leg over him, getting closer, running her hand over his chest, lost in a dreamlike state. Faster than she could blink, Colin lifted her up on top of him, impaling her with his heavy, thick cock.

"You're ready again, so soon?"

"Oh darlin', I've only just started, there are so many ways I'm going to make you come tonight, you won't be able to walk in the morning."

He proceeded to prove it to her over the next several hours as they made love in the bed, on the floor and up against the wall, the silk wall coverings sensuously sliding up and down against her back. He was amazing. She'd only been with a few guys—was a late bloomer; none came close to what he made her feel. What was the silly expression she'd always rolled her eyes when she heard it?...oh yeah, a hard man is good to find. It was oh so true, though he was also a good man, even if he lived by his own set of rules, not society's laws.

Lowering her from the wall, where she'd had another blistering orgasm, he picked her up, gently carrying her back to bed as he dipped a washcloth in the wash basin and proceeded to clean her off. Emily thought she should be mortified at this intimate act—instead she felt contentment. She didn't know what scared her more: how quickly she was falling for Colin, knowing at this point she'd get hurt—badly—if things didn't work out, or the thought she'd have to leave him, go back home, an entire ocean away from him, in less than a week. After all, she had a job, friends, a life back in Charleston, while he battled Day Walkers here in Scotland protecting humanity—it wasn't like he could ask for a transfer.

"Um Colin? We didn't use protection...I'm not on anything..." her voice trailed away.

"Emily lass, we don't have any diseases, part of the perks of being immortal. We could wade through pits of plague victims and never catch a thing; not even the sniffles. I can't get you with child, no Walker can procreate." *Children. What would it be like to have a child with Colin?*

Pouring them both a cognac, Colin climbed into bed next to Emily, pulling the sheets around them. He asked about her life in America.

"My parents were killed in a boating accident when I was a sophomore in college. My brother is great, he's not home often.

He's a professional fisherman so he's always out on the water somewhere. I miss them...some days more than others. They always knew the right thing to say in any situation. Holidays are the worst, it's when I feel lonely." He was so easy to talk to, Emily found herself telling him about Kat and Fred, her stressful job and her hometown, all trivial things.

"What traditions do you miss about the holidays? You said Thanksgiving was a favorite." Wanting to know all about Colin, she started to ask him about his childhood when she looked over and saw him fast asleep. Smiling, she curled up to him, yawning once before falling into a deep sleep.

Still half asleep, she struck out, trying to wake from her nightmare.

"Oof." He rubbed his stomach.

"What? Sorry. I...it was...a bad dream."

Gathering her in his arms, Colin held her close, whispering to her, calming her as she came fully awake. Dim early morning light filtered in through the window, doing nothing to dispel the gloom.

"Tell me what ye were dreaming of."

Still sobbing, Emily accepted the glass of water from Colin. It was so realistic, the dream brought everything back.

"I dreamt of the accident, except this time instead of being trapped in the stream, the car caught on fire. I couldn't get out. It was burning and while I screamed out for help, Charlie stood there and laughed...I was burning. Was such a realistic dream." She shook, holding on to Colin as tight as she could.

"'Twas a nightmare, it's all right, I'm here and I won't let anything happen to you. Breathe easy, try and go back to sleep, I'll watch over you and keep the nightmares away." He stroked her hair, holding her close as she drifted back to sleep. *The woman appeared out of the ocean, dolphins jumping and swimming around her as a beam of sunlight illuminated her long silver sparkling hair, it looked as if fashioned from silver and diamonds. Emily recognized her...the goddess Terya. She felt peace being in her presence. "Child, you have found your path. Keep strong for there are many obstacles ahead. You will be tested...if you fail, not only will you be destined to be alone for all eternity, but you will be responsible for dooming another soul to the in-between, and the world will be pushed one step closer to the abyss of eternal darkness." The goddess started to fade away.*

"Wait, don't go, I have so many questions."

"Trust your heart, be willing to try again."

With that cryptic advice, Terya was gone.

❦ 14 ❦

T*uesday, November 3rd*

Waking slowly, groggy, Emily tried to recall her dreams. She remembered the nightmare about Charlie; it was the other one...with the goddess, telling her to trust herself.

Talk about your subconscious sending you a message.

Surrounded by warmth, she stretched, feeling more rested than she had in days, it took her a moment to remember, she was in bed...with Colin. What a magical night. "Did you sleep well?" Lying on her side, looking at this magnificent warrior, she flung the covers back, heedless of their nakedness so intent on looking at him, checking the wounds on his arm and thigh. "Your injuries don't look infected, they should heal if you take it easy for the next week,"

"Aye lass, I slept well. Dinna worry about the injuries, they'll heal soon enough. Though if you keep running your hands over my body, we'll end up making love all morning, breakfast will get cold, and you'll be cranky later when you haven't eaten...though if you're giving me a choice, I'm all for the sex, forget the breakfast."

"Breakfast? Thank goodness, I'm starved. I thought I

smelled something heavenly. I didn't hear anyone knock." Jumping out of bed, throwing his shirt on, she went to the silver-covered trays. "I think I've died and gone to heaven...eggs, oatmeal, biscuits, fruit...oh my gosh, a cold Pepsi with ice, no one gives you ice here and the soda is lukewarm—you have to have it icy cold with ice and a straw, it's the proper way to drink it. I could kiss whoever brought me this."

"Easy lass, it came earlier. Robert thought we'd want to sleep in. I'll spare ye the rest of what he said. He also found a clean shirt and pants from one of the cabin boys, which should fit you fine."

Clean clothes, food and Pepsi—she was happy. Breakfast, then a shower. It was going to be a great day. Content, she loaded plates for both of them, bringing them back to bed so they could stay in bed, eating together.

Over a leisurely breakfast they talked of their lives learning more about each other. "Oh, that was fantastic! I'm so full I can hardly move." Leaning over, she kissed him on the lips. Growling, he pulled her tight against him, kissing her senseless.

After breakfast, she showered first. The tiny shower wouldn't accommodate them both. As Colin showered, she finished dressing. Would be glad to buy some clothes when they docked. Her breath caught when Colin walked into the room with a towel slung low around his hips.

"Keep looking at me like I'm a second breakfast, and we'll never leave this room."

Blushing, she smiled as he took her in his arms, kissing her until she was breathless.

He looked down at her, kissed her again. "Shall we go up on deck? We'll be coming into the harbor soon."

Walking around the deck, watching the village come into view, she looked up at the clear blue sky, listening to the gulls cry, smelling the tang of the ocean breeze. Thankful...for a shower, hot meal, and most of all for Colin. Touching her fingers again, she was truly amazed at the things she was finding out were possible and actually existed in the ordered, corporate-driven world she lived in. Unconsciously, she touched her lips, still bruised from their night together. Sore as well, the ache that tells you it was a fantastic night. She was still afraid of getting hurt but determined to keep knocking down her walls.

"Look, an otter, he's adorable. Can I give him a fish?"

Indulging her, Colin plucked a fish from the catch, tossing it to the otter. They watched him jumping and splashing in the water near the dock, content in companionable silence.

Hearing boots on deck, Emily turned, "Is it you I have to thank for the Pepsi?" Smiling, brushing her hair out of her eyes, she gave Robert a hug.

"Aye, my bonny lass, I heard you mention you liked them. Then I remembered hearing most Yanks liked their drinks icy cold so I had the lads bring some aboard, keeping it in the cold water for you. I'm glad you liked it."

Clapping Robert on the back, Colin was magnificent in his white shirt and kilt. She was amazed so many Scotsmen still wore them, but wasn't complaining. The kilt was rugged and sexy as all get out, especially worn with black Doc Marten boots.

"So where are we and where are we going again?" she asked them.

Colin answered, pulling a ribbon from his pocket, tying her hair back for her. "We thought it safer to disembark in Inverness."

After gathering his troops, Rawlins appeared outside the doors to Dayne's throne room on a pop of air which left gold dust floating like dust mites in the sun. The realm of Light was where they were offered the choice to become a Day Walker—you know, show them the glamour, leaving out the nasty bits—don't show the ugliness until you've signed on the dotted line, so to speak. As far as he knew, no one had ever turned Dayne down.

He made sure he was impeccably dressed. The god had a bitch of a temper, you never knew if you were getting pissed-off Dayne or very pissed-off Dayne, best to keep any distractions to a minimum.

The doors swung open; made of gold, they were twenty feet tall and just as wide, had to weigh tons, he was glad he wasn't there to be punished. Those who were in the doghouse were punished in a variety of creative ways—two of the fae had collars around their necks attached to the pulley's on the doors. Damn, had to give you a real pain in the neck opening his damned doors all day.

None of their powers worked in the realm, you could dematerialize in but once there, Dayne had to give you permission to leave, it always made him twitchy when summoned; worried he'd be in the shite and stuck there for decades or centuries while the god had his latest hissy fit.

Striding quickly into the room, wasn't good to linger in the hallways, there were all manner of nasty supernatural creatures wandering around, all having sworn loyalty to Dayne. The goblins were the worst, they would eat you as soon as speak to you. Not to mention, their skin was like pebbled gray leather, with horns and yellow-slitted goat eyes. Oh yeah, and they were about two feet tall. Don't let the height fool you, these guys could destroy an army—they were ferocious.

Sitting on an ostentatious gold throne carved with more sun symbols and inlaid with enough gems to make a pirate fall to his knees weeping, Dayne looked every inch the haughty god, sprawled across his throne as if he didn't have a care in the world. To his left another imprisoned fae, knelt, his white hair shorn off, chained in submission. On his right, a three-headed midnight black hound sat at attention, taking away a bit of the studied nonchalance.

The hound was legend. Came from one of the deep circles of the Nether realm; loved to tear humans, Walkers, and other creatures to pieces, playing with them before devouring them, preferably with wasabi sauce. Was said the beast had the power to keep you alive so you knew you were being consumed. Even worse, the beast actually talked.

"Captain Rawlins Huntington, how goes the battle?" Idly, Dayne kicked the fae, watching him shield his face, waiting for the next blow.

"Milord, 'tis always a pleasure. I've sent Alexander after Robert, and I have men tracking Colin along with the woman traveling with him," Rawlins said as he bowed.

Having been imprisoned in the Nether realm for eons as punishment for murdering the ancient sun god, no one knew who had freed Dayne.

At six foot six, with short red-spiked hair, midnight black eyes, and golden skin covered with black and purple tattoos which shifted and changed in the light, depending on his mood, he was a fearsome sight to behold.

It was difficult to look at him; he was frighteningly beautiful, with a sculpted face and broad shoulders. He favored black Armani suits and wraparound mirrored sunglasses. Sometimes he hid his skin color and let the tattoos show, others, he hid all of it. With the gift of eloquence, spoken in a rough Greek accent, women fell all over themselves to get close to him and bed him when he visited the human realms.

"Ah, good, Alexander is one of my better fighters. He's crafty enough to trick Robert into letting his guard down. I'd prefer him alive if possible; Fury"—he said this as he patted one of the dog's heads—"got indigestion after he ate the last Shadow Walker."

"Seriously, dude, needed to be oven-roasted first next time, stringy, very stringy." The middle head finished, looking over Rawlins. "You look tastier."

Grimacing in distaste, Rawlins told the demon, "I'll send over a case of wasabi sauce, if I remember you like a particular brand from New Orleans."

Fury nodded, pleased, and went back to watching the room.

He was a three-headed dog who also took form of a raven or of a man though in reality he was a very nasty demon in service to the bitchy god.

"Why are you bothering with the woman? I'm sure there are plenty of willing or unwilling women as the case may be, to bed and eat or just eat, what's so special about this one? If you're wasting my time, maybe a few decades wandering the maze would teach you some manners." He narrowed his gaze on Rawlins.

Rawlins cleared his throat, feeling the fae looking up at him from his kneeling position. That damned three-headed dog, Fury was watching him intently, waiting for him to cock it up.

"The woman's name is Emily; she can see us." Rawlins paused, letting his words sink in, seeing the realization of what that meant, cross Dayne's face.

"She's been to Shadow and back then."

"There's more, we believe she might be able to break the curse he's under."

"Don't you find it rather humorous the 'good guys' are cursed while all of you simply serve me? Much easier and no chance of getting out of the agreement."

"Yes, milord. The woman is traveling with him. He's taking her up the coast, probably to a safe house. We'll find them and kill her just in case she can break the curse." Standing his ground but ready to jump out of the way, Rawlins watched Dayne closely to determine the jerk's mood. Argh, these gods were bitchy little girls and more vindictive than a PMSing, pissed-off, high school mean girl.

"I'm not even going to ask why she isn't dead already. I don't want to hear her name again until it's done. If I have to waste my time getting involved, you'll be spending the next millennium in my maze of fun," Dayne sneered.

"Have Alexander take his men, I want Thorne's pets destroyed, every blasted one of them. On the upside, once we destroy the last Shadow Walker, the walls between the human realm and our realm will open; we can take back power and rule the worlds.

Don't make me unleash Fury. I will if you fail. After he was done feasting and wreaking havoc on the humans, I'd have enough dead humans to create thousands of armies—not to mention, we can always use more workers down here. I have lots of projects to complete."

"I'll take care of it," Rawlins told him. Fury looked pleased at this information but wisely kept his yap shut. He might have three heads, but Rawlins was willing to chop them all off, he could only take so much smart mouthitis in one day.

He was thinking about keeping Emily alive, farming her out to the minions. She'd be able to spot the Shadow Walkers when the minions couldn't. They lost a lot of workers; Shadow Walkers catching them unaware. She could warn them, and if she behaved, he might keep her for himself instead of killing or imprisoning her. Bowing, he tried to dematerialize back to the human realm and found he was unable. Eyebrow arched in inquiry, he started to ask 'what the hell?' as Dayne nonchalantly waved a hand, "Oh, right, you're free to go."

Bastard. He was all for power and ruling but wasn't so sure about these human "farms" Dayne was setting up. The big bright idea was to enslave humans, keeping them alive to take their energy, bit by bit until they died. All around the world, Dayne had started farms, set up in abandoned warehouses, buildings, underground bunkers, and farms, where he had Day Walkers stealing humans.

Mostly those who wouldn't be missed anyway—the homeless, runaways, druggies, hookers, the forgotten. They were taken to heavily guarded locations where the humans' only purpose was to provide sustenance and an extra energy boost to the Day Walkers. Dayne didn't need the energy; he was a god, came with plenty of juice.

The newest plan was to take over adoption agencies and orphanages—take the kids, they had a bigger energy signature—

ever see a three-year-old running around at full speed? This way there'd be more slaves to keep providing energy, until such time as humanity could be destroyed.

Was rather humorous when you thought about it—people eating animals, now turned into "cows" themselves to feed the power hungry Day Walkers.

Some of the other creatures, like the goblins, would be brought over to guard the humans though Rawlins thought it was a bit like the fox guarding the henhouse. Oh well, whatevs, Dayne would do what he bloody well wanted to. He made a mental note to check in on the two farms in Inverness. If the goblins were eating the stock, he'd be blamed, better to make sure all was well.

15

Robert bid them farewell. After picking up his next cargo load, he was sailing back to Edinburgh. Colin dragged Emily into the closest store to purchase clothing. The clerk gaped at them, well at Emily, wearing a man's linen shirt without a bra and men's linen pants with ill-fitting slippers. It was either the men's clothing or some questionable attire left behind by some floozy of Robert's. Of course the female clerk was staring at Colin in a different manner–like she wanted to lick him from head to toe. If that hussy didn't knock if off, Emily was going to scratch her eyes out.

"Obviously she can see you just fine," she huffed.

"It would look a bit strange if you were here by yourself talking to the air, they'd think you were daft. We can choose to allow people to see us. Don't worry lass, she's not my type—seems I like prickly Yanks." The corner of Colin's mouth quirked up.

The clerk simpered over to Colin, fussing over him, asking what she could do for him, anything at all. The bitch—batting her lashes, tugging her neckline down to show off her considerable cleavage, puckering her overblown lips. She had a lot to show, looked like one of those women who thought they could get ahead in life or at work by showing the girls. As a mark in Colin's favor, he seemed not to notice; telling the simpering idiot Emily needed assistance. He told the clerk some bald-faced lie of how they'd been mugged and lost the luggage while putting his arm around Emily to show the clerk he was taken.

Momentarily appeased, she let the girl lead her off to the dressing room.

"I'LL PICK UP A FEW THINGS YE'LL NEED WHILE YOU'RE TRYING on your wee clothes." Colin picked up a change of socks, gloves, a scarf, hat, a coat in soft dove gray to match her eyes, and a duffel bag to put it all in. The temperature was dropping fast. Changes in temperature didn't bother Walkers, one of the bennies but it looked strange if they were visible and people saw them walking around in a tee shirt in the snow.

He usually went invisi—what no one told you, you found out the hard way, going invisible took energy, not very much but you didn't want to be caught after a long day slaying Walkers, close to dark, at your lowest power by a pack of those miserable bastards. They healed and recharged at night, right before sunset was their weakest time. For Day Walkers, was the opposite—right before sunrise was their weakest time. During the short time of sunrise and sunset, all Walkers were powerless, a sort of leveling of the playing field—you had only your skills to rely on, which he didn't mind as he liked kicking ass, was damn good at it.

Course being seen on purpose, you had to stop and think sometimes when a lovely lady gave you the eye or were in a bar, picking up company for the night, to remember you had willed it, not get all girly thinking she might be a cursebreaker.

It was supposed to start snowing, earlier this year than the last...he'd seen firsthand the changes from global warming. Colin wanted to make sure they were prepared in case they had to hole up at Ravensmore for a few days.

There would be food there, his staff needing to eat. Didn't need clothes for him, normally used energy to manifest clothing as needed. Emily came out dressed in jeans and a heavy white fisherman's sweater. The thick wool socks and warm boots he picked out looked nice on her.

Handing his credit card over to the sales clerk, he hurried her along, "Are you finally done trying on clothes? We need to grab lunch and hit the road."

"Okay grouchy gus. It takes women longer. I didn't expect you to pay for this stuff. I have my own money. The bank is wiring funds to the hotel for me."

He cut her off, "Emily, that's the problem with you modern-day women, always wanting to show you can pay your own way. I know you can, I want to do this for you...so say 'thanks' and let's move on, shall we?"

"Thank you, Colin."

Stopping in a pub for lunch, they were seated by the fire as they looked over the menu. Their waitress, an older stout woman with gray hair and kind eyes took their orders. "It's cold outside, lass, ye need to fortify yourself, best to have a nip o'whisky with your tea to keep ye warm."

Laughing she agreed and ordered the fish and chips. Colin had two burgers with fries and ale. A fire was crackling in the large fireplace; he watched Emily warm her hands, letting the heat work its way through her bones. "How are your legs not cold in that kilt? It's so cold outside I swear icicles are forming on the ends of my hair."

"We don't feel cold or hot, temperature doesn't bother us. I grew up wearing kilts, my legs never did get cold," he shrugged.

"Did you notice all the missing persons flyers posted around town? I saw them in Edinburgh as well. I know there's usually more crime in bigger cities but seems like an extraordinary amount of people missing. Know what else is really weird? There doesn't seem to be the same homeless problem here that I've seen in other cities."

"Aye, we've been talking about it. It's happening all over—Scotland, England, Ireland, Wales, Greece, France, and Italy. There's bound to be more we haven't heard of yet." He frowned, thinking of the missing—not only the ones on the flyers but the street people. Didn't seem to be a corresponding increase in Day Walkers so he wasn't sure what was going on but he'd planned to ask Thorne the next time he saw him. The god appeared whenever it pleased him, off doing god stuff he supposed.

Finishing lunch, they came outside to snow falling. Emily laughed, twirling around. Colin shook his head—she found joy in the simplest of things, it was refreshing, like the crisp smell of evergreens in a wooded snowy forest.

"What? We don't get snow in Charleston. I'll meet you at the rental car place, I want to fill our thermos with hot chocolate and pick up snacks for the drive." He laughed, she had to have road trip food and drink, looked at him in horror when he'd asked why. She told him it was fun to take a road trip to a planned or unplanned destination, singing to the radio, eating junk, and enjoying the scenery.

Nodding to her, he handed her a wad of cash and strode off to rent the car.

Emily had seen a bakery and convenience store down a side street they'd passed on their walk from the harbor. Pulling the cash Colin had given her out of the deep coat pockets, she had a pang of sadness—even her Lilly Pulitzer purse and wallet had been destroyed in the tunnel. She hit the mom and pop convenience store first, stocking up on all kinds of road trip goodies. It was tragic Colin hadn't taken road trips for fun; he was so serious, always fighting evil, saving the day, the man needed to have a bit of silliness and fun. She'd show him there were good parts of the world, you simply had to look a bit harder nowadays. The bakery had some scrumptious-looking cake, tarts, potato pies, and cookies. Not knowing what he preferred, she bought some of each. The proprietor was happy to fill the thermos with hot chocolate; they wouldn't fill your own container in the states, very strict rules regarding sanitation and all that crud. Here in Scotland, safety seemed to be "use commonsense," and they were a bit more laid-back, nice change from home.

Walking towards the rental place, she wondered how her brother was doing. She made a quick call on her disposable phone and left a message letting him know she was fine, having a great time on vacation. He was away on a deep sea fishing tournament, and they hadn't talked in a couple of weeks. It wasn't unusual for them to go a few weeks at a time without touching base, but they always knew they were there for each other and both always made sure to leave some way to get in touch if any kind of emergency cropped up.

Spotting Colin, her mouth hit the snowy ground...she'd expected your average rental or maybe an SUV, but this...not only was it totally impractical, but it couldn't be great to drive in the snow, could it?...boys and their toys. She rolled her eyes. It was a midnight-blue Porsche. Well, this was certainly discreet... not. He seemed so pleased, she didn't have the heart to tell him how crazy she thought he was, vowing not to say "I told you so" when they got stuck. Emily wondered if she should buy more snacks and beverages, heck maybe a down comforter...on second thought, they'd be lucky to fit in what they had with them, into the small trunk of this machine...it was beautiful, impractical, but oh yes, gorgeous, she thought opening the door, smelling the leather interior.

Loading up the car, they headed towards Ravensmore. "Hmmrph, do you think you bought enough 'road trip snacks'? Granted we won't arrive until after dinner, but I don't think we'll starve by then, lass. I may be powerless and require food but I think we could feed half of Scotland on what you purchased."

Smacking his arm, she sniffed, "You'll be happy when your stomach rumbles in an hour or so. Anyway, it's snowing harder. We could get stuck and then you'll be grateful I have plenty of snacks. One should always be prepared on a road trip. So not only do we have snacks, we have bottled water, hot chocolate, potato pies, sandwiches, and a wool blanket. Don't look at me like that, the blanket is a gift for my brother, but if we get stuck, I hate to be cold."

"Lass, I dinna know whether to be offended or laugh...do ye really think I'd let us be stranded? But if it makes you happy to have provisions, by all means. Cars and horses aren't so very different."

"I didn't know you could rent a Porsche, especially in this weather. It looks and smells brand new. I love the smell of a new car." She groaned, sinking back into the leather seats, which by the way, were heated, hello.

Looking over at her, he came clean. "Well, that's because it is new, it's not a rental—Gus keeps a car for me at his place in case I need it."

"Um, exactly how many cars do you have that you can leave them waiting at various ports of call? And why do you need cars, can't you just 'pop' wherever you want?"

Chuckling, he shifted, picking up speed, navigating the roads with ease. She didn't cover her eyes but snow made her nervous. Weren't the weather people always telling everyone to stay home when it snowed?

"Don't be nervous. I've been driving on snow covered roads since cars were invented. To answer your question, a lot...I have a lot of cars. I used to have lots of horses, the finest breeds, now it's cars. I like the high-performance ones best. And no, I don't 'need' them, but I have quite a fondness for them. While I dematerialize frequently, sometimes I like to drive, enjoy the feel of the road, the sound of the engine." Seeing her expression, he told her, "Don't worry, I won't talk about cars the entire way. I need to make one quick stop before dark."

The snow came down harder as the sky turned the color of gunmetal, nothing but countryside around them, passing through the occasional tiny town or catching a glimpse of one of the cute shaggy highland cows alongside the road, it was warm inside the car. The lulling rumble of the engine, the warmth of the car, and fatigue from the last few days caught up to her as she fell fast asleep.

❦

GLANCING OVER AT EMILY, COLIN WAS STRUCK BY HOW peaceful she looked sleeping. Her head tilted to the side, using her scarf as a pillow, her full lips parted slightly as if she had fallen asleep mid-sentence. She approached life the same way, meeting whatever challenges came her way head on, listening to what she was told, weighing the facts before deciding to believe or not...she believed him. He surprised himself by realizing it mattered what she thought.

He hoped Rawlins and his merry band of misfits wouldn't bother them—granted it was as likely as pigs flying but still, a man could hope. The fact he was after Emily meant he had to know about her ability. Possible he also knew about the curse... that was more troubling. Rawlins wouldn't think Colin would go to Ravensmore, since it was the obvious choice, he hoped that thinking would buy them some time, time to get Emily safe, prepare for whatever was going to happen. He'd called Thorne, but it went straight to voice mail. Speeding up, the tires grabbed the road, the car purring as they sped along the deserted, snowy roads.

Pulling over to refill since they'd likely not see another open petrol station; Emily woke up as the car came to a stop. Watching her stretch, desire flared to life. He pulled her across the seat, crushing his mouth to hers, his kiss demanding, hungry.

Blinking at the rapping on the window, they broke apart, Colin jumped out of the car.

"Easy lad, didn't mean to interrupt your snogging. I'm getting ready to close so if you need petrol, better fill her up now." Running a hand down the side of the Porsche, the attendant whistled, "Now that is one fine piece of machinery."

Emily had gone inside to use the ladies room and stretch her legs.

The snow was coming down in big, fluffy flakes. Slipping, Colin caught her arm, holding the door for her.

"Can't believe I'm going to admit this, you were right, I'm hungry. Think you might share your wee road trip food with me?" He gave her his most charming smile. Could admit when he was wrong, wasn't a complete dolt.

"Won't even say I told you so." Emily handed him food and hot chocolate. He'd never admit to anyone but he liked the chocolate drink. As his stomach rumbled, she passed him a potato pie. "Would you tell me about your home? I've never been to a castle before." She'd turned in her seat to watch him. The small gesture pleased him.

"Ravensmore has been owned by a Campbell since it was built back in the thirteen hundreds. It burned to the ground at one point but was rebuilt, though uninhabited for a long time. It's made of gray stone and sits on the edge of a cliff. Behind the castle is the sea, in front, open ground sweeping down to the forest. The walls have never been breached. It has over a hundred rooms. Some of the wings aren't used so they're closed off unless we need them. You'll meet the staff; they keep it running and clean when I'm away. This is where I prefer to spend most of my time though I have a place in Edinburgh."

"I can't wait to see it. I've always been fascinated with castles. Will it be terribly cold inside like Edinburgh Castle?"

"'Tis cold but nothing like most old castles. The Roman's figured out how to run water through ceramic pipes, heating the floor, so your toes won't be cold."

"I remember the guide at the museum saying you were ahead of your time partially due to the castle being built upon an old Roman fort? Is that where the heated floors came from?"

"Aye, the Romans were so advanced in their construction and building techniques. They had figured out heat, running water, and bathing chambers. These were all intact and the castle built utilizing them. My ancestors were thrifty and didn't want to waste anything that might be useful. Ravensmore has gardens, both flowers and edible things such as vegetables, fruits and herbs. The castle boasts a large greenhouse or as it used to be called an orangerie, where oranges, lemons, and other fruits difficult to grow in Scotland flourish. You'll see the old mosaics in the bathing pool and yes, we have electricity and hot water along with toilets. We're not complete savages." He told her. "See it was expensive even then to maintain such a large holding. My father had squandered the family fortune, so there wasn't money for repairs and upkeep. I couldn't bear to let go of the place. It has secret passages and rooms that as a boy were exciting to explore. One passage leads from one of the old garrison buildings down to the sea."

She interrupted him, "Is that where the smuggling took place?"

"Aye, there's a hidden cove where small ships could dock without being seen and load the whisky. There's another passage leading down from the kitchen, it goes to three chambers. One was used for refrigeration, one for freezing and the last for ice. It was so cold in the rock, the way the sea water came in, created these ideal temperatures. Wine was stored there along with homemade cheese. It truly is a wonderful place. I'm planning to bring back the wine and cheese making—as you know, the whisky is still being produced. Many of the families who relied on me then..." His voice was strangled. She saw the emotions play across his face as he composed himself.

"They had a rough time of it after I was gone. One of the first things I did when I came back was to make sure they were being taken care of. Hamish stopped all whisky production, turning the families—rather what was left of them...he'd had most of the men hanged—the rest he put out into the streets. I tracked down every one I could find, set them up in an abandoned hunting lodge owned by my family but forgotten, on the outskirts of Edinburgh. Told them I survived, had to keep my existence a secret. Eventually, I told some of them the truth. To this day, descendants of those families still work for me."

"The guide said Hamish was killed at Castle Gloom while Abigail was away. Did they ever figure out what happened?"

Looking down at her hand on his arm, he clasped her hand tight. "Abigail was to blame. She'd decided she was done with Hamish, having spent his gold, had no further use for him. She had him murdered while she left, bound for the West Indies to marry a wealthy plantation owner. She never made it, the ship was attacked by pirates and said all perished...though it was Robert who attacked the ship. He was going to sell Abigail to a whorehouse for what she did. As much as I hated her, I couldn't let that fate befall her. Instead, she was sold to be a maid in a fine house."

Emily snorted, "You were nicer than I would have been, I don't know what I would have done, but a maid in a grand house was much too nice for her after what she did."

Pulling in to a snow-covered drive; a well-lit, cozy cottage came into view. Parking in front of the door, Colin came around to let Emily out.

"The snow's getting bad, we won't stay long. This is the MacGregor family. They've worked with me since the beginning; all three sons are part of the business. I wanted to drop their check off since I know they've wanted to put a down payment on a new boat."

The door opened, Alistair greeted him. He was growing up fast. Sixteen looking twenty.

"Colin, you didn't have to stop by tonight, it could have waited. Come in. Mam's got tea on."

The boy gave Emily an appraising glance as she came in, taking off her coat. Catching Colin's look, he blushed and looked away.

Mrs. MacGregor came bustling into the room, a plump woman, in her late forties, with gray streaked liberally through her auburn hair which was in a messy bun, wisps escaping.

"Welcome Colin! Come, come, sit by the fire, warm your bones while I fix some tea. 'Tis a lovely snowy night, isn't it?" She fussed in the kitchen, getting tea and cookies ready while he and Emily made themselves comfortable.

"Emily, this is Mrs. MacGregor, her sons—Alistair, he's sixteen. Hugh is eighteen, and Colum is twenty."

"Pleasure to meet ya'll."

Colin suppressed a guffaw at the dumbstruck looks on the lads faces. All smitten by the looks of it.

Finishing their tea, Mrs. MacGregor thanked him for the check, patted Emily's cheek, telling Colin, "You've got a good one here, even if she is a Yank. Now be off with you before the snow gets worse. I've packed you a full thermos of hot tea and there's rolls, still warm from the oven."

Heading out, the snow scraped against the low-slung car. "We're an hour, maybe two with the snow, from Ravensmore."

"I'll cross my fingers we don't get stuck. Take my mind off the weather, you said the MacGregor's all work for you, do they all make whisky?"

"Nay, Alistair has the knack for it while Hugh works on the vineyards, and Colum works on ways to continue to modernize operations and the castle. He's an engineer, always tinkering with some new gadget."

"I'm curious, what's the boat for?"

"Alistair wants to also transport goods for Robert. A small boat comes in handy for some of the locales. The family shares in the profits of Ravensmore Whisky. I decided a long time ago; all profits would go to the families who were betrayed along with me."

Seeing her shocked look, he continued, "The distillery makes a decent profit, helps them, and I don't need the money." Cut off from telling her anything else, he swore, swerving hard to the right to avoid a red Range Rover bearing down on them as the sound of gunfire shattered the stillness.

✾ 16 ✾

"Tell me that was a car backfiring." Emily slunk down in the seat.

"The glass is bulletproof; make sure your seatbelt is tight." He narrowly avoided the oncoming car, only to hear a loud pop, as the car hit something, puncturing a tire. Coming to a stop in the deserted road, he warned her, "No matter what, stay in the car, keep the doors locked. Do you know how to use a gun?"

"Yes...I learned to shoot when I was five," she stuttered.

"Safety's on, gun loaded. Shoot to kill. It's after sunset, the Day Walkers will be weakened. Hitting us after dark, they must be desperate."

Getting out of the car, he hit the door locks, striding to the Rover as four men jumped out. Colin didn't know whether to be relieved they weren't Day Walkers and this wouldn't take long or offended that only minions had been sent after him.

Throwing his dagger at the first man, he caught him in the throat, dropping him by the still-open SUV door. The second dove for cover in the vehicle. The other two hunkered down and started shooting. Pulling out his Glock, Colin dropped the guy crouching by the passenger door when he stood to fire, posing like he was some kind of cheesy action star. His cohort fired at Colin, the bullet grazing his upper arm and nicking his side before Colin reached the third man. Popping a blade out of the toe of his boot, he kicked up, catching the loser minion across the throat, blood soaking the white snow on the ground.

Now this is what sucked about killing minions, they didn't disintegrate into dust, you had to clean up the mess or the authorities would start nosing around.

Grumbling, Colin opened the hatch to throw the bodies into the back of the Rover when he was kicked in the chest as the last coward jumped out of the SUV and started running. Must have been the guy who dove for cover when the shooting started. Easily catching the weasel, he decided to question him first.

Grabbing the minion by the neck, lifting him several feet in the air, the guy's face was turning red, his feet ineffectually kicking, hands clawing at his throat.

"Stop. Tell me what I want to know and I'll let you go."

The man's eyes were wild; he stank of fear and desperation. Prison tats covered his face and arms; Colin figured he had been somebody's bitch on the inside by the way he cowered in the back of the Rover instead of fighting with his partners.

As the man motioned to his mouth, Colin eased his grip enough for the fool to speak. "Man, we was just following orders. Said to kill you and bring the girl back alive, that's all I know, I swear."

"Take Emily back to whom?" he demanded, squeezing the man's throat for emphasis.

"Rawlins wants her. Said we better not touch a hair on her head. He didn't tell us anything else." Colin's gut heaved. This *was* about Emily. Rawlins was indeed after her. Somehow he'd learned of her ability to see Walkers, putting her in danger. He swore, sending up a plea to the gods Emily had stayed in the Porsche with the doors locked. Before he could check on her, he had to finish dealing with this situation.

Hearing a sizzling sound, he looked down, seeing piss drip

from the man's pants, steam rising up from the warm stream hitting the snow. Disgusted, he threw him to the ground, wasn't worth killing but if he didn't, the loser would scurry back to tell Rawlins which would point the way to Ravensmore.

Breaking the man's neck with one quick clean snap, he heaved him into the Rover with the others. Colin got in, thankful the keys were still in the ignition. He drove up the road a ways toward the cliffs, jumped out, stripping off his bloody clothes and throwing them into the back before he put his shoulder to the SUV and pushed...the vehicle went over the edge, tumbling end over end, hitting the rocks and exploding. By the time anyone investigated, the bodies would be burnt to cinders and it would be chalked up to an accident due to the weather conditions.

Jogging back to the car naked, dangly bits bouncing, he rapped on the window. "Emily, are ye all aright?"

She screamed, her face was pale as the moon on a winter night. "Colin! You're naked—and bleeding, again. I heard gunshots...are we okay?"

Her teeth were chattering and peering closer at her, Colin could see her eyes looked glazed as she struggled to process what had happened. She was in shock. "The men won't bother us again. I took my bloody clothes off to destroy them with the bodies. Had to be done. Roll the window back up. I need to change the tire and we'll be on our way."

Colin quickly replaced the flat, slipping in the snow, cursing as he worked. Finished, he opened the trunk, pulling on a change of clothes. He kept clothing stashed around his homes and cars in case he needed them on his death anniversary.

Tapping softly on the window so he wouldn't scare her again; Emily looked out at him, her face blank. Popping the locks for him, her hands shook.

"What is it with men trying to kill you? I've never seen so many bodies, I feel like I'm in the middle of an action movie or maybe a horror flick."

Starting the car, he put the heat on high to warm her and poured a cup of tea.

"Drink, Emily. Will help warm you." Running a hand over his face, he exhaled hard, "I know it's difficult to see. I've killed so many men over the centuries it doesn't register. We are always at war, always fighting, I'm sorry you had to go through this. And yes, my clothes were spattered with blood, best to burn them."

"Are you hurt? You're covered in blood."

"Aye, nicked me in the side and grazed my arm. 'Twill be fine. Were you ogling my hot bod?"

"I'm so not going there. And I'm sure you think the wounds are minor, but I want to bandage them when we stop."

"As you wish."

The car was working hard against the deep snow. Colin downshifted, the car protesting as they pushed onward, almost there. The lights of Ravensmore blinked in the distance. The car came to a thudding stop at the outer wall; snow too high to drive through, the Porsche wasn't a snowplow but a high-performance machine. Not meant to plow the damn stuff.

"We'll have to walk from here." The snow was knee deep and still coming down hard. They'd have a foot by morning.

Banging on the heavy wooden doors, Emily looked around at the forbidding castle.

"Wow, I'd hate to be the kid dared to ring your doorbell on a dark and stormy night. It's a little scary, like the turrets are looming over us. I'm waiting for a wolf to howl or a raven to fly by." Emily shivered as the wind blew through her jacket, ruffling her hair.

His breath caught. Emily looked like some ancient goddess set against the silvery light of the moon with the snow falling on her.

The doors opened. "Who's there, banging away this time of night?"

Colin started seeing the old man in the doorway. Worthington had aged a great deal over the past few years. The butler had been born at Ravensmore, taking over once his father passed. It was lonely—always being the one left behind. Worthington peered through the fluffy flakes, scowl changing to a genuine smile when he spotted Colin.

"Ah Milord, come in out of the cold, we weren't sure you were coming. Let me make sure your room is ready," Worthington told them, frank curiosity on his face at seeing Emily. "Come in lass, warm yourself by the fire, you look ready to fall over. There is a visitor in the kitchen, a policeman from Edinburgh, named Monroe, unexpectedly arrived a few hours ago, looking for you and the lass, said he'd wait." The butler stood nervously looking at Colin.

"A police officer is here? Whatever could he want?" He was puzzled. How did the cop even know who he was? He kept a low profile. What did he want with Emily? Maybe there was some clue that had come to light regarding their room being ransacked at the hotel or when her friend Kat was pushed—he doubted it as he suspected the cause of both—didn't expect a mortal cop to know anything. He'd find out soon enough.

Meg came rushing in, fussing over them, "Oh dearies, ye look half dead. Come in to the kitchen and get warm. Worthington's told ye about the visitor, has he? I made the lovely officer some tea. He'll need to stay the night; the snow's too deep to drive back to Edinburgh."

Meg had taken care of him for years, worrying over him, she knew what he was, what he did, her family had taken care of his since the beginning. Her hair was gray, streaked with white. The lines on her face deeper than he remembered. He blew out a sigh, hated to see those he cared for age and die while he continued on, never changing.

"We'll make sure the driveway is plowed in the morning so the officer can be on his way. Now let's have some of your wonderful stew for dinner, there's some left isn't there?"

While Worthington took Emily's bag upstairs and set about

getting the rooms ready, Colin introduced Emily to Meg as the housekeeper fussed around them on the way to the kitchen.

Entering the large stone room, Emily looked around, "It feels so nice and warm in here. Oh wow, you could fit three people in the fireplace. The kitchen is very welcoming. I love the old farm table and chintz chairs, reminds me of home."

"Och, ye know everyone ends up in the kitchen don't they?" Meg tittered.

Emily returned to admiring the cozy kitchen, starting as she caught sight of Monroe hidden in shadow, sitting in a chair in the corner by the fire.

"Something smells delicious Meg. I'm starved. Officer Monroe. Isn't this a lovely surprise. What brings you here; do you know Colin?" Emily turned on all of her considerable Southern charm as she watched his face. He looked angry.

Eyes narrowed, Monroe advanced, "Damn woman, I've been looking all over bloody Edinburgh for you, thought something had happened to you when you hadn't been seen at your hotel for days. What's going on?" Before Monroe could continue yelling at her, he found himself dumped in a chair, facing Colin.

"Speak to Emily in that tone again, and I'll plant my fist in your face. Have a seat and by all means, explain what is going on." Colin spoke in a low silky tone, every inch the imperious titled aristocracy. His blood was boiling, wanted to slug this cop hard, put him in his place, as a sense of protectiveness rolled over him, threatening to unleash the beast inside.

Before a fistfight broke out, Emily waded in, "Colin, Monroe, please, sit down. Meg has tea ready. We can all sit and talk like civilized human beings." Meg bustled around the kitchen, setting out tea while she prepared dinner, spooning stew out of the cauldron bubbling over the fire. Seeing Emily's look, she laughed, "No worries, dearie, we have modern appliances but there's something about stew over a fire, brings out the flavor. Relax while I take out the bread—baked it this afternoon."

"I think we could all use some wine. Might help with all the glaring." Emily yawned.

"Shall I pour?" Emily and Monroe nodded as Colin served the wine. He wanted this meddling officer gone. Emily was emotionally and physically exhausted from the earlier events of the evening. Watching her, he was afraid she was still in shock, trying to process more men dying in front of her. She needed to eat, take a bath, and get a good night's sleep. He glared at Monroe while Emily spoke to the officer.

"Monroe, it was a long drive here. I'm afraid I'm a bit out of sorts, not used to driving in snow so forgive me if I seem scattered. Thank you for coming all this way. Does this mean you have a lead on our hotel room or Kat's accident? By the way, how did you find me? I'm sorry for causing any concern; I didn't realize anyone would be looking for me. I've spoken with Kat. She's home and healing nicely," She babbled.

A stern look on his face, Monroe took her questions one at a time while he watched Colin. "It's rather strange Baron Campbell, but there isn't much information on you."

"I prefer a quiet life. Rather a bit of a recluse I suppose."

Emily choked on her wine, coughing as Colin pounded her on the back. He shot her a stern look before turning his attention back to the cop.

"Right, whatever you say. Emily, the hotel said your room is paid for through the week. I was assured your room and belongings are fine and there have been no further issues. We're looking into the incident at the hotel but no, we don't have anything new at this time."

"I'm very sorry, it was, er, um...spontaneous." She shrugged, widening her eyes, gesturing with her hands as if to look innocent.

"I don't have anything specific, but I have to wonder why you are being targeted. You are a visitor here; don't know anyone, so why would someone target you and your friend Kat? Unless there is some kind of connection to the missing persons and murders taking place in Edinburgh. Would you know anything about that, Lord Campbell?" Monroe said the last with distaste.

"I believe *you* are the officer here. How would I know what is happening to missing persons? Wouldn't that be the purview of the police department?" Colin sprawled in the comfy kitchen chair. Interesting. The officer didn't care for aristocrats, looked at him like he was some rich, idle bastard. If only he knew.

Ignoring Colin's reply, Monroe addressed Emily. "As to how I found you, I asked around and someone finally remembered seeing you both board a ship, a very distinctive ship. I checked the ports of call and in Inverness, found a waitress who overheard you both talking about coming to Ravensmore, so here I am. By the way. Why...Lord Campbell do you carry daggers? Do you feel a need to be armed?"

Colin interjected before Emily could answer. "One never knows what might happen, I prefer to be prepared for anything. The country roads can be treacherous."

The officer continued with his line of questioning. "Want to tell me how you two know each other and what's going on?"

As to Emily, we met in Edinburgh. What's going on is really none of your concern." Colin retorted, crossing his arms over his chest. *Cheeky Bastard.*

Before Monroe could retort, Meg asked if they wanted to eat in the dining room. Colin started to say yes, but upon seeing how tired and spent Emily looked, he didn't want to make her move. He was afraid she'd fall asleep in her dinner as it was. "No, we'll stay put, we're all comfortable."

Meg quickly set the table, bringing the food over. Emily's stomach growled loudly as Colin cut his eyes to her. "Now I see why you needed so many road trip snacks. Your stomach is always hungry. Are you sure you don't have a tapeworm?"

Pointing her nose in the air, she put on an affected air, telling him in a falsetto voice, "Dahling, we southern women—our stomachs do not growl, we do not sweat, we glisten, and we never utter any other bodily noises." Cringing in mock horror, a tired smile crossed her face.

Monroe roared with laughter as Colin chuckled. "All right then Miss Southern Emily, it must have been Monroe here; he doesn't seem nearly as refined as you."

"Let's eat before you kings and queens decide it's time to guillotine the peasants, which would be me, I suppose." Monroe leveled a glare at Colin who merely shrugged.

The room was quiet as each tended to their meal, eating and enjoying, warm against the bitter wind and cold outside. Meg came to check on them. "The rooms have been made ready for ye. Can I get you anything else?"

"It's so delicious, and the bread is the best I've ever tasted." Meg blushed under Emily's praise as Colin and Monroe chimed in, accepting heaping seconds.

"Yes, Monroe, you must stay the night. It seems the roads are quite impassable and can be treacherous in the dark to those unfamiliar with them. In the morning, we'll have the driveway plowed. If the snow has stopped, you can be on your way. I'm guessing the black Mercedes SUV outside is yours? They do quite well in the snow. Nice machine on a cop's salary." Colin raised a brow in inquiry.

"Yes it's mine; she's great in the snow. And my finances are none of your concern."

Colin watched Emily while he and Monroe talked automotive wonders. She stared ahead with glassy eyes, half asleep. He stood up bidding Monroe good night and picked Emily up.

"Put me down, I can walk to my room." The protest came out half-hearted.

"Your nose was in your soup bowl, and I know fine Southern women don't make 'noises,' but I swear I heard snoring. I warned Worthington that a bear must have gotten in to the castle to hibernate for winter, we'll have to look for him in the morning," he teased her.

Colin didn't put her down, liked the way she felt in his arms.

On the way out of the kitchen, he pointed out the great hall and library. Telling her he'd show her the rest of the castle in the morning. His arm and side were burning where he'd been hit. It was a bitch healing the old-fashioned way. Made him realize how much he enjoyed his powers.

Monroe trailed them, "Must cost a mint to keep this place up and running? What did you say you did again?"

"Didn't say. There are a number of business ventures I dabble in."

They followed Worthington up the stairs. He showed Monroe to a guest bedroom on the second floor.

"The lavatory is down the hall. Fresh towels are on the sideboard. Breakfast is served at eight."

Bidding everyone goodnight, Monroe turned in.

Reaching the third floor, Worthington opened the door as Colin carried Emily into the master bedroom at the end of the hall.

"This must be your room, very masculine. All the blues and greens match your kilt. I live in the wrong country, these huge fireplaces are fantastic."

He inclined his head to her. "I'm pleased you like it. I don't need any of it, but it pleases me to have things as they were." Showing her to one of the chairs facing the fire, he watched her look over his room. 'Twas strange to see a woman in his private chambers; no woman had set foot in his domain since Abigail. Emily looked as if she belonged in his room, standing there and warming her hands over the fire. She moved to look at the furnishings, admiring the towering armoire which could hold four people.

"Wow! This has to be the biggest bed I've ever seen. Bet ten people could sleep in this thing. I love four poster beds though I've never seen one with working curtains. Guess you needed them to keep the cold out?"

"Aye, 'Tis been my bed since I came of age. The curtains were meant to keep the occupants warm and to shut the world out."

Colin turned to her, "I shouldn't have assumed. If you prefer, you can have your own room, but I would like very much for you to stay with me." He didn't look at her; instead he faced the fire, couldn't bear her rejection.

Emily crossed the room to where he was standing, placing her hand on his arm, answering him, "I want to stay with you. I want you."

His control shattered, his gaze pinned her to the spot as he swept her up in his arms, took three strides to the bed, pressing her into the mattress. "Don't be gentle, I don't want gentle and nice. Take me, I need you inside me."

Swearing in Gaelic, he crushed his mouth to hers Trying to get rid of the barrier of cloth between them; a ripping noise broke the silence of the room as Colin tore his shirt, buttons popping. Emily's hands found his chest, her hands tracing his nipples, circling them with her tongue. He lifted her shirt off, popping her bra with one hand, tracing a line between her breasts, her nipples puckering as the cold air hit them. He groaned as he bent his head, tongue flashing out to lick her, sending her body arching, desperate with need.

He slid her jeans off, leaving her panties on. Tracing the lace with his finger, she thrashed side to side, spreading her thighs to allow him access.

Colin chuckled, licking his way down her body to put his mouth on her over the lace of her panties, the friction rubbing against her core. He could feel the tension in her body as she edged closer to the cliff, her thighs shaking, ready to explode for him.

Emily moaned, "Please, I want..."

The beast within roared...MINE, as he ripped the flimsy lace off, lowering his head, taking her crashing over the edge.

17

W*ednesday, November 4th*

"Meg, everything tastes wonderful." Emily was full and content. She'd finished off eggs, fruit, potato pancakes, toast, jam, tea, and amen sister—cold Pepsi. The dining room was ornate with silk wallpaper and wainscoting in the blue and green from Colin's kilt. The table was gigantic; it must have seated a hundred people easily. The chairs were deeply padded with rich green brocade. The silver gleamed and the china looked like a Rosenthal pattern Emily had seen in an antique shop back home.

She almost giggled, imagining the look on Worthington's face if she were to roll one of the hardboiled eggs all the way down the table, simply to see if she could, without it falling off. Nope, he'd probably have a heart attack and her grandmother would come back from the dead to scold her.

Meg told her Monroe was up at dawn, had an early breakfast and departed. He wanted her to tell Emily and Colin he'd be in touch, was going to follow up on a couple of leads. Emily liked the irascible man, though she knew she'd never be cut out for a job like his. All the misery, death, and worst side of humanity coming out, she'd turn into a cynical, jaded person. Nope, she made a mental note to make a donation to the police fund here and back home. She wasn't the volunteering type, more the write-a-check type.

"The driveway has been plowed. Monroe was able to leave, though he may have a time of it on some of the roads leading back to Edinburgh. I've spoken to the stable master; he's getting the sleigh ready. I thought we'd go for a drive around the grounds; show you Ravensmore, dressed up in snow. Would you like that?" He said the last bit as if he wasn't sure she'd like going out in the snow.

"Oh yes, it sounds like fun." Emily's eyes glittered with joy and she decided to have another cup of hot tea before they left.

"Meg packed hot chocolate and road trip goodies for us. I'm assuming one doesn't have to be in a vehicle to partake of these goodies you're so fond of?"

"Nope, you can bring road trip goodies in a car, boat, plane, bike, golf cart, horse, or sleigh, anything that takes you on an adventure."

They'd visited the orangerie earlier that morning, enjoying the humid air, the orange blossoms filling the air with a wonderful scent. Colin's kisses left her breathless, laying her down on a chaise, surrounded by flowers, her senses left her when he unzipped her jeans enough to reach inside, rubbing her, thrusting his fingers in, bringing her to the brink before he pulled her jeans down, sucking hungrily on her bud, sending her crashing over the edge, screaming out his name. Pulling herself together, she greedily returned the favor.

Unzipping his fly, freeing his erection, she took the head in her mouth circling it with her tongue before taking him in, sucking, swirling, gently rolling his sac. Feeling his hips buck, she sucked harder, sliding her mouth along his shaft up to the tip, blowing air across the sensitive head and then taking him back in, up and down, circling as she licked and used her other hand to stroke him.

"Gods, you're amazing." Colin ground out, coming hard. Grabbing her shoulders to hold her tight to him as she milked him dry, licking her lips.

On the way out to the stables, Colin showed Emily the library and told her she was free to explore to her heart's content.

"I've arranged for the hotel to send your things to Ravensmore. Should be delivered later today."

"Talk about choices—exploring the library, wandering around the castle and outbuildings or a fairytale-sleigh ride? Let's go on the sleigh ride. Plenty of time for exploring when we get back."

Walking across the snowy courtyard, she could almost imagine she'd stepped back in time. The only sounds in the silence were the horses and people working to clear the rest of the snow. The sleigh looked like something out of a fairy tale. It was painted a deep indigo blue with white trim. Inside, the bench seats were covered in the same blue and green wool plaid. A picnic basket was on the floor filled with sandwiches, cookies, and hot chocolate. There was a pile of cozy-looking blankets to wrap up in as the sleigh was open on top. Four horses stood waiting, jet black, huge beasts.

"Aren't you a beauty." She cooed to each horse, pulling treats out of her pocket to make friends. "Would you like a tasty carrot? And here's a sugar cube for each of you." She bet they could fly and hoped she would get a chance to ride one when the snow was gone—if it ever melted. Kat would love these magnificent animals. She adored horses. Emily's throat closed up. She missed her friend, hoped she was healing. Making a mental note to email her when they got back for the day, she admired her surroundings. It was so cold outside; she could see her breath on the air. The weak sun glinted on the icicle laden branches, casting the barren landscape into a magical scene out of a book. She expected to see Jack Frost or the Ice Queen come riding across the rolling hills.

"Colin, the sleigh is amazing. It looks like an antique, so beautiful."

"Aye, we've had it since the mid fifteen-hundreds. 'Tis a great way to get around the estate during the winters. I'm glad ye like it. We could have taken one of the trucks, but I thought you'd enjoy the crisp, winter day and an old-fashioned ride in the sleigh. There are plenty of blankets to keep warm, of course, I plan to kiss you until you turn pink and steam comes off your lips. You know, when you are in the midst of pleasure, your skin turns a pale shade of pink, the tips of your breasts darken, 'tis a beautiful sight." He gave her a look full of longing, promising an erotic ride over the estate.

Turning pink with embarrassment, Emily stammered something unintelligible, hoping the stable boy hadn't heard. From the grin on his face, he had and was looking at her with a great deal of interest.

"Being at Ravensmore, I feel as if I've stepped back in time so I don't want to take a car to see the estate, the sleigh is perfect...not to mention I smell some of those molasses cookies Meg was making."

"That's my Emily, always thinking with her stomach. As much as you eat, I don't know where you put it, you're a tiny thing."

"Flattery will get you everywhere," she told him waggling her eyebrows, leering at him. Colin chuckled, easily lifting her up into the sleigh. He climbed in beside her, tucking them both in, a warm cocoon, his arm around her. "All right Callum, lead on. Let's take Emily on a tour."

"Can I see the place you told me about, the old chapel where you create whisky? I'm curious as to how it's made." The chapel was a single-story stone building, weathered, with blue and green triangular panes of stained glass. The middle of each pane contained initials, different ones in each window, belonging to previous barons and baronesses. It was very romantic. A scene opened before her of she and Colin married, watching their initials set into one of the windows. Blinking out of her daydream and back to reality, she sobered. He liked being with her, liked having sex with her, but he hadn't mentioned a future together, had never said those three little words. Of course she hadn't either but she'd realized upon waking up, not only was she falling for him...she was hopelessly in love with him. She prayed to whoever was listening, she wasn't making another colossal mistake. After all, they hadn't even talked about her going back which she would have to do soon. She thought about staying but what about her job, her friends, her brother—why was she thinking about leaving Charleston when he hadn't even asked her to. This might be nothing more than a fling to him. He said he'd never get serious again, never let anyone in. Sighing at being a hopeless romantic, falling for him after she said she was swearing off men, she decided to enjoy what time they had. If it was meant to be, it would work out, right?

Walking inside the chapel, now whisky distillery, she was grateful for the warmth, the smell of warm, baking bread from the malting process, wrapped around her, making her hungry. She met the workers, part of those long ago families.

He showed her the copper kettles, liquid dripping out into barrels while in another room, the barrels were stacked up. In that same room, was a trap door, open into the floor. Seeing her curiosity, he told her, "It leads down to the cove I told you about. Would you like to see? I promise no cave-ins this time."

She cringed, thinking about their ordeal but had to admit she was curious to see the tunnel and cove where his smuggling activities had taken place all those years ago.

Squaring her shoulders, taking a deep breath, she told him, "Please, I'd really like to see the cove; it's not too narrow is it?"

"No, it's actually rather wide, we used to use horses and a flatbed wagon to transport the barrels, now we have an electric flatbed with seats, you'll ride in style milady, no getting dirty for you today...well, not that kind of dirty anyway." He smirked.

They walked down the ramp leading into the tunnel. "No

stairs for the horses, this way they could walk down." Climbing into the seats, Colin started the engine. It was dimly lit, with lanterns instead of torches in the walls, she could feel the air growing colder as they traveled under the ground. Moving so quickly the wide corridor didn't make her feel too claustrophobic and with Colin beside her, telling her the history, she relaxed. Sitting up straighter in her seat, she tried to see ahead, she could smell the ocean, it was such a wonderful smell, salty, fresh, full of possibilities. The water was healing, always had been. It got lighter, she could see row upon row of barrels, the fresh air swirling around her, she inhaled deeply.

"Wow, that's a lot of whisky. How long did it take to make it?"

"Some barrels are more than twenty years old. We keep some here and other barrels are moved to another building to keep the risk lower in case of fire or theft. It's legal now so I no longer smuggle, but there are always those who wish you ill will. Though those who mess with my business usually end up dead."

She didn't know whether to laugh or take him seriously. For all she knew, he actually did murder any who messed with his business but since he was supposed to protect humanity, she hoped he only scared them.

The large, cavernous room, led to another room, it was even larger, the water lapping gently against the stone.

"The boat would come in, the bell on the church would ring, giving warning when needed to alert the workers."

She could see posts to tie a boat to. The smaller boat then would load up, going out to the bigger boat, keeping nosy eyes from seeing a large boat at the coast, giving away their location.

Colin settled her in the cart for the ride back. Along the way Emily said goodbye to each man by name, offering them Meg's hot chocolate.

"You've got them in the palm of your hand. They'll be ruined wanting hot chocolate whenever it's cold out." Colin rolled his eyes.

Lifting her back up in the sleigh, he paused, kissing her, a long lingering kiss, before settling her on the bench, wrapping her in blankets.

The horses led on, bells jingling. Could it be any more picture perfect? Kat would die with envy. Emily smiled, happy with the day, enjoying the cold, crisp air. Her stomach protested loudly, Colin laughing at her when Callum, their driver, turned around to ask, "Milady, was that you?" He looked incredulous, Emily and Colin both laughed. The found a spot by a waterfall, the water partially frozen, creating a beautiful ice sculpture, tinkling over the rocks.

Removing the blankets from the sleigh, Colin spread a couple on the ground, saving the rest to bundle them up in. He wasn't wearing his kilt today, he'd put on jeans and a thick, chunky wool sweater with his usual Doc Marten boots. He looked like he'd walked off the cover of Mr. Outdoor. Emily felt a bolt of desire pool in her center, wanting to throw herself in his arms.

Callum took two sandwiches, handfuls of cookies and two beers before he unhooked the horses, leading them off to an area of grass for them to graze on. "Milord? If ye don't need anything else, I'll be on my way."

"No, you can go. Thank you for driving us." Colin bundled them up under the remaining blankets, spreading the bounty in front of them, pouring Emily warm, spiced wine, a beer for him.

"We're in the middle of nowhere. Where will he go?"

"Did ye not see the lad putting on snowshoes? He'll head back to the castle."

She gaped at him, "It's so far!"

"The folk here are outdoors most of the time. They walk everywhere or ride. I offered him a horse, but he was fine with his snowshoes. Let's eat before your stomach rumbles again."

They fell upon the food as if they hadn't eaten in a week, the cold air giving them a hearty appetite. Colin finished off four sandwiches to Emily's one. He also ate most of the cookies; thank goodness she'd taken a couple and put them aside by her meal. He eyed them, and she snatched them away, "Oh no you don't, these cookies are fantastic, you've eaten at least a dozen, I'm not sharing the last two."

"You are heartless."

After cleaning up, he sat back down beside her, "Alone at last," he pulled her close, kissing her soundly, his hand reaching up under her sweater, pulling the cup of her bra aside to reach what he wanted. His palm was cold against her breast and Emily gasped, her nipple hardening. A slight moan escaped her as he rubbed circles around her nipple, laying her back, covering them with the blankets, trapping the warmth inside as he pulled up her sweater, licking her stomach. Kissing his way to her aching nipples, he took one in his mouth, suckling it as his other hand drew lazy circles on her other breast. Emily reached under his sweater, unbuttoning his jeans. *Damn, why did he have to have button-fly jeans on today, seriously.*

Working the buttons, she freed him; he didn't wear underwear, his proud erection sprang free, bobbing against her hand. She circled her hand around the width of him, marveling at the velvety softness of skin against the hard shaft. Up and down she stroked him, running her hand over the top of his cock, feeling the bead of moisture on the head. He moaned deep in his throat, switching his mouth to her other nipple, his hand trailing to her waistband, undoing her jeans, reaching inside her panties.

"Gods, you're so wet and ready for me."

He tapped her bud; sending fissions of pleasure through her, her body vibrating with need. She stroked him harder and faster, hearing his breathing become ragged. She smiled at the power she held in this moment, bringing him pleasure. Before he could bring her to completion, she shifted, breaking contact, licking her way down his chest, her tongue circling his nipples, paying attention to each of his six pack abs, nibbling a path to what she was seeking. She took his balls in her mouth, rolling them around gently, sucking. Licking short hard licks at that part where the base of his cock met the sac, she felt him hiss, his hands tangling in her hair, fisting it. Kissing her way up his shaft, she took the engorged head in her mouth, running her tongue around the crown as his cock jerked. She took him in, sucking and licking up and down as he thrust his hips up to meet her. Feeling him breathing harder, his cock pulsing as his warm seed spilled down her throat. Lapping at the head of his cock, it was purple, still hard with need. Growling, he grabbed her, sliding her along his body, flipping her over on her back, his cock poised over her, jutting straight out from his body.

"My God, I want you Emily." He said it reverently as if praising her, his eyes hooded. His hair had come undone from the tie holding it back. He looked like an ancient god there above her, ready to devour her in some ancient fertility rite.

"Take me," she pleaded.

Pushing her knees up, spreading her legs wide, he stared at her. "You are so beautiful, look how ready you are for me. I want to lick you until you scream." He looked feral, every inch the ancient warrior as he leaned down, licking her, causing her to buck, lifting her hips up as his tongue swirled around, she moaned. Sucking on her clit, he inserted two fingers as he felt her start to clench around him. She cried out, falling, the waves crashing home.

With a very satisfied male smile, he entered her, his head rubbing her clit, making her whimper, lifting her hips, wanting more, "Colin, please, I want you inside me."

Thrusting, he buried himself to the hilt, groaning, "Ah, you're so tight and wet." Pulling out almost all the way, he paused, slamming back into her. Leaning down, he suckled her nipples, Emily felt the waves building inside her, ready to crash to the shore when he pulled out. Starting to cry out at the feeling of emptiness, she was lifted up and flipped over on her stomach. Rising up on her hands and knees, he took her from behind, filling her, touching her core as she rocked back, meeting his thrusts, his balls slapping against her. He reached a hand around, stroking her nipples, pinching enough to make her insides clench at the delicious sensations. His hand stroked down her stomach, searching, finding her bud, stroking, circling, tapping out a rhythm as he pounded into her. The cold air puckered her nipples. Harder and harder, he slammed into her, relentless, savage with need as she shattered. Removing his finger, he grabbed her hips as he came again, calling her name.

Maybe she should be shocked at herself. Having sex outside, but no one was around, so no reason to be embarrassed. He pulled her on top of him, her head resting on his chest.

Emily dressed under the warm blankets ready for a nap before dinner. Colin wrapped blankets around her and tucked her into his side as they started back to Ravensmore. Pointing out a crumbling ruined castle in the distance, he stopped so she could enjoy the view. Castle Gloom he told her, belonged to Hamish. After his brother died strange things started happening and it was rumored to be haunted. The castle fell into ruin.

"It looks so desolate, lonely...I think buildings can feel unloved; you can feel the melancholy in the air around..." She trailed off.

"Becoming a Scot already are ye?"

"The end of the week is almost here...I'm supposed to go home."

"Ah, well, I'm sure we'll have taken care of whoever is after you by then. You can go back to your life in Charleston. I'm sure your brother and friends are missing you. Probably miss work as well. Good to get back to something familiar, forget all of this."

Wait a minute? Did he want her to stay or not? He hadn't said but seemed to like being with her, was it fishing if she asked? Why couldn't he just tell her? Angry, she decided to say nothing, if he didn't feel anything for her other than sex well then, fine.

Both silent, lost in thought, Emily watched the winter afternoon light casting shadows across the highlands, then she caught a scent, swore she smelled gardenias. The smell hit her so strongly, for a moment she couldn't breathe. It reminded her of being at her grandmother's in Georgia, the early morning smell of the air, grass and sunshine, telling you it would be a wonderful day. Struck by how clear the memory was, she was overcome with emotion, her eyes started to tear up, and her throat clogged. Not sad but happy, as if her grandmother were passing on a message, what—she didn't know, but a message nonetheless. Emily smiled, remembering her. She was a great lady.

She thought about the power of memory...of scent. Maybe for others it wasn't scent at all but a certain movie, TV show, song, or world event to trigger memory. Smell did it for her. She'd bet she could find Colin in the dark by his scent alone. Remembering a few weeks before she left for this trip, walking through a department store, catching the scent of White Shoulders perfume; she didn't know they still made it but immediately could see her grandmother, full makeup on, clothes and hair done, perfume wafting around her...at the breakfast table.

Her grandmother insisted they dress for breakfast. It still made her smile when she was home in her pajamas with wild hair and no makeup. Or one time in the airport, waiting to board her flight...a guy walked by who smelled like Rainbath shower gel and in that instant she was transported back to school, sitting next to a boy she was crazy about who always smelled of that particular shower gel...he turned out to be less than desirable but to this day, she recognized the scent anywhere.

A part of her knew, all of her memories reminded her of where she came from and those collections of memories helped define the woman she'd become today. To this day Emily couldn't stand the smell of deli sandwich meat...it brought back the memory of lunch the day of her parents' funeral and reminded her how much she missed them.

"You're awfully quiet. Is everything OK?"

She refused to tell him what was wrong. How could he be so kind one moment and so cruel the next?

"A bit tired I suppose. I'm fine." It was childish, but she planned to give him the silent treatment for a while until she got over the hurt of his careless words.

18

Almost to the city, Monroe thought back to last night. He'd gotten his laptop out to make notes before going to bed. His room was richly appointed, done in dark burgundy and gold. Thick, heavy curtains on the windows to keep out the chill, a fire crackling in the fireplace, the floor warm under his feet, heavy quilts on the large bed, with a trunk at the end. Two chairs flanked the fireplace; he sat in one to finish his thoughts. Lord Campbell must be raking in the money. There was still something suspicious he couldn't quite put his finger on. The baron wasn't what he seemed. Monroe had done well for himself. Saved every pound, had a small inheritance from his mother he'd invested, and while his apartment was a hovel, he thanked whoever might be listening for his Mercedes SUV. It was a beast in the snow, worth every bloody bit of the expensive price tag. His one concession to vanity.

Worthington had given him the code to access the internet. He could check email on his mobile but preferred the larger laptop screen if possible. He'd received intel from a source he'd dealt with before. The guy was in the import/export business, right, most likely illegal, but he hadn't done anything yet, seemingly content to live and let live, occasionally giving Monroe a tip.

The informant pointed Monroe to an abandoned warehouse where a high-end red Ducati motorcycle had been spotted a couple of times, same color as one seen leaving a recent crime scene. He figured the guy wanted the warehouse and giving a cop the tip, might ensure the bad guy was taken out of the picture, freeing up his source to pick up the warehouse for a steal.

He'd woken early, left at first light thankful the drive had been plowed. The roads were dicey in places but steadily improved as he made his way back to his beloved Edinburgh.

The snow was much lighter in the city, only a few inches blanketed the ground. The abandoned warehouse near the water on the outskirts of town was the same location Monroe checked when Alice was killed; it couldn't be coincidence to end up here again. The killer had to have used this place, something tied him here. All he had to go on was the expensive bike, smell, and gold dust. Hell, it was more than he'd had in the past ten years.

Being his day off, he didn't have backup but was used to poking around the more unsavory parts of town. Entering the warehouse, it looked empty and unused. He'd search it inch by inch to be sure. Heading into the interior, the grime encrusted windows cast a dim light. His flashlight pointed the way, glinting off the metal door at the back of the building.

Slowly sweeping his beam back and forth across the floor, he moved closer to the metal door. Odd—it looked new, no rust. Trying the handle, it swung open easily, leading him into blackness.

Monroe fell to his knees, the now-familiar smell filling his nostrils, invading his lungs, choking him, clawing its way to his brain.

There was noise up ahead, the sound of metal clanging. Using the wall for leverage, he pushed up, steadying himself, and moved towards the noise.

Raised voices. He moved faster, coming into a lighted room, skidding to an abrupt halt as he gaped at two huge sonofabitches fighting.

Geez, had giants started populating Edinburgh? These guys were easily over six feet, at least seventeen stone each. Bugger me, there was a guy wearing black leathers, dressed as some badass movie reject with... swords strapped to his side. He tripped over a piece of metal, causing it to clatter to the floor, as both men stopped mid-swing, staring at the newcomer.

"Well, well, well, who do we have here?" drawled a bored voice.

"Put your hands in the air. What are you doing here?"

"This guy is funny. Though not as hysterical as that getup you're wearing, pirate." The guy pointed his sword at Monroe. "Back off, human."

"Fighting with swords? I'm taking you both in to answer some questions." Monroe sneered, wishing he had backup.

"Look cop, leave now, go on about your business, nothing to see here." The other guy was leaning against his sword watching the scene play out. Monroe narrowed his eyes, "How do you know I'm a cop?"

"The whole 'put your hands in the air' thing, plus you smell like one. Really, you think you're going to take me in for questioning or some such rot? I'm bored, you have two minutes to leave then I'm killing you because you're interrupting my day. I already have one idiot to kill, right Robert?—easy enough to make it two." The giant brushed dirt off his pants.

Monroe growled through clenched teeth, "You're the same bastard who murdered my girlfriend...I've been looking for you for ten years. How many people have you killed and gotten away with it? No more."

"I've destroyed hundreds of you pathetic humans, I certainly can't be bothered to learn their names or remember them. I'm busy here, leave now. Last chance." With a bored huff, the man landed a solid kick to Monroe's chest, sending him halfway across the warehouse. Everything went black.

ROBERT WAS TRYING TO DECIDE HOW TO FINISH THE FIGHT with Alexander without involving the human cop. It was against their code to let humans see if they could prevent it. He knew they should have gone invisi to fight, so much for keeping the human out of it. Jumping into the fray, Robert cold-cocked Alexander; the human cop looked unconscious but breathing.

Suddenly, three more Day Walkers flashed into the cavernous room. "Look, more girls come to the tea party. Well come on then." Robert jeered. He'd faced worse odds. Ducking, he narrowly avoided his head being severed from his body. At least no one had guns out. Well, not yet, it would draw too much attention from the surrounding buildings, someone might get curious, call the cops. Right, the cop was already here.

He managed to take one Walker out, slicing his hamstrings, bringing the guy crashing down to the floor. Robert cut out his heart. One down, three to go. Pulling out his second sword he came up from a kneeling position, slashing, cutting the heads off the two Day Walkers. They could wait before he took their hearts, as it was a bit hard to recover from losing your head. You'd be dead. But to make sure, you still took the hearts ensuring Dayne would have to make new Day Walkers and couldn't piece his toys back together.

Taking a dagger to the thigh from Alexander, Robert stood wincing, and taunted him. "Have to have your girlfriends' help you fight eh? What, can't do it on your own?"

Enraged, Alexander dematerialized, appearing behind him, swinging his sword and meeting air. He had flashed to the other side of the building in the nick of time. Laughing at the expression on Alexander's face, reveling in the fight, Robert missed the warning sign.

"Look out," Monroe bellowed, pushing Robert out of the way, taking the energy blast meant for Robert in his gut. Robert manifested an ice dagger, threw it at Alexander, hitting him in the shoulder at the same time that Monroe picked up a gun from the floor and emptied the clip into the bastard, hitting him in the chest, and in the heart.

Robert had another ice dagger ready to finish the Day Walker off, when he felt a hand on his arm. "Wait, let me do it. This needs to end now. I know it was him."

"Cop, you don't know..." Robert was interrupted.

"It is. Look at his ear, the earring with the 'A' on it. If it belonged to Alice it will have 'Love M' carved on the back. I gave them to her for her birthday...check." Pulling the earring out, Robert turned it over; it was as the cop said. Why had the Day Walker kept it? He was usually never sentimental over any human, never took trophies. There must have been something about her or some reason they'd never know. Robert knelt down, handing the earring to the cop. Monroe was badly injured, bleeding like a sieve from the gut wound.

Grunting, Monroe grabbed a piece of rebar lying close by and used it to lever his body up. Handing the cop a dagger, Robert said quietly, "To finish it you have to cut out the heart and stab it."

He watched as Monroe gathered his strength to finish Alexander off. He saw understanding dawning on the guys face as the Day Walker turned to gold dust and was no more. The cop had encountered their kind before, interesting. Before Monroe could ask a million annoying questions, he was horizontal, looking up at Robert not knowing how he got there.

"Now you have closure; you're lucky. Most of us don't get that luxury. Hold on cop," He told him, pulling out his mobile and dialing emergency services for an ambulance.

"Quit calling me cop, it's Monroe."

"Right." The guy was losing a lot of blood, Robert wasn't sure he'd live but Monroe showed strength and honor so he'd do him a favor and make the call.

"You're wasting your time; I'm dying, won't get here in time." Monroe rasped, blood leaking out of his mouth.

He was taking a chance, the cop would get nosy and dig

around if he survived. Looking into Monroe's eyes, "You can't tell anyone about us; anyway who would believe people disappearing or turning into dust? Tell them you were passing by, heard a noise, encountered a drug deal gone bad. Trying to stop it, you were stabbed with a knife and must have been electrocuted, the men got away."

Hearing sirens, Robert vanished with the cop's blood on his shirt. A human saved his life, which had never happened in all the years he'd walked these streets as a Shadow Walker. The cop held his own against Alexander for a bit, right proud work.

Thorne was going to be pissed. He didn't like loose ends. The god had a fearsome temper and while he didn't show up often, all the Shadow Walkers knew he could obliterate them on the spot if he was in a mood.

19

Thursday, November 5th

Dressing for dinner, Colin could have punched himself in the face. Idiot. Had the perfect opportunity but no. What a lame thing to say, should have told her you care, bloody wanker, instead you tell her it's good to go back, to forget everything here. Tell her you're crazy about her, want her to stay...dolt. He wasn't ready to say it out loud; if he did it would be out there for all to see, for him to try again, to let her betray him as Abigail had done. He knew she wasn't like Abigail—still he carried the fear deep within the blackness of his heart, that as soon as he opened up, she'd gut him like a fish, leave him gasping for air, flopping on the wooden dock, trying to breathe as the life drained out of him. Throwing his whisky glass against the fireplace, gratified to hear it shatter, he made his way down to dinner...a condemned man marching to the gallows.

Dinner was stilted. Colin didn't know how to tell her he wanted her to stay, couldn't find the words. Emily was quiet, picking at her food. He'd come to bed late, knowing she feigned sleep. He felt her tossing and turning through the night.

Getting up early, he knew he was a coward avoiding her. But

if he allowed her some distance maybe he could figure out what to say to her. Find a way to make it right, get rid of the hollow feeling in his gut. Leaving the bedroom, he looked back over his shoulder. Her body was a straight line, rigid, the tension swirling around her. Closing the door quietly, he ran down the stairs. Needed hard work to take his mind off a certain southern belle in his bed.

After spending the early morning, visiting tenants, making sure they were OK in the snow; he'd stopped by to see Mrs. Burns. She was a widow, both her sons worked for Colin and they lived in a cottage on the estate. Her cow was stuck in a deep snowdrift and both boys were on a ship bound for France to deliver a shipment of wine. The cow was mooing, frantically trying to get out. It would have been hilarious if the woman wasn't so upset. Colin freed the beast, slipping in the muck, cursing. Washing up inside, he accepted a cup of tea before leaving. As he was heading back to the castle, Mrs. Burns threw her arms around Colin, hugging him tight, kissing him on the cheek. "Thank you, milord, I don't know what I would have done if ye hadn't gotten Bessie free, thank you."

He went in to breakfast, determined to fix things with Emily. "Meg, where's Emily?"

"Milord, she's already eaten, said she was going to explore the castle and grounds today. She'll be back in time for lunch. She was awful quiet this morn. Everything all right between you two?"

Colin didn't answer as he headed outside to check on the horses. He'd talk to her over lunch, clear the air.

WAKING, EMILY SLOWLY TURNED OVER...YEP HE'D ALREADY left. Disappointment washed over her. Frowning, she got out of bed, jumped in the shower and got dressed. She'd go exploring to take her mind off things. Maybe Colin would be waiting in the dining room and they could clear the air. Right, cause the big guy was all about sharing his feelings. Not bloody likely to use his words. OK, get over yourself, be a grown up and talk to him during breakfast. Heading down the stairs trailing her fingers along the rough stone walls, she followed her nose to the dining room. Empty. He wasn't there.

"Emily dear, come in and eat." Meg bustled around bringing her breakfast.

"Has Colin already eaten?"

"No, he hasn't been in yet. I would've thought he'd come in with you. Everything OK?" Emily felt her face growing warm with embarrassment. Was it obvious they weren't speaking? "Oh, everything's fine. He must of told me and I forgot. Thought I'd explore the rest of the castle today." Finishing, she grabbed a banana for a snack and hoped her mood would improve by lunch. Men. Gah, how was it possible to be sad and angry at Colin at the same time? "Meg, I'll be back around lunch. Taking a banana in case I get hungry. Thanks for breakfast."

"Have fun lass but be careful, the west wing is haunted." Meg shivered. "You would think a wee ghostie wouldn't bother me knowing about Colin but there's something verra strange wandering those halls."

Ravensmore was truly amazing. As Emily explored the unused wings, marveling at the furnishings, the weaponry laid out as if waiting for its owner to come in from a long day, she let her thoughts wander. Approaching the west wing, she meandered down the hall until she came to what must have been the lady of the manor's room. She was drawn to a large window with an inviting window seat, filled with pillows—covered in dust but still lovely. Climbing onto the window seat, she peered out. Wow, what a view. As she admired the landscape, she noticed a man coming out of one of the adorable cottages, a woman followed, throwing herself into the man's arms, hugging him, kissing him. Smiling at the couple, she watched them, wishing she knew how to fix things with Colin. Starting to turn away, a voice stopped her cold.

"I wouldn't turn away yet milady, might want to see who the second half of that lover's couple is." Turning to the voice, she saw a man dressed in silk as if he'd stepped out of a costume ball. Her stomach clenched, he was slightly transparent and floating a few feet off the ground. Remembering what Colin told her, she didn't think he was a Day Walker or Shadow Walker since he didn't have any substance.

Curiosity overruled fear. "Who are you?"

"I was the lady's servant and continue to watch over all the ladies of the castle as they come and go. Frederick, at your service ma'am." He bowed. "Look out the window, milady."

Frowning, Emily looked out, seeing the man from the cottage come closer. Watching him approach, she gasped, one hand going to her heart, the other splayed on the frigid stone wall to steady her. Her heartbeat filled the room, so loud it drowned out what the ghost was saying. It was Colin. There had to be an explanation. She'd march downstairs, find him and ask him to clear it up. Starting to leave, the man's next words stopped her in her tracks, sending icy fingers crawling up her arms.

"Ah yes, Baron Campbell, quite the ladies' man. Leaving one of the many mistresses he keeps on the grounds. There are others...in Edinburgh, also in France and England. He does admire the ladies."

"What are you talking about? Colin isn't involved with anyone; told me he wasn't." She was sick to her stomach, this couldn't be true, he wouldn't lie to her.

"You watched them embrace, caught him coming out of the cottage after having his way with her. Has he promised you to be his wife? Asked you to live with him as mistress of Ravensmore?" Seeing the hurt on Emily's face, the ghost pressed on. "He won't, still loves Abigail. Yes, the mistress betrayed him, but he's never gotten over her, never will. He slakes his lust with others but will never give any of you his heart. I'm sorry, milady. Best you know now before you fall too hard for the charmer."

The ghostly figure threw in one last parting shot. "Did he tell you some fantastical story about a curse? He tells all of you the same story and you fall for it, thinking you'll be the one to save him. There is no curse. He uses it to bed all of you. I couldn't bear to see another young woman hurt by him. Leave, go back home, forget this place, and forget him. There's nothing for you here...nothing except betrayal and heartbreak."

The figure faded away without a sound. Emily sunk into the window seat, dust floating up from the pillows. Face white, trembling, she tried to stop the tears from falling to no avail. She cried, huge, noisy sobs wracking her body as she berated herself for trusting again, for believing in love. Was she that desperate for someone, she believed anything? Hours passed as she cried until there was nothing left. Wiping her eyes, she felt empty, hollow.

He'd lied. In her book not being honest was a deal breaker. Furious, she decided she was taking control of her own life. Let him play his little games, she'd had enough. She wasn't staying here one more second, she was going home. Dropping her half eaten banana, she fled, heading for the bedroom. Turning around, taking in the room, her eyes stopped on her suitcase. The rest of her things had been delivered, it figured. She couldn't bear to haul her bags down the stairs like some pathetic, rejected lover. Shaking her head, she decided to leave it all. Checking to make sure she had her passport and emergency cash she'd had stashed in her suitcase, she grabbed her coat, pausing by the bed. It was rumpled from their lovemaking the night before. Her stomach rolled. Brusquely walking out, she pulled the door shut.

Moving quickly down the hallway, she heard voices. Not wanting anyone to see her leave, to avoid the knowing looks, the pity on their faces, she headed for the passageway Colin had shown her. Darting in to the ladies solar, quietly closing the door, she moved to the fireplace, looking for the lever. Pressing it, she headed into the passageway that would take her outside. At least it was well-lit; thank goodness for electricity. Quickly making her way through, she came to the door. Cracking it open, she peered out. She could see the old garrison, now a garage across the courtyard; no one seemed to be outside. Pushing hard against the door to dislodge the snow, she put all of her weight into it, hearing the door groan and creak as it opened enough for her to squeeze through.

Scurrying to the garage, she looked over the choices—not a sports car, too impractical if there were still icy spots on the roads. Spotting an old Land Rover, slightly dented, it looked like a car for the staff to run errands or to use for driving around the grounds. No one would pay any attention to it on the road. Looking at the cupboard holding the keys, she tried to find the right one, her hands shaking with anger over Colin's duplicity.

Suddenly a large hand covered her mouth, muffling her scream, the other pinning her arms to her sides, pushing her against the wall, preventing her from kicking out.

"Well, well milady, we meet again." She had heard the voice before. "Why couldn't you mind your own business? I tried to scare you off, had your hotel room tossed, your dear friend pushed down the steps, and still you keep nosing around. You should have left with her, staying has caused me a great deal of difficulty."

After gagging her and securing her hands and feet, he turned Emily to face him. "Captain Rawlins Huntington at your service, milady. You can call me Rawlins."

This was so not good. He was a Day Walker. If Colin was to be believed, he would kill her, draining her dry. It sounded like a terrible way to die. But if he was going to kill her why tie her up? Trying to talk, thrashing, Rawlins placed a cloth over her face. Before she passed out she had the fleeting thought it was chloroform like on TV shows; they described it as cloyingly sweet. She succumbed to the gray nothingness.

Waking up, Emily's head pounded, her vision a bit blurry as

she tried to figure out where she was—Rawlins had her. She had no idea how long she'd been unconscious. Startled, she sat up quickly, retching from the drug in her system. Taking in her surroundings, she was in a stone room, sitting on a bed piled with blankets. There weren't any windows, the lanterns on the outside wall cast weak light into the cell. The door was heavy wood, with iron bars, a small window through which she could see the lanterns. It was so cold. Reaching for a blanket, she wrapped a couple around her for warmth. Finishing her appraisal of the room, she noted a pitcher of water next to the bed and a chamber pot in the corner.

Oh hell no, I'm in a freaking dungeon. It looks different from Edinburgh Castle, maybe Ravensmore has a dungeon? She felt groggy. Head full of cotton. Taking a drink of water to ease her dry, scratchy throat, she called out, "Anybody there? Hello?" Surely Colin would be looking for her, wouldn't he? Pacing around, she tried the door to no avail. She examined every corner and crevice of the room, trying to find a way out, or anything to help her escape. Frustrated, she sat back down on the bed. Great, now she had to pee—no way was she going in a chamber pot, she wanted a real bathroom or at least something with a door.

Standing up, she pounded on the door, yelling, "Hey, need some assistance here. Can anyone hear me?"

Rawlins appeared in front of her out of thin air. "No need to shout."

"Where am I? Where's Colin?"

"Welcome to picturesque Castle Gloom. Colin is going about his business not missing your lovely presence. I'm thinking he has better things to do than worry over you."

She wanted to think Colin would rush to her rescue; he cared for her...she remembered the mean ghost telling her all kinds of awful things about Colin. If they were true maybe he wouldn't come for her, would think she'd left on her own, still angry with him. No. There was no way Colin would leave her in the hands of a Day Walker. Rawlins was trying to get inside her head. She wouldn't take the bait. "Wait a minute, I saw the castle, it's nothing more than a ruin."

"The main castle is in ruins. However the dungeons survived, not many know it, and I find them useful from time to time.

"You can't keep me here."

"There's where you are wrong. I can keep you here or wherever I please, as long as I please. Who's going to stop me, your precious Colin? I think not." He leaned insolently against the door, watching her like a hawk watches a mouse.

"I need to go to the bathroom." The despicable man pointed to the wretched bowl. "Use the chamber pot. Be grateful you have that much."

"Why am I here?" She finished, coughing from the effects of the drug.

"Why—because I felt like it. Annoy me further and I'll take twenty years of your life from you in less than a minute," he finished, turning to leave.

"Wait, how long have I been here?" Her voice trembled, afraid to ask her real question—what was he going to do with her, she didn't want to die and she certainly didn't want to grow old before her time.

"It's late afternoon. Get comfortable, you're not going anywhere. Oh, scream all you like, no one will hear you." With that Rawlins vanished, leaving Emily alone with her thoughts.

A while later, not knowing how much time had passed, only that her stomach was growling ferociously, she heard someone. It couldn't be Rawlins since he simply appeared at will. A man rapped on the door, telling her to stand back against the far wall. She did, looking for a way to get past the man entering the room. He had a tray of food with a teapot. She eased to the left, ready to run for it when another man blocked the doorway pointing a gun at her.

"Now, now, ducky, don't even think about it. We don't want to harm you, but we will shoot you if you try to run. Where will you go? It's snowing again, no one will find you, and you'd freeze to death before you made it back to Ravensmore. Eat or we won't bring you anything else. Don't really care if you're hungry or not."

Emily was scared. These men looked like some kind of prison rejects, all mean faces and weasel eyes. She had to hope Colin would look for her, he was sworn to protect humanity...surely that meant he'd come after her, see her things left behind, no car missing.

Dejected, she sank back on the bed. She decided to eat; wanting to keep her strength up. There had to be a way to escape. The food was bland but palatable, the tea hot, the water cold. She ate everything, drank all the tea, saved the water for later. Looking to make sure no one was watching, embarrassed to the core, cheeks flaming, she used the chamber pot, wrinkling her nose and disgusted to not have any toilet paper. She would have never survived in the past; she liked her little luxuries—toilet paper, toothpaste, showers, heat, electricity, running water. Sighing, shoulders slumping, she rinsed her mouth out with water and climbed into the tiny bed, pulling the covers tight around her, trying to keep warm. Lying there, the tears silently ran down her face. *Please Colin, come for me. Terya? If you can hear me, please help me, tell Colin where to find me, I need him.* She drifted into a restless sleep.

"WHERE THE DEVIL IS SHE?" COLIN BELLOWED. WHEN EMILY didn't show up for lunch he'd thought she was punishing him, still angry. Then when she wasn't in her room, he checked every outbuilding, asked everyone, no one had seen her.

He'd searched their room; all her things were there except her passport. No vehicles were missing, no taxis had shown up, the bloody woman wouldn't have tried to leave on foot in the snow, would she?

Worthington had seen her heading to the unused west wing

mid-morning. Colin took the steps three at a time, telling himself she'd gotten distracted and didn't notice she'd missed lunch, and after he yelled at her for worrying him, he'd kiss her senseless, tell her he was an idiot, he wanted her to stay.

Checking every bloody room, he came to the last room—Abigail's room. Tentatively he pushed the door open. Walking in, he looked around curiously; he'd never been in here. She'd moved in when she married Hamish. The room smelled of Abigail, it was overpowering, not the fresh scent of sunshine and peaches like Emily.

There were marks in the dust on the table, someone had moved things. Looking closely, he saw footprints in the dust which had to be hers. It looked like she'd sat in the window seat from the disarray of the pillows. A half-eaten banana behind a pillow told him she'd indeed been in the room. She couldn't have disappeared...all the vehicles were there...where was she? Frustrated, he ran his hands through his hair, swearing, alarm bells ringing in his head, warning him she was in danger.

Slamming the heavy wooden door to the room closed, he thundered down the hallway pausing as he felt someone touch his sleeve. Stopping, he turned. There in the corridor was one of the castles infamous ghosts, Billy. Before Colin's time Billy had appeared whenever there was danger. It was said he had worked as a servant, bringing firewood to the rooms before he fell down the stairs one night and broke his neck. The lord of the castle had adored him and had a small statue commissioned and placed in the kitchen garden as a memorial. Billy was buried in the family graveyard.

He was a low-level ghost; transparent and couldn't communicate other than nodding or gesturing. The hackles on Colin's neck rose; if Billy had shown up, he or someone he cared about was in imminent danger—Emily.

"Billy, my lad, have you seen Emily? The American who came to Ravensmore with me?" Billy nodded, gesturing frantically. "Wait a moment, I'm trying to understand."

The little ghost floated towards the stairs, motioning Colin to follow him. He led Colin to the garage, pointing wildly. He didn't see anything—taking a deep breath, he reached out with all his senses. The seconds ticked by—he smelled Emily and something else—he knew the scent from somewhere but couldn't quite place it. He stiffened, letting a string of curses flow as he recognized the other scent...Day Walker...one who had recently fed.

Only one Day Walker would be so brazen to come into Colin's territory, take something of his...it had to be Rawlins. He was going to rip Rawlins open and feed his entrails to the ravens while he watched. Colin had put her in so much danger and now she was alone, thinking he'd deserted her, failed to protect her.

"Billy, do you know where he took her?" With slumped shoulders, Billy shook his head no and from the gesturing, Colin guessed he'd dematerialized with Emily, which was hard unless you'd fed heavily and were juiced up. Now where would he take her? It had to be a trap, where would he go?

"Thank you, lad." Billy smiled and faded away. Colin headed to the study, pouring a large drink. He needed to think before he acted, come up with a list of places where she might be. He'd have to ask Robert to try Rawlins's home, now-falling-apart Huntington Castle in England, then Edinburgh Castle, the Vaults, and the secret rooms under Rosslyn Chapel as he still didn't have his powers back. Those would be the most likely places.

A sliver of fear snaked up his spine as he thought of one other place—the Day Walker realm—filled with horrible creatures who would rip Emily to pieces. He'd leave it for last, needing a Day Walker to take him in if he couldn't get Thorne to visit Dayne for him.

Had to find her, time was running out. Rawlins couldn't know about the curse, gods help Emily if he did. They would both be doomed when the clock struck midnight on Friday night.

20

Waking up, she stiffened, goosebumps rising on her arms as she felt someone watching her. Getting up and looking through the small window in the door, squinting in the darkness, she could barely make out two guards on duty and screamed when a voice spoke next to her ear.

"Good evening to you Emily." A lantern flared, Rawlins was in her cell, standing much too close. Hastily, she backed up, feet propelling her backwards until her knees hit the bed and she sat down hard.

He gestured to dinner, set on a heavy desk with a velvet covered chair. "Eat, you've missed dinner, don't want to be accused of starving you." The desk wasn't there before, she never heard them bring it in, it was massive and had to weigh a ton. "Where did that come from? It wasn't here before."

"I am civilized. Couldn't have you eating in bed like a common American...oh, yes, you are American, well still, now you have a proper place to eat. Don't fret; it was easy enough to do without waking you."

She threw her fork at him. He caught it, eyes narrowing, "Don't test my patience. I will tie you to the bed and spoon feed you if I must." Scowling, she ate, would keep up her strength, try to figure out a way to escape. Would Colin think to look in this ruin? He might not know the dungeon was still intact under the rubble.

Rawlins poofed outside to talk with his men. She hated when he did it, was also a bit envious of the ability. It would be fun to pop in and out of places, always on time, no traffic or parking spots or filling the car with gas. Never worrying about the weather or ever getting sick, there were some nifty perks but being immortal must be lonely, everyone you cared about dying and still you go on.

Did the jerk Rawlins lose someone he cared about? What made people do the things they did? Emily finished her dinner. She knew it could be worse, they could have abused or tortured her. At least they had been civil so far.

Her jailers came in, taking her tray and chamber pot. She smirked knowing they had to empty it, she hoped it smelled terrible and splashed on their shoes. The men were supposed to stay and watch her, but she heard them talking, they were going into town to have a drink. Arguing amongst themselves, telling one another she couldn't get out, so why sit and watch her in the cold? They could be in a warm pub with the match on the telly.

Sleep evaded her as she tossed and turned. Propping up the pillow, she sat up, wondering what she could do. As a last-ditch effort, she spoke out loud, "If anyone's there, can you help me, please?" She pleaded, feeling a little silly calling out to a ghost.

She knew it was a long shot but that awful spirit at Ravensmore was there, maybe one was hanging around here, the castle name certainly seemed like it should have restless spirits, but hopefully not mean ones.

The room was growing colder, when she felt the air stir, "Is someone there?" A faint blue light started to glow, within it, she could see a girl. She had long blond hair, her dress was tattered, her face tear stained as she hovered near Emily.

"You can see me, miss? No one comes here, and those who

do can never see me, except for the big, blond man, he scares me so I hide when he shows up."

"Can you help me get out of here?" The girl wrung her hands, shuddering. "This is a sad place. No one leaves the dungeons of Castle Gloom unless they take you to the rivers of Doom and Sorrow to drown you, so many dead."

Speaking in low soothing tones to the ghostly girl, "Is that what happened to you?" Tears ran down the girl's face. "I was in love with Lord Hamish, he'd promised to marry me. I worked in the kitchens. When I found out I was with child, I told him, happy we could be married. Hc asked me to meet him at the river of Sorrow to discuss our wedding.

"We met by the light of the moon, it was a lovely warm summer eve. I didn't know until it was too late, he pushed me in...held me under...until I saw the light. It was my fault my baby died. The light took my baby to the other side, I tried but couldn't cross over, I don't know why."

It was a heartbreaking tale. "It wasn't your fault, you do know that? It was Hamish's fault. He murdered you and your unborn child. You bear no guilt in this. Forgive yourself."

The girl looked up at Emily, "The mean man is planning to lure Lord Colin here and kill him when he tries to free you."

"No! We have to warn him. Is there anything you can do?" Emily pleaded.

HELLFIRE. ROBERT PHONED COLIN, FINDING NOTHING AT Rawlins's home other than a handful of minions who he dispatched. No sign of Emily at Edinburgh Castle and nothing at the Vaults.

"Colin, you didn't tell me about the secret rooms under Rosslyn Chapel. The grail, gems, and gold all belonging to the old Knights Templar, I'm guessing? Still hidden away after all this time."

"Aye, Robert. I knew ye'd haul it away, and ye dinna need any more money."

"Hmmprh, I'll go back for the lot once I know you have your Emily safe."

"Appreciate it. Might want to think twice about stealing the booty—I'm guessing you didn't encounter the dragon guarding the treasure?"

"Maybe the beast was out hunting. Well, I'll think on it. Worth the adventure, I think," he laughed.

It was deep into the night, the clock was counting down, and Colin was no closer to finding her. Why was Rawlins waiting to contact him? If he had Emily and wanted a fight, why not tell him where to show up? He'd left a message for Rawlins on his mobile, yes, he was an enemy but he still knew the bastard's number. It went straight to bloody voice mail.

Pacing in front of the fire, drinking a bottle of wine, he was getting ready to call Thorne when a timid, wisp of a girl appeared surrounded by a faint blue light, weeping and wringing her hands.

"Lass, what ails you?" She was filthy, dripping water on the rug, mud clinging to her gown.

"Milord, be you Lord Colin?"

Seeing his nod, she continued. "That awful man has her, your woman. She's locked in the dungeon at Castle Gloom, but there are men waiting for you, 'tis a trap. I don't have the power to free her. I can't do anything."

By the gods, why didn't he think of Gloom? It made sense in a sick, twisted way. Colin thanked the spirit, "What you've done may save Emily's life. I am indebted to you—if there is anything I can do to help you, call for me and I will come."

The girl flickered in and out before disappearing to tell Emily she'd found Colin, he was coming to save her.

BLOODY HELL. RAWLINS, DRAINED HUMAN WOMEN DRY ALL the time without a single intrusion of conscience yet now, so close, was having difficulty dispatching Emily. Knew killing her would put them one step closer to winning this war, but kept thinking back to the night Colin died, seeing the look upon his face when he realized the depth of the betrayal perpetrated by those he loved, all those years ago in Edinburgh Castle.

He'd never been in love, couldn't fathom the feelings or the position of weakness it put you in, yet he'd felt pity that day for the strong warrior. Saw now the depth of his feeling for Emily, knew it would take away Colin's will, make it easy to kill him—he didn't want to win if Colin wasn't at full strength. He wanted a sporting fight. He'd wall her up alive.

Over a hundred years ago Rawlins had captured a Shadow Walker. After months of nonstop torture the Walker told him about the curse. Now Rawlins would find out the truth. If indeed it proved to be true, he and Dayne could use this knowledge to destroy every Shadow Walker they could find.

By the time Colin found Emily it would be too late, the curse would run its course, Colin would turn wraith. But first, he'd relish a worthy fight. These humans nowadays, they were soft, couldn't fight, relied on a gun and when it failed, bawled like babes for mercy which he never granted.

Annoyed he'd felt something other than anger, he dematerialized to Inverness to slake his frustration on the humans. He'd drain a dozen or so, a good dose of energy ought to banish the melancholy thoughts.

THE MEN ENTERED EMILY'S CELL, GRABBING HER BEFORE SHE could run past them. They bound her hands and feet, as she struggled, screaming herself hoarse before they gagged her. Both copped feels, roughly kneading her breasts as she clenched her legs together with everything she had, fearing they would rape her.

Taking her to the end of the passageway where the cells ended, she could see stone and mortar stacked on the ground by the bright lantern light—oh great, plenty of light so she could see what was going to happen to her.

Walled-up alive. Oh. My. God. Her palms were clammy as sweat ran down between her breasts. If the spirit didn't find Colin, if he didn't get here in time, she'd die in the wall. She wouldn't die of starvation as many must have, she'd have a heart attack, her worst claustrophobic nightmare coming to life in high-definition color. Gagging, she made herself swallow a couple of times. If she threw up now, she'd choke and die.

Iron rings were set in the wall making her flashback to seeing Colin held in the dungeon of Edinburgh Castle. Moaning in terror, she thrashed, trying to get free as the two men holding her dropped her on the ground. Wriggling, rolling away from the stone, a hand snaked around her foot, dragging her back. Her head snapped back, as one of the men punched her in the face. Seeing stars; she took another hit to the jaw, biting the inside of her cheek as blood trickled out of her mouth running down her chin. Frantically reaching for anything to defend herself, her hand grasped a shard of stone. Striking out blindly, she heard a yelp as it made contact with the second man's thigh. Screaming in pain, he kicked her as a shot rang out, reverberating on the damp, cold, stone walls. He shot her point blank. The bullet hit her side, pain exploded through her body. Barely registering the vicious kicks, vaguely the sickening snap of her rib penetrated her brain as she gasped for breath. Welcoming the blackness she passed out cold.

Slowly coming to, she winced in pain, her entire body ached. Could barely breathe. Her nose must be broken. Intense pain radiated down her side. At least the gag had fallen out so she could take shallow breaths through her mouth. It was pitch black, so cold. Her arms felt like they were being pulled out of their sockets and something was biting into her wrists. Why couldn't she move? Terror consumed her, claustrophobia kicked in, spots appearing in front of her eyes as it dawned on her—she'd been entombed in the wall.

Uncontrollably shaking, sobs wracked her body, tears blurring her vision. A faint blue light filled the space, she heard a whisper—the young girl was back.

"Milady, what have they done to you? Hold on. I found Lord Colin, he's coming. Because of both of you, the light is back, pulling me towards it—I couldn't pass on to the next realm without telling you first." With that, the ghost faded.

"Thank you for helping me. I'm happy for you." In a detached, numb state, Emily wondered if Colin didn't make it in time would she die of fright or from heart failure or starvation and lack of water? They were all terrible—she didn't want to die, had she been given a second chance only to have it end this way? She hadn't saved Colin, still had to help him, he could be redeemed, he was a good man.

Pressing against the stone with her knees, it wouldn't give. There was no way out.

Never having told Colin she was in love with him, didn't matter if he didn't love her back, she wanted him to know how she felt, wished she could have helped him. Tears trickled down her cheeks as she accepted she was going to die here, alone.

SADDLING A HORSE WAS THE FASTEST WAY TO GET TO CASTLE Gloom. A car would take twice as long to go around on the roads. Colin searched for Emily. Rounding the far corner of the ruined castle, he saw two minions coming up the old stairs where the dungeon was located. Reining in the horse, he tied him to a tree and made his way around the building. Filled with fury, unleashing a primal anger, letting loose the beast within, he set the uncontrollable side of himself free. Pulling the driver from the car, he gutted him from neck to groin, finishing him off by running his blade through the asshole's eye. The thrust was so forceful, his blade came out the back of the guy's head, hitting metal, the point of the blade breaking off.

The second man, frozen in fear, was babbling. Disgusted, Colin reached in, cutting the pansy's throat with one vicious cut so deep, his head rolled off, rolling down the steep hill. Who knew where it would end up?

Starting to wipe the blood from his hands, he stopped. Why bother? He was drenched to the elbow, his shirt soaked. He tossed the broken blade. Jumping down the steps, he landed with a thud, sending a cloud swirling around him.

"Emily," he roared her name. Nothing. She had to be here. He checked every cell, alarm mounting with each wasted moment. *Calm the hell down.* Breathing deep, he saw blood on the stone. She was close. Drag marks in the dirt and dust ended at a wall. The stone didn't fit with the passageway. Pressing his ear against the wall he heard faint scrabbling noises.

Those fucking bastards walled her up. She would be out of her mind with fear; he knew her weakness for enclosed spaces. "Emily! Thank the gods." Pulling his other dagger from his boot, he jammed it into the mortar. It wasn't completely dry. He pried carefully not knowing how close she might be to the stone on the other side. Digging out the mortar around the stone, bit by bit.

Scanning the darkness, he could barely make out a shirt. "I'm here, love."

In reply, he heard a muffled sob. She was alive. Putting all his strength into tearing down the recent wall, he pulled with his hands, tumbling stone after stone to the ground. Could see her feet were bound.

"Hold on a few moments longer while I remove the last bit of stone." Moving quickly, seeing fresh blood on her jeans and shirt, he pulled harder, a large section of the hastily put up wall came tumbling down, stones striking him as they fell. He didn't notice, kept his eyes on her face. Covered in grime, clean where her tears had run down, she tried to speak. Her mouth moved but no sound escaped. Her eyes were full of terror, the pupils so big her eyes looked black.

"Dinna worry lass, you're safe, I've got you." He caressed her bruised cheek, noting the broken nose, black eye, and blood running down her chin.

Momentarily stopping, a fury so bright burned through him, he thought he would light up all of Scotland. They had hurt her, fastened her to the damn wall...he knew what it felt like, the agonizing pain of your arms stretched too wide, shoulders protesting trying to hold the weight, the numbness in your wrists. The intense pain inflicted upon her body.

Tamping his anger down only so he wouldn't frighten her, he vowed to kill Rawlins for his part. Swore to kill every minion and Day Walker he could find. He ripped the iron rings from the partially set mortar, releasing her arms, catching her as she fell. Her gasp of pain and sobs broke his heart as she tried to tell him what had happened to her, stumbling over the words.

"We're going home. I won't ever let go."

"I knew you'd come for me." As he shifted her weight, she cried out. He cradled her in his arms, lifting her onto the horse in front of him. "The horse was the quickest way here. I am sorry for any pain the ride may cause."

"Doesn't matter, take me home." She closed her eyes. He urged the horse into a gallop, flying over the sodden ground back to Ravensmore. Passing under the portcullis, Colin bellowed for the stable boy. He dismounted, carrying Emily as if she were made of glass, taking the stairs two at a time to their bedroom. Stumbling as he gently placed her on the bed, Colin called for help.

A fierce storm was brewing, icy rain pelting the windows, thunder rumbling across the sky as the fire crackled, warming the room.

Colin thundered for hot water, clean cloths, and clothes to be brought to him. Meg came running; Worthington behind her arms laden with food and drink.

"Milord, shall I call for the doctor?"

"There's no time, Meg. We'll have to make do." Nodding, Meg went into the bathroom. Colin heard running water. Carrying Emily, jostling her broken ribs as little as possible, he held her on his knees to remove her clothes. Needed to clean the wounds, see how bad they were. Lifting his arm to tie his hair back, he frowned—his arm was bloody...he wasn't bleeding. Looking down at her, he saw fresh blood blooming on her shirt and jeans. He stripped off her clothes.

Emily flinched, a tear running down her face. She looked up at him, searching his face. He held his breath, lost in her gaze. Colin started to raise his hand when pain sliced through him. All the battles, all the injuries...they were inconsequential compared to the agony he felt watching that lone tear trail down her cheek.

Her torso was a mass of black and blue bruises where she'd been repeatedly kicked. Above her hip, a spot he'd kissed a hundred times, was more damage...a bullet wound, blood dripping onto the stone floor. So much blood, how much had she lost? The cold air would have slowed the loss. He didn't want to take the time but had to be sure there weren't any other serious injuries.

Placing her in the warm water, washing her, he checked her injuries. She was in shock, not speaking, eyes glazed with pain. Her face was so pale the freckles stood out in stark contrast, the circles under her eyes, purple, gray eyes stared blankly into space.

"Not long now. We'll get your wounds bandaged and then you can rest." He choked on the words.

She had three broken ribs, a cracked cheekbone, broken nose, both wrists were sprained and the blasted bullet wound. He noted the powder burns, a point blank shot—thank the gods it was a clean shot, through the flesh of her left side narrowly missing her hip bone and other vital organs. The water turned rose-colored as he cleaned the blood, dirt, and grime off her. He washed her hair, feeling another cut on the back of her scalp, most likely from banging it against the stone wall, fighting as they walled her up like a common criminal.

His gut twisted in knots, he lifted her out of the tub, placing her on the table that had been set up in front of the fire. Covering her with a quilt, she was unconscious from the pain; he reached deep within himself for every ounce of strength remaining in his body, focusing on saving her. Giving everything to her.

It wasn't enough.

Emily's eyes flew open, fixing on Colin. She shuddered, letting out a gasp, her body limp.

"Hold on lass, no! Emily, come back to me." Shaking her frantically, reaching for power that was wasn't there, he had nothing left. Falling to his knees, letting out a primal scream full of gut-wrenching pain, his soul screamed out for its mate, a black yawning emptiness filled his soul, longing coursed through him... as he realized too late...he loved this woman. Didn't want to be a wraith, wanted to protect her, keep her safe, love her for eternity. He never told her. Emily would never know how he felt.

His heart shattering at the loss, Colin leapt to his feet, destroying the room, throwing furniture against the walls, splintering anything he could get his hands on. Anything to dull the pain. She was still as a statue, gone. Grabbing the whisky, he drained the bottle. Smashing it against the hearth, he collapsed to the floor, screaming her name over and over.

21

"Dude, you look like something the cat wouldn't bother dragging in." Robert was breaking the rules to visit the cop in the hospital—screw the rules. He'd been breaking them since he signed on his first ship at the tender age of seven.

"Head's killing me. Was I run over by a truck?"

"Close. The truck was a big sonofabitch."

"It's about time you showed up. I have questions and I want answers."

"Right. Don't think you're really in a position to be demanding anything." Robert pointed out the obvious.

"Don't worry. I sold everyone that crap story you made up. I need to get out of here." Monroe scowled, straining, causing all the monitors to start beeping at the same time.

"Oy, human—you need to calm the hell down before you rip your stomach open again." The chart at the foot of the bed caught his eye. The bloke had died for three minutes and come back. Monroe could now interact with Walkers.

There would be hell to pay when Thorne found out what Robert was about to do. He was going to tell the cop, let the chips fall where they may—if Monroe started yapping, he'd kill him. Something told Robert they'd be seeing a lot more of this guy.

Pulling a chair close to the bed, Robert told him about Day Walkers, Shadow Walkers and the quest to protect humanity. He told him about how they killed each other, when they are strongest/weakest and how they became Walkers.

"It's like I'm in some crazy science fiction movie—only the monsters are real. I want answers. Ever since Alice was murdered I've needed more, crossed lines, and taken a lot of risks to find out what's really going on. I can't go back. I know it's time to move on. So can I call out to this head guy in charge, Thorne?"

"No. You have to be dying when you call out. Maybe he'll answer, maybe not; he's a fickle bastard. You can't wake up one morning and decide to join us. It doesn't work that way, cop."

"Does Thorne have a mobile? Can't we call him and talk about me coming on board?"

"Not even going there. Look, I'm going to get the shite kicked out of me for telling you any of this, which is fine, I can take an ass kicking but you need to give me your word you won't mention our conversation. Not to anybody, not your partner, shrink, priest, anyone. Period. Got it?"

The cop looked thoughtful turning his gaze on Robert, "You have my word." Holding up a hand to stop Robert from speaking, he continued, "I want to help. These assholes are running around my city killing people. This goes on much longer and the dead bodies that are young but look old will create a panic. I need to be involved."

Robert knew he'd have to talk to Thorne. Hell, this is what he got for having one moment of being a good Samaritan. Comes back and kicks you in the face. Shrugging, he looked at the cop. It'd be nice to have some help—if the guy could survive long enough. "I'll talk to my boss, see what he says. In the meantime, shut the hell up and get better."

For kicks and grins, Robert vanished from the room, leaving Monroe gaping.

22

Friday, November 6th - The last day of the curse...*

Hours passed by, the clock chimed two in the morning, dragging to his feet, Colin thundered: "Thorne, get the fuck down here."

The room shimmered, from within the silvery light, a man, who was something more appeared. "You'd better have a damn good reason for using that tone with me boy." Thorne stood there, silver light reflecting off and through him. The ancient god looked pissed to be dragged out of his realm—well too bloody bad.

Standing there giving off a "this better be good or I'm feeding you to Fang for disturbing me" look, the god lowered his RayBan Aviator shades, icy blue eyes boring straight into his soul and glared at Colin. Fang was Thorne's pet—a saber-tooth tiger, huge and ferocious, said to eat those the god was displeased with. Like all ancient creatures, the tiger could talk and was a sarcastic asshole.

Today Thorne had on the Shadow Walker's favored uniform of black Doc Marten boots, faded Levis 501 jeans, and a white t-shirt showing off his ripped body. The casual clothes enhanced the lethal vibe he threw off. At six foot seven with long silver hair, and silver skin covered with blue tattoos, which flashed across his skin like lightning and rain, changing in the light, he was beyond intimidating. Colin and all the Shadow Walkers respected him and had a very healthy dose of fear around him—you never knew what an ancient god would do. Thorne's moods were mercurial, he controlled weather and would toast your ass with a lightning bolt if you looked at him the wrong way.

That being said, the guy could hide his skin color and tats if he wanted, appear in any guise. Thorne loved the women, especially human women, usually had three or four in his bed at a time if Colin remembered correctly. Then Thorne would send them back, wiping their memories, letting them think it was an erotic dream.

The god noted the room, smashed to bits, his eyes coming to rest on Emily's prone form. Thorne opened his mouth and out came his stuffy British accent, "Yes, well she's dead and gone. You know the rules. Why did you call me here? In a rush to become a wraith and leave my service so soon?"

Stepping up on the god, Colin took a swing, finding himself thrown against the wall as Thorne flicked a small lightning bolt at him. Shaking his head, getting to his feet, his voice cracked, hoarse, "Please save her."

Arching an eyebrow, Thorne stared hard at the Scottish warrior standing in front of him. "I would suggest you think long and hard on your request. I don't want to lose you to the Wraith realm but what you ask...the price is steep."

Hands clenched at his sides, he pounded out the words. "I. Will. Pay. The. Bloody. Price."

"You don't even know what it is, so don't be so quick to accept." Raising a hand, Thorne sent Colin across the room, the force of his will pushing him down in the chair. Sitting across from him, the god spelled it out.

"There is always a price. There must be balance. In taking from death, you must pay with life—if I do this, you will agree to give up your immortal soul, to never see this woman again. She will forget you, fall in love with someone else...not you. You will never love anyone. You will die alone, with no friends, you will become mortal, to live a mortal's life, your memory will be wiped and when you die—no matter natural causes or murder—you will become a wraith, doomed for all eternity."

Thorne paused, looking at Colin, waiting for the answer. "I accept. I gladly pay the price but for one thing..." he was stopped by the god standing up, getting in Colin's grill.

"You dare to ask for anything?" he softly growled as the room swirled with electricity. Colin drank it in, feeling stronger, the broken furniture in the room lifted from the floor.

"Give me one last night with her before you wipe our memories, wait until tomorrow...please." Colin stared back at Thorne meeting his gaze. Let him be damned, he was anyway but none of this had ever been Emily's choice. He wanted to give her a chance at happiness, even if it was with someone else. The beast within wanted to rage, Colin quieted it down, telling it better for her to be alive than dead, she deserves to be loved.

The god's gaze was unfocused as if he were speaking with someone or watching something only he could see.

"As it's after midnight—I will give you from the coming dawn until the clock strikes midnight. Tell her she came back, survived. And in believing in you broke the curse. Nothing more. As far as she's concerned you're still immortal."

Nodding in agreement, Colin motioned for Thorne to continue. "After tonight, when she wakes in the morning, she'll be back at her hotel, won't remember anything other than enjoying a lovely holiday. Her friend simply fell down the stairs and went home early. When she's asked about the mysterious Colin, Emily will laugh, saying what a funny joke played on her. She will believe you to be some crazy re-enactor who went around having fun with tourists.

"This is all she will remember of you—a joke to be told to her friends, family...husband...children. There's more. In asking for this, when the clock strikes midnight you will die, turn wraith and be condemned instead of living out your life as a mortal. Colin—are you quite sure you want to do this?"

"My miserable life is nothing compared to hers, I give it freely." Colin felt a weight lift, something changed inside, the ice around his heart splintered, shattering, he was free. The remaining day with her was completely and utterly worth his soul.

"So be it." Thorne vanished, the air in the room settled, the furniture reassembled, hitting the floor with a loud bang. Emily's startled cry ripped through the silence. Colin turned. She was sitting up, the coverlet falling to her waist, wounds healed, the skin shiny and pink, the bruising gone.

Crossing the room in quick strides, he knelt at her side. "Thank the gods." He held her face in his hands, searching. "You scared the hell out of me Emily, don't ever do it again. I think you've given me gray hair."

"You can't get gray hair, you're immortal. Why don't I hurt? Did you heal me? I knew you would rescue me." She leaned forward and kissed him.

"You saved me." His voice was rough as he took possession of her mouth, kissing her as a drowning man gasping for air.

"Why did you leave Ravensmore?" He picked her up from the table, carrying her to the bed, crawling in beside her.

"I was exploring the castle. In Abigail's old room a ghost appeared. He told me to look outside. I saw you embracing another woman, kissing her when you came out of her house. He said awful things about you having lots of women, said she was one of your many mistresses, you would never commit to anyone, least of all me, and you were only using me. I was angry so I ran. In the garage, I looked for a car to take, one that could handle the snow, that's when Rawlins showed up. He put something over my face and when I woke up, I was in the dungeon at Castle Gloom."

"I couldn't find you anywhere. You've no bloody idea how worried I was."

"How long have I been out?" Trying to sit up, she was healed but still tired from her ordeal. Colin eased her back, propping the pillows behind her, handing her a cold Pepsi.

"Next time you're mad at me. Ask. 'Twas a simple explanation—the woman was Mrs. Burns, a widow, her cow was stuck in the snow and mud, I freed it. I went inside to wash the muck off my hands, when I came out, she hugged me, kissed me on the cheek to thank me. That damnable ghost was always causing trouble when Abigail was alive; he was from France, loved gossip and causing problems. It must have pleased him to turn you against me. He hated me, thought I was barbaric, not good enough for her. I'll find him; send him to another realm. I may not be able to destroy him, but I can banish him."

"I overreacted. I'm truly sorry." She blew out a sigh.

"Given what happened to you, it would have been easy to jump to conclusions, especially after the way I reacted when you talked about staying. I was so bloody stupid. I want you to stay here with me. I need you." He wanted to say those three little words to her...yet...even after losing her, a part of him was still afraid.

Emily smiled up at him, tears swimming in her eyes. "I love you. I think I have since the moment I found your button in my pocket."

As the fire crackled, they drank wine, and he spent the rest of the deep night showing her how much he loved her the only way he knew how...with his body.

23

The curtains were drawn around the bed. Colin was fast asleep when something woke him. With a start, he sat up, reaching for his dagger under the pillow.

Every sense on alert, he pulled on his kilt and boots, careful not to wake Emily. Drawing the curtain open, he peered out. Something wasn't right, every sense screamed for him to be wary.

"Well, it's about bloody time you got out of bed. Granted it is almost time for breakfast, however while some start the day with coffee, I prefer killing Shadow Walkers—find it puts a lively skip in my step for the rest of the day, really starts you off on the right foot." Rawlins was relaxed in a chair in front of the fire, hand casually resting on his sword, gun at his other hip, daggers in his boots. "I see you found dear Emily, did she enjoy her accommodations?"

"She could have died. What the bloody hell were you thinking? Why would you take a woman and not come straight at me? And to Gloom, my bastard brother's hovel of a castle?" Colin's voice was low, deadly.

"It pained you to see Hamish's castle again didn't it? Hurt you to know I had your woman, that she might die by my hand with nothing you could do to stop me? I'm going to kill you once and for all—you've been an annoyance to me for over four hundred years and I'm tired of the game, I have other things to do."

With that the Day Walker leapt up from the chair, dropping into a fighting stance. "Let's do this the old-fashioned way, yes? Bullets are so tiresome; I much prefer the cut of a blade." Brandishing his sword, he gestured at Colin.

Filled with anger at his last day with Emily being interrupted by that bloody bugger, he lunged forward...missing Rawlins by a foot. Rawlins had a surprised look on his face as he taunted, "Being with a woman has made you slow Shadow Walker."

Colin had forgotten how fast he was as a Shadow Walker. He'd been the best warrior of his time, and Colin would be damned if he'd let Rawlins kill him before he had the rest of his time with Emily.

Feinting to the left, he caught the Englishman on the sleeve, a red stain appearing on the white fabric of his shirt. "Bring it, ye English whoreson. I've things to do with my lady and I don't want to waste my time with the likes of you—let's finish this once and for all."

Grudgingly, Colin had to admit, Rawlins had also been a great warrior, with his Day Walker power, he might have the edge but Colin had willpower, and in many cases a warrior's will could help him win the day when he was outmatched.

"You almost killed Emily. Her blood is on your hands. Your minions beat her, broke her ribs, and shot her before walling her up alive. I will not let that treachery go unpunished."

"I should have taken her for my own, had a taste before I left. Oh well, another time, mate." Striking faster than the eye could follow, Rawlins slit Colin's leg from thigh to knee, spinning around, dancing back. "As to my men, well, you know how soldiers are, they need to be kept in line or they get unruly."

Pain lancing through his leg, Colin stumbled before regaining his balance. "I remember how much you relish a fight, especially when the odds are in your favor."

"Rather slow this morning," Rawlins taunted, cutting him across the chest as the red stain spread, the blood running down in rivulets to the floor.

Scoring Rawlins across his back, he opened a large gash across the Day Walker's shoulder. "You stood and watched while my brother killed me, made a deal with him to betray me, killed my men, and destroyed their families, no longer," he roared, bringing his blade down, catching Rawlins on his bicep with this strike.

❦

EMILY WOKE WITH A START, SHE'D BEEN DREAMING OF swordfights. Rubbing sleep out of her eyes, alarms went off in her brain as she reached over for Colin and found the bed empty. She pulled on his shirt, jumping out of bed, horror on her face at the scene playing out in front of her.

That awful Rawlins was back, in their bedroom no less, fighting with Colin. Would it ever stop? She was so tired of blood and swords and guns, she wanted peace and quiet. Her adrenaline flowing, she tried to tiptoe over to the door to summon help. They were so focused on killing each other, neither noticed her. As she reached the door that damned ghost, Frederick, pushed her. She tripped, hitting the table, knocking a vase to the floor, sounding like an explosion, shattering against the stone floor.

Both men froze, mid-strike, looking at her. Rawlins tipped his head to the ghost who promptly vanished. He then stalked towards Emily, sword raised, ready to strike. Emily screamed, back against the door, nowhere to run. As the sword was about to take her head off, she slammed her eyes shut, hoping it would be quick and painless. Hearing a dull thud, she cracked one eye open.

"No!" she screamed, seeing Colin on the ground, Rawlins standing over him. His blade, razor sharp, cut through Colin's shoulder. "'Twas a good fight Colin. You were a worthwhile opponent, there are so few nowadays, we are a dying breed. I'll miss you as an adversary. Wanted you to know old chap, I never condoned what Hamish and Abigail did to you all those years ago, it went beyond the code of honorable men. Know you understand—I have to finish you off or Dayne will have my head, literally. Die well."

Kneeling to take Colin's heart, Rawlins didn't notice Emily. Tiptoeing along the wall, she picked up the heavy iron fireplace poker. Sending a silent plea out, smelling freshly mown grass, she raised the heavy iron bar, arms shaking, and struck. She'd never know how but by fate or divine intervention she'd managed to stab Rawlins in the chest. Gasping with surprise, he looked up at her. "Well done, milady."

Rawlins yanked the poker from his chest and vanished.

Falling to her knees, Emily couldn't stop the bleeding. Blood was trickling out of Colin's mouth. He was immortal; of course he would live.

"Colin, look at me. Tell me what to do." She spoke softly, stumbling over the words, stroking his face.

A croak came out, "The Fates have a hell of a sense of humor. I'm dying, ye must..." Colin grasped her hand in his, pulling her close.

"No, that simply isn't possible, you're immortal, he didn't take your heart, you will heal. I need you, don't leave me." Her voice was hysterical, rising with every word until she was sure, every animal within a hundred miles winced from the shrill pitch.

"Shhh, lass." Coughing as blood bubbled on his lips, running down the side of his mouth, Colin seemed to reach deep within for the strength to tell her something.

"I was lost the moment ye tried to help me in the Vaults, the compassion in your lovely gray eyes, the color of a stormy sea—

so beautiful, so kind. I wanted to grow old with you, give you the big family you always wanted."

"Don't talk darlin'. You are the strongest, bravest man I've ever known, you're not leaving me, not after I've finally found you." Tears streamed down her face.

"I love you. You gave me peace after a lifetime of war. I didn't think it was possible. Wanted us to dance in the shadows, bathe in the moonlight while every star smiled down on us, for all eternity." Colin took one last breath, smiled weakly and was gone.

Screaming out in fury, mad with grief, she pounded on Colin, tears running down her face. "Please, don't leave me. I love you, Colin." Looking up towards the sky, she cried out, "Terya, please, I beg you, please help him, I will give anything, I entreat you."

Rocking back and forth, she sobbed, terrible animal-like sounds wrenching out of her, a deep keening noise emanated from deep within, grief overwhelming her.

A warm breeze caressed her face, sunlight streamed in through the window, bringing the smell of a woodland forest and freshly cut grass. Emily looked around, there were honeybees flying around Colin. The room started shaking, the floor cracking open as a tree grew out of the stone, reaching up towards the high ceiling, its branches reaching out across the room, splintering furniture to pieces as the oak tree filled the room. Larger around than any tree she'd ever seen, the bark was dark chestnut with copper running through it. The leaves every shade of green imaginable, covering she and Colin, giving the impression of cradling them within as the room was filled with silver and gold light. A carpet of green grass appeared filled with all types of flowers, the scent filling the room.

The air shimmered as Terya appeared. She wore a gossamer gown of the palest blue, her silver hair sparkling and unbound, skimming the floor, bare feet walked towards and then stopped in front of Colin.

Crawling on hands and knees, Emily wrapped her arms around the goddesses' legs, kissing her feet, weeping. "Please, bring him back to me. I can't live without him." she gazed up through eyelashes sprinkled with tears sparkling like diamonds.

"My child, what would you give to have your brave warrior back? Would you give your soul, your heart, the very breath in your body?"

"I don't want to live without him. He fills the empty space in my heart I thought would never be filled. I will give whatever you ask of me to have him back."

Terya reached down, her fingers under Emily's chin, tilting her head up to look in her eyes.

"There must be balance. I cannot give life without taking in return. To return Colin to life, you must willingly give your own life—this is the price which must be paid." The goddess gazed at Emily with ancient, all-knowing eyes.

Without hesitation, Emily stood, facing Terya, squaring her shoulders, "I gladly give my life for his. I understand—when I died and came back after the accident, it was so I could save Colin at this moment in time. Every moment I've had since the accident was a gift, I know now what it is to truly love...for that I am indebted to Colin, if this is how I repay him, I willingly offer my heart, soul, and breath. Would you tell him how much I love him?"

Casting a benevolent gaze upon Emily, Terya told her Colin would know. Content, Emily laid down next to Colin, curling up to him, running her hands through his hair, tracing the scar on his face, and gently kissed his lips for the last time. She nodded to Terya, "I'm ready."

Wrapping her arms around Colin, burying her face in his chest, she closed her eyes. *How long would it take—will I fall asleep and not wake up, will it hurt? Why was someone banging a drum, am I dead already? Gah, I don't want drums in the afterlife, I hate drums, and why am I so freaking hot?*

Bolting upright, something wasn't adding up. His heartbeat was strong...but how could that be? She was dead. Maybe she hadn't moved on and was a ghost? Opening her eyes, Colin was looking at her.

He. Was. Alive!

Before he could utter a word, Emily pulled him close, kissing him. His chuckle was a deep rumble as he kissed her back. "Somebody want to tell me why there is a giant tree in our bedroom?" Colin saw the goddess.

Pulling away, Emily stood, launching herself at Terya. Might not be the smartest move but she couldn't help it, she was filled with joy. "I don't understand what happened, why am I alive?" she stammered.

Caressing Emily's cheek, Terya motioned for her to sit as a branch from the tree reached down, providing a bench for the goddess. She sat facing them.

"My darling child, you died from your injuries. Colin made a bargain with Thorne to bring you back. In doing so he sacrificed his soul so you could live and in so doing, doomed himself to existing as a wraith for all eternity."

The goddess continued. "You are full of life, full of spirit, able to love again after being so grievously hurt. More like you, those who would put others before themselves, are needed to heal this wounded world."

Speechless, Emily turned to Colin, embracing him, a tear of joy running down her face as he held her tight, gently kissing her eyes, her cheeks, her lips as if afraid she would disappear.

Colin spoke, "I should not be here before you, I am damned."

The goddess turned her gaze to Colin and Emily held her breath. Nodding as if satisfied by what she saw, "Brave warrior—it is true, you did die. Emily begged for my assistance, offered her life, her soul, her very breath so you might live. In committing a selfless act for true love, you each paid the price, therefore the balance is kept, the debt is settled."

A tinkling laugh, made Colin look up. "Don't think so hard

warrior. Trust in yourself. In Emily. You each have a choice to make."

Emily and Colin looked to the goddess. "You both are now human. You can be together, with no memory of any of this. Your memories replaced with a different life. You will be happy, have many children, grow old and die together, when the time comes. There is another path, another choice I offer—I will give you back your immortality and Emily, I will grant you immortality to be with Colin. Colin would continue fighting for the Shadow Walkers. However, immortality carries its own price. You will not be able to have children, and if one of you is killed, the other will die at the same time as you will share one heart. I grant you until midnight tonight to make your choice. Here in this room, speak your choice before the clock strikes twelve and so it will be. Think hard on your answer for there is no going back."

With that she vanished. The flowers, grass, bees, and tree remained. Colin started to ask Emily what she wanted when she placed her hand over his mouth. "I'm exhausted. Let's enjoy the day, not talk about this until tonight. Right now I want you to ravish me, and then breakfast. I'm starved."

"As you wish, milady." Colin spent the next several hours gladly fulfilling her request.

24

The missing person flyers filled the tube stations all over the UK. It was only part of the story; the fringe elements of society were also quickly becoming less apparent. In every city, the politicians took credit for cleaning up the streets, getting people off government run social assistance; when in reality they had been drained by the Day Walkers or taken to the farms, enslaved.

In Inverness, an old ruined abbey was sold to the highest bidder. All of the historic landmarks were going to be on the market, sold to the highest bidders if the economy didn't turn around soon.

The abbey was perfect. It had outbuildings, plenty of land around it and was remote enough to discourage visitors. These old sites usually had underground buildings and passages as well, ideal for the farming activities.

Dayne was inspecting this newest addition. The site was large enough to farm the humans for energy and have a separate area for an orphanage.

His new right-hand man, well demon actually, was named Solien. Vicious to the core, he hated humanity, his parents had been killed by humans thousands of years ago, he'd never forgotten or forgiven. He was a sadistic, brutal jailer, perfect to oversee the farms.

"How are we doing? I want the farms up and running soon. I'm all for killing every human on the planet but we must think strategically. Work discreetly, take the dregs of society, then the small towns no one will miss, then I'll throw in a few plagues to cover our larger takes. Soon enough, my friend, there won't be a free human left in the world."

Dayne had to be discreet. If Thorne got wind of what they were doing, he'd call every creature he'd allied with over the millennia to fight them. Stealth was better. Keep it quiet, then when his brother found out, it would be too late to do anything. His precious humans would be gone, the Day Walkers stronger than his pathetic Shadow Walkers, and they could eliminate them one by one, at their leisure, until Dayne ruled them all.

The abbey had held witch hunts in its heyday and had a large number of underground holding cells. These had been cleaned out and were currently full of humans. The humans tasted better if you didn't scare them first, the fear tainted the energy, gave it a sour taste. Better to take them from the cell to another building, then take a little, send them back or fully drain them and remove the corpse. The old cemetery was being put to good use, they'd dug a large mass grave and simply threw the discarded human shells in the pit, covering them with lime. Once the hole was full, they'd dig another, dust to dust and all that rot.

A few towns around the abbey were deserted. To officials, rumor of the Black Plague making a comeback was the reason. In reality, most of them had been sent to the farms or drained immediately.

Dayne didn't need any of the humans' energy; he simply wanted the more powerful army and didn't care if he destroyed all of humanity to get it. A few weeks ago, he visited an abandoned industrial site in Glasgow; it was perfect for large-scale urban farming. They had room for thousands. The site came with ten corporate apartments; these were perfect for some of the men to live on the grounds.

The orphanages took more planning. Dayne thought in hundreds of years instead of five or ten; he knew it would take time to defeat Thorne, cost him many armies. The prisons were ripe for the picking. He was pleased the worldwide financial system was in such ruin, prisons were all going private. He had good lawyers, mainly demons in human guise, they were the best at law, buy the prisons anonymously and then Dayne had entire armies at his disposal to convert to Day Walkers. Easy enough to turn the inspectors as well so no one wondered why the prisoners were disappearing, the cells replaced with human cattle. It was the perfect cover. He was acquiring his first prison next month, couldn't wait to see the results. He could have huge farms and armies in production in one fell swoop. He was brilliant, patiently waiting to take Thorne down once and for all.

The orphanages were an experiment, if it worked great, if not, the humans could be drained, either way, win, win in his book. As the children grew, slaves from childhood, created to provide energy sources, he pondered the food issue. He did have to feed the disgusting humans. Maybe he'd acquire a few fast food establishments as Rawlins suggested, the cheaper the food to feed them, the better for his bottom line. Funny, as humans cut corners to feed farm animals as cheaply as possible, now the people were "cows" feeding his armies, fed and housed as cheaply as possible.

"Milord, I've brought over three of the goblins to guard the orphanage and a group of demons to guard the food. I've told them they cannot eat any healthy children. Sick ones, or those dying, may be eaten at any time." Solien smiled.

"Excellent work." Dayne was thoughtful. Keeping a secret this big from Thorne would be tricky but so worthwhile. His dear brother, trying to save the humans, while Dayne was destroying them at a much faster rate than they could ever be saved. Delicious.

"I had a rather interesting call from Rawlins. He visited the farm in Inverness, said a couple of the goblins you placed there have been eating the stock, the healthy ones. Rawlins killed the two responsible, he's back in our realm healing, took quite a few rather nasty wounds. We did discuss this—no eating the healthy stock whenever the fancy strikes, at this point we need them to get up and running. Give them a healthy one once a week, that ought to satisfy and keep them from depleting our reserves."

"I'll take care of it, milord."

25

Colin went to his study and pressing on a rosette next to the fireplace, the wall swung open, the lights coming on. Nice not to have to keep torches lit anymore, electricity was a fantastic invention.

The stairs led down to a vault where most of the castle treasure was stored. Hamish had never found it, couldn't waste it, neither had Abigail found the secret rooms. The treasure was still there waiting when he came back, finally took back Ravensmore. There was gold and silver, all worth a fortune to today's collectors. Many jewels, tucked away in chests...he was looking for something particular. Something the first Baroness of Ravensmore had owned.

Pausing, he let out a breath. He'd never thought to give these jewels to Abigail. She demanded new jewels and he gladly indulged her, thinking these were too old-fashioned. How things change with the right woman. He knew Emily would appreciate them, not only for their beauty but for the history behind them and what they represented.

He came across a set of fine china, must have gotten it from Robert at some point. He made a mental note to bring it up, give it to her as a wedding present. Sitting down he had a moment of panic, what if she didn't want to marry him? He was asking her to give up everything, her brother, her friends, her job, her life in the States. Would he be enough for her? He knew he loved her, would cherish her as long as they both lived.

Which posed an interesting question—he knew Emily wanted children, wanted to give them to her, might she be interested in adoption? If so, he'd fill Ravensmore to give her the large rowdy brood she wanted. Colin knew deep in his soul he wanted to continue fighting, he believed in keeping humanity safe, loved the fight, wasn't sure he could give it up.

Taking a page from Emily's book, he decided to quit moping, enjoy the day with her and discuss it over dinner. Coming across the chest he'd been looking for, his heart sped up; the wooden box had turned nearly black from age. Opening it, the brilliance of the jewels caught the light throwing prisms of color across the room. There was a stunning choker, set with fire opals and diamonds in a vine pattern which would look beautiful against her skin. A matching bracelet, earrings and ring finished the set. These would be the perfect wedding present to go with the china. There was one last box, it was small, it should be here... there, sitting on a solid gold plate, waiting for him.

Opening the box, he smiled. She'd think it was too big—the first baroness had worn this ring every day of her life, passing it down to each subsequent generation. It was a stunning emerald cut diamond, easily twenty carats, with smaller diamonds flanking each side. He'd have a wedding band made with emerald cut diamonds to match.

Taking the stairs two at a time, he placed a call to a jeweler he knew in Edinburgh. The jeweler had old notes regarding the ring, the firm had originally fashioned it, so it should be simple enough to tell him what he needed.

Emily and Colin spent the rest of the day together. After eating lunch in the orangerie they headed upstairs to be alone, curled up by the fire in their room. On the soft grass blanketing the floor, Emily fell asleep, he watched the firelight play over her features, memorized every detail, couldn't believe after all these years he'd found her.

Waking up, Emily leaned up and kissed him, "It's nice to wake up next to you. You generate a lot of heat."

He waggled his eyebrows at her leering, "I'll show you some heat." Growling, he lifted her on top of him, stroking her thighs, making love to her.

Afterwards, Colin had tea served while Emily relaxed. He was so nervous he paced the room. Couldn't remember feeling this ill ever in his life, not even before his first battle. He'd gladly face a thousand Day Walkers rather than face her rejection—what if she wouldn't have him? She'd said she loved him but forever was a long time. Maybe she'd want to enjoy her immortality, not be tied down.

"Colin, what's wrong? You're scaring me." Stopping in front of her, dropping to one knee, he laid his heart bare at her feet. Emily's eyes were wide as she watched him.

"I was lost in shadow, devoid of hope until you appeared and blazed a shining path through the darkness. I want you to stay in Scotland with me. I love you, for all eternity. Will you do me the honor of becoming my wife?"

He looked at her with love in his eyes, waiting for her answer. Emily lunged forward almost knocking him backwards. "Yes, Colin, yes, I'll marry you! Yes, I'll stay in Scotland. I love you, with you I'm whole."

Holding out the box to her, he watched her open it, gasping, her hand flying to her mouth. Thank the gods she was pleased. Colin slid it on her finger; it fit perfectly as if it had been waiting all these years for her and her alone.

"It belonged to the first Baroness Campbell. Do you like it? It isn't new, if you'd rather something..."

"Are you kidding? It's beautiful. The sparkles remind me of the stars and the story you told me on the ship. I love it. We have to make a trip to Charleston, I'm showing you off and walking around with my hand waving around in the air so everyone can see it. I think this is the biggest diamond I've ever seen."

There was a knock at the door. Worthington stood there, his eyes briefly widening as he took in the tree and meadow that had sprung up in the middle of the room, "Will you be attending dinner, milord, milady?" he sniffed.

"Aye, we'll be there, thank you Worthington." Colin suppressed a guffaw. How it must look with a meadow in their room. Worthington probably wondered how he would have it cleaned and did someone have to mow the bloody grass?

26

Thorne, god of shadow, approached the graveyard in the realm of shadows. There were many, every ancient god and goddess had a temple here, lost to the world, forgotten. There were no priests or priestesses, no flowers, no visitors except him. He didn't know if his brother came or if their mother ever showed up, today he didn't care, he came seeking solace.

Luna's temple was made of silver and white marble. Hauntingly beautiful, eerie in this barren landscape, where no living creature dwelled. Entering, his footsteps were loud to his ears in the stillness. He knew Luna wasn't here; she had been turned into the moon after her death...after he killed her. This empty temple stood to mock him over what he had done in a fit of jealous rage so many eons ago.

Thorne remembered. He had heard a human cry out as the human died. The human consumed by guilt and self-hatred. As self-inflicted penance for killing Luna, Thorne vowed to protect humanity from his brother's scheming; he answered the angry lost human...and created the first Shadow Walker.

Shoulders slumped, Thorne was weary of the constant

battles, weary of controlling his temper and from holding back his rage and destroying the world. He wanted solace, peace.

Sitting on a white couch in front of a life size painting of Luna, he willed himself to relax. In front of him, the painting was offset by the stars, the temple opened to the heavens, stars sparkling down at all times, weeping for her.

Thorne had asked for forgiveness many times, never receiving an answer. He knew she could hear him, even in her moon form, yet she refused to answer. The painting mocked him, she was still the most beautiful woman he'd ever laid eyes on. He fell in love with her with a simple glance across the room. Luna was already in love with Solus. He didn't care, ancients were fickle, he thought she'd tire of him and they would be together, instead they fell deeper and deeper in love.

Wincing at the memories, replaying the night he murdered her, Thorne slammed shut the door in his head, putting his head in his hands.

"Why won't you forgive me? You know I regret what happened, how sorry I am, that I still love you."

No answer. Well, at least she was consistent. Thorne wasn't sure if he showed up here because he thought one day she'd answer and forgive him, or because he knew Luna would never deign to answer him.

27

Walking in to the dining room for dinner, Emily kept looking at the massive ring on her hand. Colin wanted to shout for joy seeing her happy.

"I can't stop looking at my ring. Wait until I tell Kat; she's going to flip. Fred will probably calculate how many Third World countries we could buy with this rock."

"Thought ye might be pleased, though the skipping part might have given it away, lass."

Pulling out her chair, he lightly smacked her arse earning a startled yelp in reply. Chuckling he sat down across from her, wanting to drink in the sight of his woman.

"Everything smells wonderful. I like your hair pulled back in a ponytail, it shows off your eyes. And please tell me you'll wear a kilt every day for the rest of our lives."

"Ye dinna care for the daggers?"

"Seriously Colin, only guys drool over the weaponry." Leaning across the table, giving him a nice view of her breasts down the front of her dress, he didn't care what she was talking about. She mock whispered, "Though I think the black silk shirt makes me want to run my hands over the silk, down to your kilt and kiss the scar on your thigh to make sure it's all better."

His cock jerked in response, ready for her. He was completely healed. The scar on his thigh Rawlins inflicted, the only thing remaining as a reminder of the sacrifice.

He grabbed her elbows, pulling her across the table, dishware clattering as he kissed her soundly.

"Milord! You're ruining my pretty table. Let the poor lass eat before you devour her." Meg scolded, bringing in the wine.

"Oh! That was some kiss."

Pleased she was breathless, he grinned while she pulled herself together. Embarrassment flushing her cheeks a fetching shade of pink. Colin poured her a large glass of red wine. Emily —his fiancée—he'd never been happier and terrified at the same time. Thinking of her safety, how Day Walkers would try to kill both of them. If he chose a mortal life, he could still see them, but they'd have the advantage with their powers. Yet, he wanted to give Emily a child, to create a life with her, as much as he wanted to keep fighting, he couldn't take that dream from her.

"You look beautiful tonight." His eyes caressed her, taking in the soft heather gray sweater dress and black boots. He wanted to slide his hand up her booted calf, up her thigh, to see if she was wearing lace or silk panties, to touch her, make her shake with need.

My god, get a hold of yourself man, you're ready to take her on the table in front of the staff, nice way to have your first meal with your fiancée. Shifting to a more comfortable position, he hoped he didn't have to stand up; his tented kilt would give evidence to his feelings.

Meg and Worthington, along with the rest of the staff, congratulated them as the meal was served. Once the staff departed, Colin shared his news. "I called in a few favors, we can have the wedding next week if you'd like? Kat and Fred, and your brother can all attend." Seeing her annoyed look, he wanted to laugh out loud but refrained. "Don't worry, I didn't tell them I've ravished you; I told them you were OK but had been in an accident and would be staying here for a while to recover. They all said they wanted to come, so it was really rather easy. When they get here you can tell them I'm keeping you here." He finished, looking quite pleased.

"You forgot making an honest woman of me. Next week can't come soon enough, and I did want all of them here. Thank you. Though I'm not sure if I can find a dress so quickly, I want a white dress and I'd like to be married here at Ravensmore."

"Lass, I'll buy the store if needed, you'll have the dress you want. It makes me verra happy you want to be married here. Are you sure you want to live here? It's a drive to the city, will you feel isolated here after the hustle and bustle of Charleston?" He wanted her to love Ravensmore as much as he did, but if she didn't, they'd live in Edinburgh if she wanted, he'd do anything for her.

"I fell in love with Scotland the moment I set foot off the plane, the stark beauty of the highlands, the colors of the sky against the land, it's breathtaking. When you brought me to Ravensmore, I finally felt like I belonged. Something about this place, it makes me feel like all is right with the world."

"Even after everything that's happened? It would be understandable if you didn't want to live here."

"We can't change what happened, and I won't let that spoil Ravensmore for me. Home for me, is wherever you are. I will be content staying mortal with you, growing old together, though I would hate not remembering everything but either way, as long as I'm with you, that's all I need. I know you want to keep fighting for what you believe in and I'll try not to, but I will worry when you fight. If I lost you again, well, it would be best I died at the same time, I don't want to live without you, and I can accept us being immortal—I'll have forever to love you." She watched his face, waiting for his response.

Sucking in his breath, Emily continued to amaze him. He was prepared to be mortal, give her lots of children, would she regret the choice?

"What about the houseful of children you want? If we choose

immortality, I don't want you to regret your choice a hundred years from now." He looked at her, searching her face for a clue to her feelings.

With a tremor in her voice she asked, "Would you be open to adopting a few kids of our own? You'd be the most amazing father."

Jumping up from his seat, Colin practically ran around the table. Laughing, he picked her up, swinging her in a circle, kissing her face. "Lass, we'll adopt a houseful, there's an agency in Inverness we can visit. This place needs to be filled with laughter and love."

Putting her back down as the dessert was brought in, he sat beside her. "Oh yum, orange sorbet, my very favorite."

"You can have it for every meal if it will keep you smiling like that, makes me want to drizzle it all over your body and lick it off," he leered at her.

"Colin Campbell—you will not waste sorbet. Now I'm fine with ice cream or honey but I'm eating every drop of this sorbet...speaking of which...if you're not eating yours, pass it over."

Roaring with laughter, he gave her his dessert, watching her eat, imagining the spoon she was licking was his shaft.

As she finished the last drop, he nearly dragged her from the room, swinging her up in his arms as he dematerialized them to their bedroom. "Let's tell the goddess so I can properly ravish you, I'm not sure I can wait much longer."

Pointedly looking at his erection tenting his kilt, she arched an eyebrow, "I think we better sit down to talk to Terya, not sure how she'd feel about you sitting there with a big ol' hard-on."

Sitting in front of the ancient oak tree in the bedroom, noticing the gold and silver dust floating in the air, sparkling on their skin, Colin asked Emily to call Terya since the goddess seemed to have a special affinity for her.

The air shimmered, the sound of a babbling brook filled the

room as Terya appeared. Barefoot as always, her hair floating in the breeze, she looked serene, all-knowing.

"Have you come to a decision?" she asked sitting on a branch of the oak tree. Colin cleared his throat. "We have. While we want children we both feel this war is important. Dayne must be defeated. I need to fight and Emily wants to help, whether gathering intelligence, working to find missing persons, or saving children. We don't want to forget everything we've been through."

Emily added, "We don't want to live without each other, we accept the price of sharing the same heart and dying together. We are filled with gratitude for what you have offered."

"Then so shall it be. You will both be immortal, sharing the same heart. Colin, you have all your Shadow Walker powers back. Emily, you retain the power to see Walkers, to talk with the dead and I grant you the power to use lightening as a weapon against the Day Walkers to protect yourself. It will serve you in your quest." Turning to go, the goddess stopped, "Child, is there something else you would tell me?"

Shyly showing the goddess her ring, the happiness evident in her voice, "We are to be married next week." Looking up at the tree, Terya smiled. "As a wedding gift, I bless you both with twins, a boy and a girl." Stunned, Emily and Colin thanked the goddess. With that, Terya vanished. Colin kneeled in front of Emily, placing his hand on her stomach. "I wonder if you are already with child, but to be safe, we should make sure."

Pulling him close, she kissed him. "I thought you'd never ask." He swept her up, laughing, tossing her on the bed as he landed next to her.

EMILY SAT UP, PULLING HIM TO HIS FEET, SHE KNELT, GENTLY removing his boots, placing his daggers, all four of them, on the table next to the bed. Next was the double shoulder holster with his guns and spare magazines, then his shirt, the silk sliding like water through her fingers as she lightly ran her fingernails down his chest, watching his nipples harden under her touch, his skin pebbling from the sensation. Undoing his kilt, her hands shook, wanting to give him everything, wanting to be his shelter, the kilt fell to the floor, his heavy erection sprang free, bobbing near her hand, wanting, seeking. She ignored it for the moment, placing soft, feathery kisses from his ankle up to his hip, across his stomach and down the other leg.

She could hear his sharp intake of breath, hear his heart beating faster as he held still, rigid with need...wanting her. So this is what sex is supposed to be like between two people, she mused, feeling as if he was the first, the only man she'd ever been with, the others falling away like fall leaves, brittle, crackling, carried away on the wind.

Watching the firelight dancing across his body, he was a magnificent predator, like a big cat, lethal, beautiful, ready to spring and devour her. Reaching on tiptoes, she pulled the tie from his hair, letting it fall, the braids swinging at his temples, the chestnut and burnished gold strands reflected in the light. He didn't have any hair on his chest, his muscles flexed under her palm as she ran her hands down his rock hard stomach. Standing there with his legs wide apart, strong thick thighs, broad shoulders and heavily muscled biceps, she felt her eyes fill that he trusted her to do as she wished with his body. This night, she would show him how much she loved him, not with words but with her body.

He watched her, his velvet green eyes, hooded, waiting for her next move, letting her explore. Placing her palms on his chest, she pushed him back to sit on the bed, backing up, slightly out of his reach. He raised an eyebrow, the corner of his lip curving into a smile as she slowly pulled the sweater dress over her head. She'd never stripped for a man before, finding it too intimate, too revealing. Crazy, she knew, considering she slept with them but something about the act, made it off limits for her, until Colin. She wanted him to know every part of her. He'd given his life for her, she knew she could trust him.

Clad only in her bra, she saw his eyes widen. "You didn't have any panties on, I should have dropped my napkin at the table, climbed down to get it and taken you in my mouth, made you come as you ate your bloody orange sorbet."

Giggling, she waggled her finger back and forth, "Now, now, no touching yet."

"Hmmprh, have your way with me but remember this game works both ways, lass."

In answer, Emily reached up and removed her bra. Turning around, she bent over giving him a view of her backside, pleased when she heard him hiss. Slowly, she unzipped and stepped out of each boot, tossing them aside.

Colin's words came out in a cough. "You enchant me. Standing before me, the fire looks like it's licking your body, illuminating and at the same time hiding every part of you as the shadows dance across your skin. Gods Emily, ye hold my heart in your hands, able to crush it with a single squeeze if ye so chose." He took a deep breath, exhaling hard.

Tears in her eyes, she held them back. Her savage warrior had been profoundly changed. She'd died for him, would love him throughout eternity. Her voice choking, "Your heart is safe in my keeping, I'll never hurt or betray you."

"Dinna cry lass." Reaching out to touch her, Colin stopped.

Seeing Colin reach out for her, her breasts grew heavy, she was ready, anticipating him, wanting him so very much. Emboldened, she moved to stand between his legs. Swallowing in anticipation, she knelt, pressing her breasts to his chest, sliding down his torso, reaching his cock, enveloping it between her breasts. Licking her lips, she took him in her mouth, kissing him, stroking him, tasting him as she lightly scraped her teeth along the underside, feeling him jerk against her, hearing a rumble of satisfaction from deep within his chest, his breathing rough as she took him in, licking and suckling.

Reveling in the feeling of power, Emily took Colin over the edge as he fisted his hands in her hair, calling out her name as he came. Kissing his sac, running her tongue in that lovely crease between his sac and thigh, he growled, reaching down to pull her up.

She stayed him with her hand. Sliding up his body, rubbing against him, stretching like a cat, enjoying the sensation of skin on skin. She straddled his hips, leaning up to kiss him. Her breasts, brushing against his chest, her nipples hardening as he reached to roll them between his fingers, stroking her as she rubbed herself along the length of his shaft.

"You're ready again?"

"Aye lass, 'tis a wonderful benefit of being a Shadow Walker, wouldn't ye say?" With a moan, he reached down, sheathing himself inside her in one quick, hard thrust. Sighing in contentment, she rode him, arching her back, letting her hair brush his calves. Leaning up to let him slide out, she twisted back down hard as he filled her to the core. Swiveling her hips, she ground against him, gasping with pleasure as he reached down, stroking her while she rode him. Rocking her hips, she could feel the waves cresting, rising, almost to her peak. Leaning back to allow him greater access, she placed her hands on his ankles, her body arched as he took her breast in his hand, kneading, stroking the nipple as his other relentlessly played her. He was so deep within her at this angle she could feel their shared heartbeat through her body, starting in her center, radiating outward as the waves crashed over her.

Spent, she rested her body on top of his, kissing him as he let out a satisfied groan. "Rest now love, I plan to have my turn next." Lying in his arms, she couldn't stop touching him; lazily tracing circles on his chest. Flipping her over, he lay between her legs, spreading them wide, dominating her.

He kissed his way down her neck, nibbling her ear, scraping his teeth against her nipple, the underside of each breast, making her skin pucker. Licking his way down her stomach, she quivered, his stubble, exquisitely rubbing against her skin. Dipping his head down, he licked her, sliding a finger in, drawing words inside her with his tongue, telling her how much he loved her as he took her in his mouth. The pressure built as he flicked his tongue against her bud, she shattered again in pleasure, her thighs tight against his head.

Pushing her knees up, he slid inside, burying himself to the hilt as she wrapped her legs around him, her hips bucking up to meet every thrust as they fell over the cliff together, the sacred bees adding the music of their buzzing wings, the leaves of Terya's oak covering them like a blanket, shutting out the world.

All that mattered was they'd found each other, would spend the rest of their days loving each other, forever.

Upon waking, the tree, meadow, grass and flowers had disappeared, leaving only two gold acorns remaining. The room was as it was before.

28

Saturday, November 7th - Edinburgh

Inside the dress shop, Emily thought of Kat; this store's selection was on par with Charleston's. Kat would be thrilled Emily had found someone. With a pang of sadness Kat wasn't here to help her pick a dress, she shook her head, reminding herself that Kat would be there for the main event.

She tried on a number of dresses, wanting something simple, classic, no big white cupcake dresses for her. Luckily the shop had everything from shoes and hairpins to dresses. She found a beautiful white sheath dress with simple lines–heck, with her giant ring, she didn't need any other type of adornment. The proprietress was an older lady in her sixties, with snow white hair and a twinkling smile. The owner fussed over Emily, bringing her shoes and gorgeous rhinestone sticks to put her hair up, placing a short veil on top. She told Emily to close her eyes, felt something being put on her dress, felt jewelry being placed on her.

"Oh lass, you are a vision—wait, don't look yet, let me straighten one thing...there, open your eyes."

Speechless, she was speechless, a sash of plaid matching

Colin's was around her waist—but oh my stars, the bling. Tentatively reaching up to touch the gorgeous stones, she was blinded by the fire opals surrounded by diamonds, throwing rainbows all across the shop as the sunlight poured in, illuminating the stones from within. "I don't understand, these are amazing, they look antique and worth an absolute fortune..." her voice trailed off.

"Yes on both counts. A wedding gift from Baron Campbell, worn by the first baroness, like your ring. He wanted to give them to you himself but wanted to make sure they went with the dress you chose and of course he couldn't be here to see the dress, lass."

"Seriously, these rocks would make a trash bag look like haute couture. The man is amazing." She couldn't stop touching the sparkling stones. A necklace, drop earrings, bracelet and ring, wow—on so many levels.

The owner told her they'd have the dress altered and would deliver it along with the accessories in time for the wedding. She handed Emily the jewelry cases as Colin came in.

Emily jumped into his arms, "I didn't want to take them off, I want to shower in them, sleep in them, they are magnificent!"

Arching a brow, he leaned in to whisper in her ear, "I'm imagining you naked in nothing but the jewels, if we don't leave now, I may take you on the bloody floor."

Blushing, she kissed him as he put her down. They thanked the owner and went to grab lunch before going back to Ravensmore. Colin started to tell her all the arrangements he'd made, to tell her he'd enlisted Kat, that he'd like to have her work with some of the men they were training, she'd whip them into shape in no time, it was daunting to say the least.

Emily laughed, "Has she completely taken over yet?"

"Are you kidding, that woman could run the country if she wanted to, I'm in awe and a bit scared of her." Colin grinned.

"She's worked with Meg and they've taken care of the flowers, cake, food, and drink. All I have to do is finish the license. She even took care of getting movers lined up. They are packing up your cottage and everything will be here in a few weeks. There's a professor who wanted to buy the place, but she told him she'd rent it, that you wouldn't want to let it go." He was watching her closely.

"I don't need anything except you, my life in Charleston seems long ago and far away. I'll let Kat know to go ahead and sell it, heck, she'll get more for it than I would have. I don't need it. Ravensmore is my home now. You are my home."

Walking down the street, Emily headed for the car. "Come on, I want to drive back to Ravensmore, I'll try and drive on the left, not my fault we drive on the normal side of the road and you all have to be different." Reaching in his pocket, she gave him a caress and laughed when he flashed his eyes at her.

"Better put your money where your mouth is. Better yet, I want your mouth on me." Colin growled.

"Emily? Is that you? What are you doing in Edinburgh? Who are you with? Yowza, you look great."

Oh my god, it was Charlie. What was he doing in Edinburgh? Oh this is too perfect, thank you Universe. I'm with my hot fiancé, looking my best and there is jerk face Charlie. Every girl in the world wishes this scenario when running into an ex-boyfriend. Only usually the girl is in sweats, with no makeup, bad hair and a big zit on her nose or forehead while said ex is with some supermodel girlfriend, happy and glowing.

"Charlie, what a surprise. This is Colin."

"You're the bloody stupid bastard who killed Emily?" Colin glared at Charlie and moved within an inch of him. "I should kick your arse right now, better yet, tell me why I shouldn't gut you from belly to nose and rid the world of some pansy-assed boy who can't take care of a woman." Colin sneered.

Realizing he was in serious trouble, Emily tried not to burst out laughing as Charlie backpedaled.

"Hey it's all good man, saying hi for old times sake. Whatever happened to let bygones be bygones, forgive and forget? Emily, help me out here," Charlie pleaded.

It was so fantastic seeing Charlie humiliated that Emily started giggling. Clapping her hand over her mouth didn't help. She started laughing so hard, tears streamed down her face and she started hiccupping.

"Colin, let's go, he's not worth your time. Anyway, he peed his pants, and you're going to be stepping in pee in a minute."

"Oh hell, you are a loser. Get out of my sight before I change my mind." Colin sounded disgusted.

At that moment, Emily thought she'd died and gone to heaven as she heard, "Honey, where are you? Charlie, I've been looking for you." A woman, who looked like she stepped out of a preppy catalog, with bobbed brunette hair, beige shoes, and beige handbag, looked down her nose at Emily and said, "Who might you be? I'm Muffy."

"Muffy, yikes, what a name, I'm Emily."

Watching the recognition cross Muffy's face, Emily laughed, "Yes, THAT Emily. You better get your boyfriend home, seems he's had an accident and pissed himself."

Muffy's eyes opened so wide she looked like an anime cartoon. Grabbing Charlie's arm, she pulled him down the street and Emily laughed as she heard Muffy screech, "Don't walk near me, how embarrassing. Walk behind me. Disgusting."

Charlie ran behind Muffy yelling, "Give me your sweater so I can cover my pants. I must be getting sick or something."

EPILOGUE

One Week Later

The orangerie was beautiful, the white flowers adding to the heady orange blossom fragrance. Kat and Fred arrived two days before. Fred took to Colin's steward immediately. They were currently closeted in the study going over ancient account books. He was fascinated with how Colin's ancestors kept track of everything on an estate the size of Ravensmore.

Fred had been easily won over with a few bottles of Ravensmore whisky he found waiting in the room for him. Kat had said he looked younger in person than that dreadful painting in the museum.

"Emily, he's perfect for you. A little scary at times, talk about an alpha male—whew! Are you terribly happy?"

Sighing, Emily smiled and hugged her best friend, "He's my one true love, corny as it sounds. I thought I loved Charlie, I was wrong...Colin showed me what love really is."

"You've been through so much, I'm glad you've moved on and found someone to share your life with. Please tell me the Charlie story again, talk about karmic justice." Wiping her eyes, she'd laughed so hard, she cried when Emily related the story of running into Charlie and Muffy.

"I would have given anything to have been there and see him pee his pants." She howled with laughter, making Emily laugh harder. Colin found the two of them in tears, cackling. Shrugging at Matt, they went outside so Colin could point out the path down to the water and a few choice fishing spots.

"Look, I know my sister is crazy about you, but if you hurt her I'll have to kick your ass." Matt looked a little sick as he said this.

"I would expect nothing less. Point taken. Now shall I show you where the fishing gear is? I hear you're quite the fisherman."

She had a moment's sadness wondering how they would explain not aging as the years passed; she'd have to ask Colin how they would handle it. She couldn't bear never seeing any of them again.

The day before the wedding, Robert arrived with Monroe in tow. Monroe looked tired and drawn after his brush with death; he'd gotten out of the hospital the day before and insisted on attending. Emily had sent flowers when she found out what had happened. "Great to see you, mate. You remember Monroe?"

Robert slapped Colin on the back and swept Emily up into a hug, kissing her on the cheek. He hastily put her down when Colin growled at him.

"Monroe, up and about I see. No criminals lurking about, why are you here?"

"I sure as hell didn't come to see your ugly mug. I'm here to wish Emily well, to see Miss Chandler again, and meet her husband."

"Monroe, I'm so glad you could make it, Are you feeling OK?" Emily fussed over him. "I know Kat will be so pleased to see you. I think she and Fred are exploring the dungeon."

"I hear congratulations are in order. Walk me to my room? This place is huge."

"Absolutely. I've seen that look on Colin's face before; let's go." Emily and Monroe turned and headed for the stairs.

❦

GRUNTING, COLIN TURNED AWAY, JERKING HIS HEAD AT Robert to follow him around the corner.

"The cop's going to be a problem. We don't need him sticking his nose where it doesn't belong. Thorne is going to rip your head off when he finds out what you did."

"The guy deserved some closure, his woman's death was eating him up from the inside. Anyway, we could use a mortal's help here and there. I'll talk to Thorne...eventually."

Colin shrugged, "It's your head." A small change in the air pressure was the only warning Colin and Robert had before Thorne materialized into the hallway. "Talk to me about what? About how you broke the simple rules I've drilled into your head. Maybe about how you involved a human in Shadow Walker matters, or maybe how you cocked it up when you told him all about our merry little band, hmmm."

Robert paled. Fuck me, he was here. This was so not good. At least Thorne had his human guise in place though at six foot seven, giving off the whole I'll kill you with a look vibe, he was the kind of guy people instinctively backed away from. Today he was wearing a black tux by Armani, his silver hair pulled back in a ponytail, his icy blue eyes, sparking with anger, looking like he'd walked off the pages of some men's fashion magazine.

"Guess that about sums it up," he shot back, cocky.

Landing against the far wall of the great hall, he decided it wasn't the best way to start the morning by getting blasted by a bolt of energy. At least it wasn't full force—if it were he'd be dust by now.

"While you made a few relevant points to Colin, how do you know we can trust this human?" Thorne raked a glare over

Robert. "I'm trying to decide whether I should send you back to the Shadow Walker realm and have you beaten for a few hundred years for your insolence or...guess what, he's your responsibility. The cop fucks up anything, talks about us to anyone, your life is forfeit. Are we clear?" Thorne was right up in his grill. Robert wanted to back away but showing weakness would only earn you a bitch slap or something worse. He stood his ground.

"Crystal."

"I'll be back for the wedding." With that the god vanished.

LATER THAT EVENING MONROE PULLED EMILY ASIDE. "LOOK, are you sure you know what you're doing? What do you know about this guy? You only met him, now you're all I do, down the aisle?"

Patting his shoulder, she told him, "No need to worry. Yes, it's fast but I'm more sure about Colin than I've ever been about anything in my life. Sometimes you go through an...event in life, it changes you. Afterwards what's important seems to be clear, the rest is noise, it falls away. Please don't worry, I'm happy."

He blew out a deep breath, "Ah, then, I'll be checking in from time to time to see if you need anything."

She bid him goodnight and crawled into bed in one of the many guestrooms. She'd refused to kick Colin out of their bedroom. It was strange sleeping alone after being with Colin every night. Emily had insisted in keeping the tradition of him not seeing her the night before or day of the wedding.

Fresh from her shower with a cold Pepsi, wrapped in a cozy robe, she thought about the night before. A feast, lots of toasts, surrounded by those she loved, all there to see her married. Colin's friends would be in attendance, he told her his boss was putting in an appearance. She only wished her parents were alive to see her married, her dad here to walk her down the aisle, her mom to help plan things. Wiping a tear away, a knock on the door made her jump, pulling her from her memories.

"It's about time you're up; we have so much to do today to get you ready. Come with me, I've taken over a room called the lady's solar. I have a hairdresser, manicurist, masseuse, waxer, and Meg all waiting to get you bride ready." Kat blew the hair out of her eyes. Standing there, Emily was overcome with emotion, jumping up and hugging her tight.

"Thank you again for coming on such short notice. I need you here, you're more than my best friend to me, you're my sister, I love you, Kat."

Wiping her eyes, Kat playfully smacked her on the arm, "Don't put my waterproof mascara to the test, it's going to get enough of a workout when you walk down the aisle. Come on sleepyhead, I brought Pop-Tarts..."

"You are an angel. You know Pop-Tarts and Pepsi are my favorite breakfast."

Screwing up her face in distaste, Kat grimaced. "See how you know I love you, I bring you horribly processed food to eat. On the bright side, if there's a siege, you can survive on Pop-Tarts. I think they're like Twinkies, they never go bad."

Half dragging her to the solar, Emily came to a full stop in the doorway to the room, her mouth open. It looked like...a spa exploded in the room. Emily took a deep breath and put herself in their hands.

A rap on the door, had everyone's head turning as Robert walked in. "Well, this is my kind of place, a room full of beautiful ladies, I think I've died and ended up in the hall of beautiful women." He flashed his pearly white teeth at them and a few of the women giggled, making eyes at him. Emily was willing to bet he wouldn't be spending the night alone.

He stopped next to Emily with a horrified look on his face, "What on earth are you eating?" Kat busted out laughing. Emily was indignant. "Do not make fun of the Pop-Tarts. These are one of the best inventions in the last hundred years." With that, she stuck her nose in the air. His hands up in front of him, Robert roared, "I'll take your word for it." Kneeling down to sit beside her, he looked a little nervous, pulling a box out of his pocket.

"I wanted you to have this; it belonged to my sister a long time ago. I know you need 'something borrowed' but consider it a wedding gift; she'd have liked you wearing it."

Opening the box with a gasp, everyone crowded around Emily for a closer look at the stunning bracelet. It was fashioned into flowers and vines. The vines were tiny emeralds, the flowers alternated between sapphires, rubies, and diamonds.

"Oh, Robert, it's stunning. I would be honored to wear it but I must give it back. You'll want to give it to the woman you marry someday."

A shadow crossed his face, leaning down so only she could hear, "No, lass. 'Tis unheard of for one of us to break our curse, I don't expect to see it happen again. I gave up on love a long, long, time ago."

Straightening up, he turned on his heel, "I'll leave you ladies to your rituals."

"Robert, wait." Emily rushed over to him, shyly handing him a box. "Would you please give this to Colin? It's his wedding band; I understand he is supposed to be wearing it when the ceremony starts after sunset tonight."

The band was a plain, wide gold band with the old Celtic symbols for love, life, eternity and energy engraved on the outside, very masculine just like her warrior. Inside the band, she'd had engraved, *My heart belongs to you.*

Her wedding band had been waiting for her when she woke up. Meg must have put it on the nightstand while she slept. The emerald-cut diamonds went all the way around and matched her engagement ring. If anyone tried to hurt her, she could blind them with all the diamonds on the rings. Inside was inscribed; *Your love gives me life.*

The day passed in a blur. She'd been waxed, had her nails and toes done in a plaid pattern to match her sash, eyebrows plucked, and ended with a massage after lunch.

"Why don't you have a nap, then we'll do your hair and help you get dressed later." Meg shooed her upstairs.

MONROE BARGED INTO THE STUDY WHERE COLIN AND ROBERT were enjoying a whisky. "Whoa cop, where's the fire?" Colin snarled.

"Whatever with the attitude, I got a call from my partner; he was called to a domestic dispute at a house next door to the orphanage in Edinburgh. Here's the interesting bit, a girl who works at the place said there are a lot of kids there one week then the next week, when she asks why there are so many missing, she's told they've been adopted. Said a big, blond guy comes once every few weeks to check on the place. He looks like some toff out of a fashion magazine, has an English accent. The other thing she told him was every few weeks it smells like burnt electrical wiring. She told her superiors but they told her not to worry. The girl wanted him to know in case the old place was going to burn down."

A look passed between Colin and Robert. Monroe continued with the tale. "Shamus only told me about it as the girl was attractive, he wanted to ask her out. He called to find out how long I'd be on medical leave, tell me what I was missing. Look, I think that strange smell is related to all the missing persons. I've smelled it before at crime scenes where grandmothers are killed, only they turn out not to be grandmothers. It's connected. I'm going to check it out."

"No cop, let us take this one. We've been hearing rumors related to the missing people, don't want to tip anyone off, we can be a bit more discreet than you, get my drift?"

Before Monroe could protest, Colin held up a hand, "We'll

share what we find out." Colin had heard orphanages across Scotland were being bought by the same corporation. He was trying to find out if it was tied to the Day Walkers. If they were killing kids, he'd tear every one of them apart. Maybe the cop could be useful after all.

Worthington interrupted them, "Milord, 'tis time." Robert clapped him on the back and even the prickly cop wished him well as the butler led them to the orangerie.

❦

KAT AND EMILY WERE THE ONLY ONES LEFT IN THE SOLAR. Zipping up the dress, Kat started to tear up, "You look so amazing, Colin is going to fall out when he sees you walking down the aisle." The dress was white silk with a slight gray blue undertone which looked gorgeous with the colors in the plaid and set off Emily's gray eyes.

Her hair was up in a messy chignon with rhinestone sticks holding it together. She'd done her own make up with a light hand, letting the dress and stunning jewelry take center stage.

Slipping her skyscraper heels on, they left the solar, Matt was waiting outside.

"Sis, you look beautiful. Mom and dad would be so proud."

She hugged him, smiling through unshed tears of happiness. Kat led the way to the orangerie while Matt took her arm, keeping her steady. There were candles everywhere, the flames making shadows dance on the glass, the night stars shining down, the moon bathing Colin in silvery light as he stood there, his gaze locked on her. Standing there in his kilt, his hair down, he was her mysterious man in the painting come to life. She mouthed "I love you," took a deep breath and walked towards him hoping she wouldn't trip in her heels.

Fred was on her left smiling and nodding as she passed by. Kat kissed her on the cheek and took her seat next to Fred, wiping her eyes as he passed her a handkerchief. On the right, she saw Meg and Worthington. Robert and Monroe stood against the wall, nodding in admiration as she passed by.

Matt released her hand and moved to sit next to Fred and Kat, kissing her cheek as he nodded to Colin. Standing next to Colin, Emily felt his breath on her ear as he leaned in to her, "I've waited an eternity for you."

She reached up, stroking his cheek, her face filled with the love she felt for him. Looking around she didn't see anyone waiting to marry them, until her eye caught on a very tall man she'd mistaken for a tree, waiting in the shadows.

The man moved to stand in front of them. He was huge, gorgeous, with silver hair. Colin bowed, "Thorne, may I present Emily Laurens. Emily love, this is Thorne." His icy blue eyes bored into her, searching as he seemed to come to some silent acceptance.

Colin presented his palm as Thorne took a silver dagger from his Armani tux. Holding it up he said, "You pledge your blood and soul to Emily Laurens for all eternity?"

"I so pledge."

"To protect her from harm?"

"I so pledge."

"To sacrifice yourself for her?"

"I so pledge."

With that, he sliced a deep cut across Colin's palm, the blood, flowing, dripping to the floor.

"Milady, your hand." Thorne smiled kindly at her.

Oh boy, blood was not her friend; Emily prayed she wouldn't faint. Taking a deep breath, she held out her hand, palm up.

"Will you love Baron Colin Campbell with your body and soul for all eternity?"

"I will."

She felt a sharp prick then something like an electrical current running through her palm as Thorne placed her palm over Colin's, pressing them together. A blue tattoo appeared, encircling Colin's wrist. The design was intricate, made up of symbols, pulsing in shades of blue and green. Thorne spoke in a low voice, nodding, "You can now throw bolts of energy without draining your power, my blessing to you warrior."

"By the energy of the blood the bond is consecrated."

Cheering broke out. She was vaguely aware of another tingling as Robert wrapped their hands. He saw her look of confusion. "Yes, the wound is already healed but can't have the guests seeing that now, can we lass?" He clapped Colin on the back and hugged Emily, congratulating them. The staff served champagne while everyone mingled, waiting for dinner.

Emily was on her way back from powdering her nose when Thorne appeared in front of her. Startled, she jumped, "Sorry, you scared me."

"Don't fear me Emily, only my men need fear me. My wedding present to you, the children you carry will be half mortal, half immortal, they will age slowly, living very long lives."

Exhaling in relief, Emily hugged him. Thorne had a shocked look on his face as if no one dared touch him, let alone hug him.

Kissing the top of Emily's head, Thorne vanished. Walking back into the orangerie in a daze she barely noticed Kat as her best friend hugged her. "Um, sweetie, you have a streak of silver in your hair, not like gray hair but silver and kind of sparkly, it's pretty, I don't remember the hairdresser doing it."

Linking her arm through Kat's, they walked towards Fred, the corner of her mouth tilting up, the silver streak was where Thorne had kissed her hair.

The wedding festivities lasted late into the night. The full moon was high in the sky when Colin pushed back his chair. He bid everyone goodnight, sweeping Emily into his arms, kissing her, she laughed, waving goodbye at everyone, pleasantly tipsy.

"I've been waiting hours, no longer; I'm taking you to bed Mrs. Colin Campbell."

"Say it again."

Smiling down at her, he growled, "Mrs. Colin Campbell, Emily Campbell, Baroness Campbell, Mine, always and forever."

Happiness radiated through her body, from her head down to her toes. So consumed with joy at knowing this warrior was her own, she didn't notice what had happened. "You blinked us here, not sure if that was a good idea, I think you'll need all your strength for the night ahead."

"Uh, wasn't me, it was you. A powerful will you have there, wife. It usually takes a few years to master dematerializing, even longer to do it taking someone with you."

Eyes wide, she couldn't believe it, what a cool power to have. She was going to have to practice and see what else she could do. She tried to summon a drink to her hand but no go. Hmm, not as easy as it seems. The shadows from the candles danced across the walls of their room. Colin undressed her, scattering the pins from her hair to the floor.

"My wife."

"Husband." She hugged him, stepping out of her shoes and returning the favor. Impatient, he quickly stripped and picked her up, carrying her to the bathing chamber. Meg had scattered rose petals and gardenia blossoms across the bed and floor leading to the bathroom. Steam was rising from the huge tub, flowers floating on the water. Bathing by candlelight, Emily leaned back against Colin still wearing the jewelry. He noticed the silver streak in her hair, "Where did this come from?"

"Thorne gave it to me. He had a gift for me." Colin tensed behind her.

"Before I tell you his gift, I want to give you my wedding present...I found out this morning, we are pregnant as Terya promised."

He sat up sloshing water out of the tub onto the stone floor, laughing with joy.

"I'm going to be a father. We have so much to do to get ready for twins."

His face radiant, Colin placed a protective palm against her stomach as if imagining his children growing within her, declaring them his.

"Darlin, we have a good nine months, don't start worrying yet. So, do you want to know what Thorne gave us?" Wary, Colin nodded. "He said our children will be half mortal, half immortal, age slowly and live very long lives."

"I'll be damned; the bloody bugger can be decent when he wants to." Pulling her tight against him, he kissed her soundly. Caressed by moonlight, they were molten silver unable to tell where one began and the other ended; they spent the rest of the endless night loving each other.

SPUTTERING AS HAMISH CAME TO, HIS SENSES SLOWLY returning, it had been so long without them. Everything was louder, brighter, smelled stronger. He was in a throne room, curled in a fetal position on black marble floors. In front of him sprawled in the huge, ornate silver throne was what he could only describe as a god. The air was icy cold, smelling of the night, filled with promise. He inhaled deeply, grateful. It had been too long to remember, lost in a gray world where he couldn't speak, smell or taste. As far as the eye could see, gray nothingness, he'd never experienced anything like it. Shuddering at the horror of that place, was it purgatory? He didn't know, but if it was, where was he now? Didn't seem to be heaven; he couldn't imagine he'd rate an audience there. It seemed too cold to be hell so where the bloody hell was he?

The being on the throne stared down at him. "Hamish Campbell, how would you like a second chance..."

THANK YOU SO MUCH FOR READING! I HOPE YOU ENJOYED Lost in Shadow. Next up is, Desired by Shadow, where you'll meet the pirate Robert. I hope you love it.

IF YOU'D LIKE TO RECEIVE AN EMAIL ABOUT MY UPCOMING new releases, please join my mailing list. Visit my website, cynthialuhrs.com

ABOUT THE AUTHOR

Cynthia Luhrs spends her time out on the deck, looking into the woods, imagining what if. She writes women's fiction, time travel romance, contemporary romance, family sagas, paranormal romance, and thrillers. Readers say her books (well not the thrillers, those are gritty) are light-hearted reads to escape reality.

She lives in the mountains of North Carolina with two rescued tiger cats, has always been a reader, and is overly fond of sparkly flip flops and pretty pens. Though now that she lives in the mountains she's going to have to find fabulous boots, mittens, and hats!

Keep up with her on her website

facebook.com/cynthialuhrsauthor
instagram.com/cynthialuhrs
bookbub.com/authors/cynthia-luhrs
goodreads.com/cynthialuhrsauthor

www.ingramcontent.com/pod-product-compliance
Lightning Source LLC
Chambersburg PA
CBHW011454170626
46814CB00009B/3046

9781939450012